Secrets Under the Sun

Nadia Marks (née Kitromilides, which in Greek means 'bitter lemons') was born in Cyprus, but grew up in London. An ex-creative director and associate editor on a number of leading British women's magazines, she is now a novelist and works as a freelance writer for several national and international publications. She has two sons and lives in North London with her partner Mike.

By Nadia Marks

Among the Lemon Trees

Secrets Under the Sun

Nadia Marks

Secrets Under the Sun

PAN BOOKS

First published in paperback 2018 by Macmillan

This edition published 2018 by Pan Books
an imprint of Pan Macmillan
20 New Wharf Road, London N1 9RR
Associated companies throughout the world
www.panmacmillan.com

ISBN 978-1-5098-1568-5

Photograph on p. ix by Leopold Glaszner from the archives of the
Glaszner family with thanks and gratitude to Irma and Panayiotis Vulgari,
great-grandchildren of Leopold Glaszner.

1 3 5 7 9 8 6 4 2

A CIP catalogue record for this book is available from the British Library.

Typeset by Palimpsest Book Production Limited, Falkirk, Stirlingshire
Printed and bound by CPI Group (UK) Ltd, Croydon, CR0 4YY

Visit **www.panmacmillan.com** to read more about all our books
and to buy them. You will also find features, author interviews and
news of any author events, and you can sign up for e-newsletters
so that you're always first to hear about our new releases.

To Mike

Josef Linser   *m*   Eva Linser
b Vienna, Austria   *b* Vienna, Austria

Franz Linser   *m*   Ernestina Caruso
b Vienna, Austria   *b* Palermo, Sicily

Olga Linser   *m*   Ivan Kovacs
b Larnaka, Cyprus   *b* Debrecen, Hungary

Sonia   *m*   Nicos   Anita   *m*   Costas
Kovacs-Linser   Constantine   Kovacs-Linser   Photiou
b Larnaka,   *b* Larnaka,   *b* Larnaka,   *b* Famagousta,
Cyprus   Cyprus   Cyprus   Cyprus

Eleni Constantine   Adonis Photiou
b Vienna, Austria   *b* Vienna, Austria

Larnaka promenade – Finikoudes – c. 1930s

Prologue

Larnaka, 1961

The sound of crying came from one of the bedrooms. Through the half-open door Olga saw her sitting bent over on the edge of the bed, head in hands, sobs wracking her body. She had never seen her cry; the sight was confusing. For a moment she stood by the door watching, unsure how to act. Finally, she crossed the room and sat by her side.

'What is it?' Olga asked, arms around the shaking shoulders. The woman raised her head, eyes pleading.

'I didn't mean to love him,' she said and covered her face with both hands. 'Please forgive me.'

1

Larnaka, 2010

Eleni stared into the open casket. Peaceful was the first word that came into her head. Then no words, just an overwhelming feeling of sadness. She placed a small bouquet of violets on the old woman's breast over her heart and wiped her tears with the back of her hand. When she was a child the mere thought that this woman might one day not be there had been inconceivable.

'Please don't die, Tante *mou*,' she'd cry, clinging onto the woman's legs.

'I won't. I promise. Not just yet, anyway,' she'd laugh, and kiss the top of Eleni's head. Death had already played a prominent role in the young girl's life. Her mother and father, both gone all at once before she could even remember them, and she couldn't bear for anyone else to leave her. Tante's laughter, a throaty chuckle, would always make her worries fade away, and for someone so young she had a few.

*

3

That morning Eleni had woken to the clatter of dishes. A beam of light was escaping through a crack between the shutters onto her legs sprawled on top of the tangled sheet. The heat was already filling the room. There was no air conditioning in the house; the two old women who had lived there had had no need for it, they always told her. This was a villa, with thick stone walls and high ceilings built to withstand the summer heat, they insisted, but Eleni thought otherwise. She opened her eyes very slowly; her head was throbbing. 'How can I have a headache while I'm asleep?' she thought, pressing her palm against her forehead for relief. 'I wonder if Adonis has a headache too . . . and Marianna . . .' The thought faded away as her eyes closed again. She lay motionless for a while, willing the headache to go, trying not to think about the previous night's events. Finally, she opened her eyes again and fixed them on the ceiling, letting her brain wander. There was so much to take in, so much to digest. She felt overwhelmed. Slowly she sat up and her feet found the floor. *First there is the funeral to deal with. Then I can think about everything else.*

She declined her cousin Adonis's offer of a lift, and braving the inferno that was the July sun, made her way on foot through the narrow streets of the old town. Given it was mid-morning, it was probably a foolish move. Her head was heavy from the previous night's revelations and drinking but she wanted some space alone.

Larnaka in 2010 was very different from the Larnaka of her youth, she thought, but in some respects it was getting better. At last, there were signs that some of the old buildings left to ruin were being renovated. There had been a time before she left when it seemed anything with character and history had to be replaced by oversized concrete mediocrity. She was thankful that St Lazarus's bell tower was still soaring above all the buildings that surrounded it in the square.

She was first to arrive at the church; she needed some time alone. The modest coffin stood by the altar, its simplicity a contrast to the opulent interior of the Byzantine cathedral. St Lazarus, named after the patron saint of Larnaka, was no larger than an average church, yet once inside, the magnificence of the iconostasis, chandeliers and frescoes left you in no doubt of its importance. Christ's friend had apparently fled to Cyprus for safety after his resurrection, and was ordained by St Paul as the first bishop of the island. He lived there for the rest of his life. Now deep in the catacombs of the church stands a sarcophagus bearing the inscription 'The friend of Jesus', in which the saint's holy relics are believed to be stored. Every year on his name day they are brought up to the church in a heavy silver casket so that the faithful can pay their respects.

The cathedral was always Tante's preferred place of

worship and she would take young Eleni there for the Sunday service. Eleni would sit obediently beside the older woman, anxious not to lose her in the crowd. Later, when Eleni was older and rebellious, the girl would reject the 'oppression' of religion and argue fiercely about it. 'I don't want to be told what to believe by anyone,' she'd sulk; nevertheless, whenever she felt the need for solitude she too would seek it in St Lazarus rather than in the Catholic church where her grandmother and aunt went to pray.

She didn't hear the other two tiptoe into the church, rather sensed them. It was always like that with the three of them. They seemed to know instinctively when one or the other was near. Now, they all needed to sit together for a while before people arrived and the service began.

The news of Katerina's death had come as a sad shock to Eleni, Adonis and Marianna. Tante, as they called her – a variation on the German word for auntie – was neither their aunt nor their blood relative, yet all three loved the old lady like family. They felt deep respect and gratitude towards her; her influence on them had helped to shape who they'd become. For her part, she'd adored all three; they were the children she never had.

They hurried back to Larnaka for her funeral: Eleni from London, Adonis from New York and Marianna from Nicosia. Unlike the other two, she didn't have far to travel, just a mere forty-minute drive, a journey which she had lately been making at least twice a month in order to visit the old woman.

For Eleni, Katerina was almost a mother. She was hardly more than a year old when her parents, Sonia and Nicos, were killed together in a car crash and it was Katerina who took care of her and cherished her as her own. It wasn't difficult: Eleni was an adorable child left traumatized by the loss of both parents. Besides, Katerina had also helped to bring up the little girl's mother and aunt years before, when the Second World War was still raging in Europe. The sisters, six and eight, were only a few years younger than Katerina when she came into the house as a maid at thirteen, but her natural maternal and domestic skills shone through.

As the Greek Orthodox Church buries its dead immediately, Eleni had had no time to lose and had left London in quite a rush. Her main concern, which proved to be relatively easy to address, was to organize someone to take over her lectures at the university where she was teaching. Home was fine: Simon, her husband, was more than capable of looking after himself and the dog. The kids, Christopher and Anthony, were both away studying – finally out of their hair, as the saying went, although if anything, Eleni liked having her boys 'in her hair'.

Even so, it was easier to have only one person to think

about instead of three at the same time. In fact, she hardly had to think about Simon at all – he was very independent and an even better cook than she was, so he was going to be fine while she was away. They'd all wanted to come to the funeral – both boys and Simon were fond of Katerina – but there was no time to make arrangements at the last minute.

Eleni knew Tante had been ill but the last time she had hurried back for a flying visit, only a few months earlier, it looked as if she was recovering well.

'Don't worry, my lovely, I'll be fine,' she had told Eleni. 'You know me . . . I'm a tough old mountain nut, it takes a lot to crack me,' she joked, and her laughter had filled the room as usual, reassuring Eleni that all would be well once again.

Now she bitterly regretted that she had not stayed longer. But Katerina had never been one to dramatize, so Eleni had flown home, reassured.

This time Simon was insisting that she should take her time.

'Stay as long as you need,' he'd said when the news arrived. 'Don't hurry back, your aunt will probably need you. And you need to be there . . . plus, since Adonis is coming from New York, you must spend some time with him.'

'You're right, I must,' Eleni agreed, knowing very well that she would need time, and that the trip was going to be an emotional one. 'I haven't seen Adonis for two years – in fact I can't remember the last time Marianna, Adonis and I spent time together. I know we Skype but it's not the same as meeting up and spending time with them.'

'The last time you saw Adonis was in London, wasn't it? When he came to visit us,' Simon said, handing Eleni a cup of coffee.

'I just don't know why we always leave it so long. Life slips by and we hardly notice.' She reached for the cup. 'We should all make more of an effort. When was the last time you saw your friend Mark in Sydney? Honestly, Simon, life is so short . . .'

They had delayed the funeral for a day to allow Adonis time to arrive from New York. Eleni drove out to the airport in her grandmother's old sports car to collect him. She parked the car, walked into the terminal and waited, reflecting how they both loved to drive that car, a host of childhood memories tied up in its fabric. Recently she had missed her cousin more than ever. They were so close in age, and though they were cousins, considered each other more as siblings. After growing up under the same roof in their grandmother's house, with Katerina looking after them, their connection was deep.

The wait for his flight to arrive and disgorge its last passengers seemed an eternity, and when Adonis eventually appeared he looked shattered and puffy-eyed. They fell into each other's arms and both burst into tears.

'Don't take any notice of me,' he finally said, tears turning into an embarrassed giggle. 'I'm just tired and emotional, and besides it doesn't do here for a grown man to be seen crying in public.' He darted a furtive glance around him.

'Don't be silly – who cares about them!' Eleni scolded him and gave him a bear hug. 'I bet you anything that all these macho Cypriot men would be the first to cry if anything happened to their mama or their favourite auntie!' And picking up his flight bag from his feet, she ushered him towards the exit.

'Let's go and see your mama, she's at the house waiting for you. Marianna is waiting to see you too.'

'So, how *is* my mother?' Adonis asked his cousin as they drove across town to the old house.

'Rather broken, I'd say,' Eleni replied. 'I don't think she knows how she's going to live without Katerina.'

'We all thought Tante was going to live forever . . . how are any of us going to manage without her?'

'I know . . .' Eleni replied. 'Just knowing she was there made me feel safe . . .'

'We all did,' he said and let out a sigh.

'Did Robert mind your leaving so suddenly?' Eleni asked. Adonis's African-American partner, Robert, whom he had wed in a civil partnership three years previously, was a psychiatrist, and as Adonis told his cousin when he announced their partnership, 'he's the most supportive life partner a person could ever wish for – and he's good for the soul, too.'

'No, he was fine, of course!' Adonis replied. 'He was a darling as always, and as you know he adored Tante too – he'd have come along if he could have. But it was all such a rush.'

'I know . . . the same with Simon and the boys. Anyway, if it's OK with you, we'll drop your bags, see your mother briefly and then meet Marianna for a coffee. I asked her to meet us before we all go back to the house. She can't wait to see you.'

'I'm in your hands, whatever you want to do,' Adonis replied, closing his eyes and sinking back into the seat.

'I know you're exhausted and probably want to lie down,' Eleni continued, 'but I've been in the house for the last twenty-four hours consoling your mother, and I need to breathe.'

'It's OK, Eleni *mou*,' Adonis laughed. 'I can use some caffeine . . . I'll sleep later, and besides I can't wait to see Marianna either; I can't remember when we were last all together.'

They met their old childhood friend in a cafe on the long stretch of promenade – The Finigoudes, 'little palm trees', named after the long row of palms planted along the seafront some hundred years ago, was a popular meeting place. Now the mop-heads of the little palm trees tower over most of the tall buildings on the strip.

No sooner had they sat down than Marianna came running across the road towards them, waving wildly. It had been some time since the three of them had met there.

The Finigoudes of their youth was quite different to how it was now. When they were growing up it was still a sleepy promenade, a place for families to stroll along the seafront, with many of the old buildings still standing and only two or three family restaurants. But sometime in the 1990s globalization hit the area with a vengeance. In a few years, reconstruction and modernization totally transformed it with bars, restaurants and cafes turning the promenade into any fashionable Mediterranean resort found in Italy, Spain or France.

'At least now we can get a decent cup of coffee,' Adonis said settling down next to a massive fan, after finally releasing Marianna from his bear hug.

'Exactly!' Eleni added. 'For those of us who don't like Nescafé or don't always feel like a Turkish coffee.'

'You mean Greek coffee!' Marianna corrected her.

'Oh please, don't you start being politically correct!' Adonis protested. 'The coffee is as Turkish as it's Greek as it's Arabic! It's ridiculous to insist on calling it *Greek* coffee.'

Eleni was amused to observe how quickly her two friends reverted to their childhood tactics of winding each other up.

'You've lived in America too long, that's your trouble,' Marianna retaliated.

'Come on, you two! Stop arguing about nothing,' she butted in. 'You know what Katerina would have told you . . . *Stamatate!* Stop! Anyway, we have bigger things to talk about.' She reached for her black Americano. 'Tonight, Auntie Anita wants us all at the house for supper. Apparently she wants to talk to the three of us about something, before the funeral!'

'Supper! My mother? Talk?' Adonis looked at the others in amazement. 'When has she ever done any of that? Especially cook!' He laughed. 'Perhaps Tante has left some food in the freezer!'

'Don't think it hasn't crossed my mind,' Eleni said. 'It's all very mysterious.'

True to character, Katerina had indeed left the freezer as she always did, full of her home cooking. She had actually alerted Anita to the fact that in the event of her demise she was leaving her with enough food to last a month and she was also bequeathing to her the cookery book she had inherited from Olga.

'There will be enough food for a while,' she'd said as she folded pastry one day, 'and after that,' Katerina looked at Anita and gave a little chuckle, 'I suggest you start studying your mother's bible . . . and by that I mean her gastronomic bible.'

'Don't talk such nonsense, you're as fit as an ox,' Anita had replied in a state of panic, denying the inevitability of Katerina's fate. 'You are much fitter than me.'

Anita of course knew well enough that her friend's cancer had spread and the end might be close. She had taken to accompanying her to the hospital and during the last visit their family doctor had been quite explicit about Katerina's condition. But Anita refused to lose hope, believing that her old friend would pull through. 'Miracles do happen, Katerina,' she insisted. 'I believe in the power of the Almighty and you have always been so strong.'

Nevertheless, since the last visit to Dr Demakis, Anita took herself every morning to the Catholic church to light a candle to the Virgin Mary and pray for her friend's recovery.

'Believe what you will, Anita *mou*, but I suggest you start reading some recipes just in case,' Katerina had teased her friend.

That day, with tightness in her heart, Anita had picked up her mother's cookery book for the first time. She knew all about Olga's 'bible', yet as much as she loved its contents she had never actually read it. She took it to the sofa by the window and started to leaf through its pages. She had a lot to learn and she knew that once Katerina had gone, she would have no choice but to start cooking and looking after herself. But then again, she thought, there were plenty of bakeries down the road that would deliver her orders. Still, whichever way it went, she knew her culinary tastes would have to change.

Now that Katerina had gone, Anita felt lost. She was the last remaining member of the old clan, and living in the big house by herself terrified her. She had never lived on her own or knew how to. In the last decade after her mother Olga died, it was Katerina who had taken care of her, as she had done all Anita's life.

Anita had made a huge effort to look her best for her son. The last time he'd visited she had been rather unwell, and most of his time there she had spent in bed. She could sense his disappointment in her, but then again she *always* sensed his disappointment in her. She had never really been much use as a mother; always ailing with something or other and mainly with her bad nerves. In truth Katerina had been much more of a mother to Adonis than she had, and she felt guilty.

For their supper on the night before the funeral Anita defrosted a huge baking tray of *pastitsio* – baked pasta with layers of aromatic meat sauce – which she knew was one of Katerina's specialities and one of 'the children's' favourites. She never stopped referring to her son and niece and their friend Marianna as 'the children'. 'I know you're grown up now, but you'll always be "the children" to me,' she'd defend herself when one or the other complained of being infantilized.

Waiting for 'the children' to arrive, she took the opportunity to lay the table with the best linen and table service. She was good at that. She might not have been a cook but she was very good at making the table sparkle. It had been a long time since she'd made such splendid preparations for dinner, she mused, possibly not since that last Christmas when they were a family and her sister was still alive. In the last years, she and Katerina had taken to eating in the kitchen where it was warm and cosy and easy to clear up. She longed for the old days, for the exquisite china to be set out, the silver and the crystal, for the wine to flow and her mother's stimulating conversation. But times had changed. She and Katerina were the only ones left and what do two old ladies have to talk about? And now Katerina too was gone. How long, she kept thinking, before her own turn came?

How would she start, how would she be able to speak to them all alone with no back-up and help from her companion?

For months Anita had pleaded with her dying friend to agree to summon the three children and speak to them together.

'Please, Katerina,' she had implored, trying to convince her to agree.

'It would be so much easier if we did it together,' she persisted. 'It's time.' But Katerina would not be persuaded.

'I have given my word of silence,' she told her, 'and besides, what good can it do now? It was all so long ago; all that is past now. Let it be, Anita. Don't stir it up.'

But Anita was troubled. She was burdened and needed to speak out.

She asked Adonis to open the bottle of single malt whisky she had bought for the occasion and handing each one of them a crystal tumbler, an heirloom from her grandfather, she began.

'My children, let's drink to our beloved Katerina. We will all miss her, but she will live on with us through our thoughts and the memories we have of her.'

Their glasses raised for the toast, Eleni, Adonis and Marianna stood in a state of confusion and anticipation beneath the sparkling crystal chandelier in the *saloni*, the large reception room usually reserved for entertaining guests.

The high ceilings and airy bright rooms of this house held so many childhood memories. Portraits of grandparents hanging on the walls smiling down on them, botanic illustrations and paintings were all as known to them as each other. The opulent red velvet sofas, heavy Linser Textiles curtains over floor-to-ceiling windows, the dark mahogany sideboards and glass cabinets full of silver and crystal, were all so familiar, and yet everything that night seemed strange. They stood in mournful silence waiting for Anita to speak.

'I have much to say,' she continued, 'but let us eat first – once again Katerina has provided a feast for us.'

Anita sat at the head of the table, the others around her. Reaching for the bottle sitting in the silver ice bucket, she filled everyone's glasses with the perfectly chilled white wine, then stretched across the table and started serving the food.

They ate in almost complete silence, each lost in thought and contemplation. After they finished eating the main course and the plates were cleared, Anita fetched a platter of fruit and placed it in the centre of the table.

'Now, before I begin our story,' she looked at the three of them, 'I would like, on this night before we say good-bye for the last time tomorrow to our beloved Katerina, to honour her memory by asking each one of you to say something about your *tante*. To share a memory, something you cherish about her, what she meant to you. I am well aware of the influence she had on each one of you and the love you all felt for her. Then, when you all finish, it will be my turn.'

Eleni, Adonis and Marianna darted bewildered glances

at each other. In all the years they had known Anita this was the first time they had seen her so articulate, and in control. She always stayed in the background in life, hiding behind her ill health and bad nerves. First it was her mother, the dynamic Olga, who reigned over the household, and then Katerina who ran the home and took care of everything including Anita.

'Eleni *mou*,' Anita said calmly, looking at her niece, 'let us start with you – after all, Katerina was like a mother to you.'

2

ELENI

'She wasn't *like* a mother to me,' Eleni said quietly, 'she was the only mother I ever knew. She made me feel safe and loved . . .'

One of Eleni's earliest memories was sitting in the warm and cosy kitchen, something simmering on the stove for lunch, watching her *tante* bake *baklava*. Sometimes Adonis was with them too but mostly she was alone with Tante. Later on when Eleni was a little older, keen to introduce the girl to the finer traditions of Cypriot home cooking, Katerina would encourage her to help.

'First we prepare our filo pastry,' Katerina would explain, 'then we slowly lay it out in the tin, layer by layer, like so, and only then do we start with the filling.' The young Eleni, holding a wooden spoon, was poised over a large bowl filled with the sweet, sticky, crunchy mixture, eager to start the next stage in the process. That part, she remembered vividly, was her favourite. The chopped walnuts, pistachios and almonds, sugar, and honey fragrant with cinnamon and ground cloves: a heavenly mixture of edible delight for the young girl. It was all she could do not to tuck in and start eating it with the wooden spoon before it was cooked. Eleni was sure that those cooking days with Tante started her lifelong love affair with cinnamon.

'After *baklava* can we make Mama Sonia's *koulourakia*?' she would ask, eager to continue in the blissful atmosphere of the kitchen with all its aromatic treats. Sonia's famed *koulourakia* were delectable almond cookies sprinkled with rose water and dusted with icing sugar, making them look as if they had been left out in the snow – not that Eleni knew much about snow, apart from a few visits to the mountains in the winter and from Christmas cards.

Katerina always talked to the girl about her mama. She talked while they baked, and Eleni wished she could remember her mother making *koulourakia* as she was doing with Katerina, but by the time she was old enough to remember, her mother and father were already dead.

'Please, Tante, can we make *koulourakia* now? Please?' the young girl would plead.

'In a few days, when the *baklava* is all gone, then we will make them too,' Katerina would promise, smiling and ruffling the girl's hair. Eleni felt safe in the kitchen, nothing could harm her there, so long as Tante was with her telling her stories, showing her how to cook, and always laughing. When Katerina laughed Eleni felt everything was all right with the world; there was no danger and no one was dead.

If she closed her eyes tight and whispered the name *Sonia* a few times, she could invoke an image that was her mama. The close-up framed photo on the sideboard helped. Everyone said that Eleni looked like Sonia, but she couldn't tell. Her mama was beautiful with red lips and gleaming black hair; her own hair was a mass of light brown curls, almost blonde by Cypriot standards. The only feature she could see that they shared was a little dimple on the chin. Eleni thought she looked more like Tante than the photograph of her mama. Katerina had big dark eyes, almost black, and so did Eleni, so she was happy enough and felt lucky that she had two mamas.

Another photograph stood on the sideboard. This one was of Sonia and Nicos, Eleni's parents, a young couple standing with arms around each other by the salt-lake. Shimmering in the distance on the edge of the lake, like a scene from *Arabian Nights* against a blue sky and palm trees, was the *Hala Sultan Tekke* holy mosque, one of Eleni's favourite places to visit as a child. When she was older she loved to listen to Katerina tell her the story of the holy place. The mosque, she'd explain, was built on the burial ground of the prophet Mohammed's beloved auntie, whose name was Umm Haram. While Umm Haram was riding a donkey during a visit to Cyprus she fell off and died on that very spot, where the mosque was built in her honour. Eleni liked the name – it was like a sound she made when she was eating mama's *koulourakia*. 'Umm,' she'd repeat to herself with pleasure. Katerina always tried to talk to the girl like a grown-up; how else would she learn anything? During winter months she would take Eleni to the holy site, especially when the pink flamingoes landed on the island to feed on the lake, rich with brine-shrimp and algae. It was an enchanting sight and the little girl would watch the hazy pink cloud hovering over the water like a mirage as the birds in their thousands dabbled their beaks through the shallow water.

She liked that picture of her parents in front of the mosque and lake. It looked exotic and glamorous, but her parents were standing far away and Nicos was wearing dark glasses so Eleni couldn't really see his face, so they were like a mirage too. He was tall and was smoking a cigarette and she thought he looked handsome. Glamorous, she thought years later when she was a student, and understood its meaning was the appropriate word to use for that photograph. Glamour, magic and sorcery were all alike, she decided, cloaking what one saw with a mysterious aura and altering reality. Who were those two people who she was told were her parents? Would she ever know?

Throughout her life her parents had remained a mystery to Eleni. While she was growing up, Nicos was hardly mentioned; she knew almost nothing of her father apart from what Katerina told her. No one else seemed to mention him. In almost all the photos of Sonia around the house she was alone – there was only that one picture where Nicos was with her. There were a few pictures of Eleni as a baby with her parents when they lived in Vienna – she was born there, they told her, but she didn't remember anything of the place; she had barely begun to toddle when they came back, and her only memories were of Larnaka.

She was growing up in a house of women where men didn't seem to feature, and of course they held a fascination for her. Obviously her cousin Adonis was there, but he was a boy not a man so he didn't count. The only man, apart from her teachers, that she saw regularly when he visited them at home, was Father Bernardino. But she never thought of him as a man either – he was the family priest and wore a dress.

Even though Nicos was apparently *persona non grata* in the Linser household, Katerina obviously felt it was important for little Eleni to have some idea of her father.

'He was tall and handsome, your papa,' she'd tell her as she stirred something or other in the aromatic kitchen. 'Your mama loved him. Eros is blind, my girl,' she would sigh and Eleni imagined a blindfolded angel with a bow and arrow.

She loved to hear stories about her mother, and Katerina had plenty of those.

'She was a rebel, your mama,' she'd tell Eleni and laugh.

'What's a rebel?' she asked, thirsty to hear more.

'She wouldn't be told what to do by anyone. She had a mind of her own, that girl,' Katerina would say, still laughing.

'Our head is our own, so isn't our mind in our head our own, too?' Eleni quizzed Katerina, perplexed.

'Of course it is.' The older woman smiled at the girl. 'But when you are young you have to listen to older people who know more than you and guide you . . . your mama thought she was born knowing everything.'

'Was I born knowing everything?'

'No, Eleni *mou*, you weren't,' she'd tell her and give her a hug. 'You are a very good girl. You listen to those who know more than you.'

Eleni loved nothing better than to hear Katerina tell her she was a good girl. She always tried her best for her.

MARIANNA

'If it wasn't for her, I wouldn't be the woman I am now,' Marianna began. She always knew that it was down to Katerina that she was now living in a nice little flat in

Nicosia, the island's capital, with a good job as a dental nurse, a nice car and understanding two other languages. Her English was not bad and when she visited Venice and Rome on holiday she had enough Italian to order in a restaurant and get around; the sound of German, too, was quite familiar since it was regularly spoken in the house that was to become her adopted home. Olga, Eleni's and Adonis's grandmother who welcomed Marianna into her home, was partly Austrian and partly Italian and encouraged her grandchildren to speak both languages. The mere fact that she had the opportunity to travel to these places and had been exposed to these other cultures filled her with gratitude at how her life had turned out. She also knew that if it hadn't been for Katerina and the Linser family, the most she could ever have hoped for was a job as a barmaid or a waitress.

The first time Marianna saw Katerina was in the kitchen of the old home, preparing lunch for the family. She was wearing a light blue apron with a pink rose motif on it and she was standing in a pool of sunshine which poured in through an open window. Marianna fancied that the woman had a halo around her head, and to her young girl's mind she was the embodiment of the perfect mother crossed with how she imagined the *Panayia*, the Holy Mother of God, would look like if she was cooking for baby Jesus.

'And who is *this*?' Katerina said looking up from her chopping board when the three children walked into the kitchen. 'Who is your friend, Eleni *mou*?' She smiled and looked at Marianna. 'What's your name, honey?' she asked again sweetly. The girl, too shy to speak, stood silent, looking at the woman with awe.

'Which one of you children would like a piece of bread and haloumi before lunch?' Katerina continued cheerfully, sensing the girl's confusion, and opened the fridge door.

Marianna couldn't remember the last time anyone had spoken so kindly to her.

It was mid-September, the autumn term at the elementary school that Eleni and Adonis were attending was well underway, and according to custom, the children went home for their lunch. That day, for the first time, the cousins had invited Marianna to come back with them. The fact that their house was only a four-minute walk from school made them the envy of their fellow pupils.

'Won't your mama mind?' Marianna had asked reluctantly when Eleni suggested she could come for lunch. 'Will there be enough food? What if your mama gets angry?'

'My mama is dead,' Eleni said in a matter-of-fact voice. 'But my *tante* won't mind at all, or my *yiayia*, or my *thia* – they all like children and we always have more food

27

than we can eat,' she told her new friend and linked arms with her as they walked on.

'Tell her, Adonis,' Eleni shouted to her cousin, who was walking ahead of them. Tell her it's OK to come home with us.'

'Yes! Come,' the boy said, turning round to look at the girls. 'Come – we can play snakes and ladders.'

It was a while after the term had started when the cousins had first noticed Marianna making her way to school alone. The two of them were laughing and joking, running and playing, as they always did on their way to class, when Eleni saw the lone girl walking near them.

'*Yia sou!*' she greeted her, breaking away from Adonis and falling into step with her. 'What's your name? Mine is Eleni and his is Adonis, do you want to walk along with us?' she chattered, hardly giving the girl a chance to reply.

'It's Marianna . . .' she finally said in a small voice and gave Eleni a shy look.

'I've seen you in the playground, you're in the other class,' said Eleni as they walked on.

'Where do you live?' Adonis asked, joining them and kicking a stone that lay in his way.

'Not far . . .' the girl replied, her voice trailing off into silence.

They walked to school together that day and every day

after that. Each morning the cousins waited for Marianna to pass their house and together the three of them made their way to school. The girls were in the same year and Adonis in the class above. When school was over Marianna would walk with them till they reached their house and then she made her way home alone. They never knew exactly where she lived. It was a long time before they found out.

After that first lunchtime visit, Marianna hardly ever went home again for her lunch. No one missed her, or if they did, nobody seemed to care, and before long she started going home with her new friends after school too, for the evening meal. As this was becoming a habit, Katerina encouraged her to stay and do her homework with the cousins under her supervision, and eventually the girl hardly ever went home at all. Marianna had finally found the warmth and tenderness she had always longed for and as long as she was welcomed she couldn't bear to part with it.

'Perhaps we should go and talk to her family,' Olga had said once it became obvious that the girl had become a fixture. One more mouth to feed was no problem for them. Besides, Olga liked the girl and thought it was good for Eleni and Adonis to have another friend, a surrogate sibling, around. She loved the idea of a large family, the house was big enough, and she had always wished there were more grandchildren. She herself had been an only child and had longed for a brother or a sister, and the untimely death of her younger daughter had left her with the wish to fill her home with the sound of children's cheerful laughter.

'Why hasn't anyone enquired where she is?' Olga asked Katerina a few weeks after Marianna's arrival. 'Do we know who her family is?'

'Yes! I do!' the other woman's reply came quickly. Olga might have been too busy to give much thought to the young visitor or ask any questions till now, but Katerina had made it her business to find out.

Marianna's home was a shabby little room on the wrong side of town, at the back of an establishment that called itself a 'cabaret' but was widely known as a brothel. She lived with her grandmother, a neglectful old woman going by the name of Sotiria, who had worked there in her youth but now, too old for the job, stayed on as the cleaner.

Soon after her conversation with Olga, Katerina went looking for Sotiria. She had recognized the signs of poverty and neglect and felt duty-bound to help the child. Marianna reminded her of her past self long ago, and now it was her turn to do as others had done for her all those years before. Marianna needed rescuing and she would now be under Katerina's protection, come what may.

She found the old woman on her knees, scrubbing the bar floor.

'If you want her you can have her,' she said when Katerina finished explaining why she was there. 'I hardly see the girl anyway. I don't know where she goes, but she's never around here, that's for sure. Makes no difference to me where she is.' She shrugged and went back to her scrubbing. After that, the girl never went back to sleep at her grandmother's, and Sotiria never bothered to seek her out.

Marianna was the illegitimate child of Sotiria's daughter, who abandoned the baby with her mother after giving birth and fled to Greece with a man who promised her fame and stardom as a dancer; or at least that was what Sotiria had always told the girl. As far as the father was concerned Marianna knew nothing about him, most probably because no one knew or cared who he was. *'Your mother is a beauty, she can sing and dance like an angel and she has the body of one too! You, my girl, could never fill her shoes.'* The old woman wove all sorts of fantasies about her absent daughter and Marianna was growing up on a diet of lies. The only tangible evidence she had of her phantom mother was an old photograph of a young woman in an exotic costume dancing on a table in a smoked-filled room surrounded by men.

Like Eleni, Marianna had a mother known to her only

by a black-and-white silvery image. A mother whom nei-ther girl remembered, whose only link to her child was a piece of bromide paper. That photograph was one of two things Marianna took with her when she left her grand-mother's house; that, and her school satchel.

'My grandmother says that my mama is a great dancer and a beauty,' Marianna had told Eleni, taking the photo out of her pocket to show her friend. 'I think one day she will come and find me!'

'My mama will never come and find me because she's dead,' Eleni replied as they compared pictures.

'They're both so beautiful, and they have the same hair,' Marianna pointed out.

'And the same smile!'

'Just like us! We have the same hair,' the girls would tell each other. 'I wish we were sisters!'

'We are almost like sisters,' Eleni said and gave her friend a hug, 'and even if we don't have our real mamas we have Tante, don't we? And she is the best mama ever!'

ADONIS

'She was the one person in my life who encouraged me to be myself,' Adonis said in a whisper. Now it was his turn to speak but the words seemed to catch in his throat; emotion was choking him. 'I know you say she was like a mother to Eleni, but in my mind she was like a mother to us all.' He turned and looked at Anita. 'I think she mothered everyone . . . including you,' he said, looking at his mother. The old woman nodded and wiped her eyes with her lace handkerchief.

'It's true,' she agreed. 'We were almost the same age, but she had the maternal instinct.'

Adonis remembered his childhood as a happy one on the whole, and Katerina had played a huge part in making it so. He had grown up in a house of women who loved him. There had been men, too, at different intervals, but by the time he was old enough to know the world, they had long gone. Olga had divorced the children's grandfather when her girls were young and Adonis's own father was by all accounts a scoundrel who went the same way as his grandfather when Adonis was still too young to remember.

If Eleni and Marianna thought of each other as sisters, then Adonis was their big brother and protector. Taller than most of the boys his age, he ensured there was never a question of anybody bullying or bothering either of the girls. If they did, they had Adonis to answer to.

For their part Eleni and Marianna adored their 'big brother' and when they were young they always included him in their games. He drew the line at playing with their dolls but everything else was acceptable, especially delving into the dressing-up trunk that Katerina kept for them in her room. The three would often disappear for hours to transform themselves into their favourite characters. Eleni would turn herself into a nurse, or sometimes the Austrian Empress Sissi, inspired by stories from her grandmother; Marianna would invariably emerge dressed up as an exotic dancer – 'like my mama', she'd tell them – and Adonis, whose fantasy was of joining the Church, would clothe himself as a Greek Orthodox priest. He would perform religious ceremonies wearing one of his grandmother's discarded long dressing gowns while chanting and blessing the home and all who lived in it. Around his neck the girls would help him hang several old crucifixes on chains and ribbons, and holding a bunch of keys on a long piece of string he would ceremoniously swing it back and forth as he walked around, the jingling sound of the keys imitating the priest's incense burner. He particularly liked the flamboyant ceremonial Greek Orthodox regalia, especially that of the archbishop. His mother and grandmother would encourage him to go outside to run around with the other boys playing cowboys and Indians, but Adonis was content in the company of his 'sisters'. The rough-and-tumble games of his school friends were not for him.

'I'm not so sure how good it is for him to play only with the girls,' Olga would tell Anita and Katerina, 'and this obsession with the Church . . . I don't know how healthy it is. He's too young.'

'There is nothing unhealthy about it,' Katerina would leap to his defence. 'A calling to the Church is no bad thing, Olga. In any case he doesn't only play with the girls, he's recently started to play football too.'

'I think we should encourage him to do more of it,' his grandmother would persist. 'He's athletic enough!' But Olga didn't have to worry for too long. As Adonis grew older his religious fascination and games with Eleni and Marianna did diminish, even if they didn't altogether cease. He gave up his ambition to become archbishop but continued to go to church with Katerina every Sunday. Olga was particularly pleased when Adonis was made captain of his football team at school, and then in his early teens with the appearance of girls other than his 'sisters' in his life. He attracted them as few boys did at that early age. There wasn't one girl in either Eleni's or Marianna's class who hadn't fallen in love with Adonis.

'I'm glad to see he has expanded his horizons,' Olga would say with relief.

'It was natural that he'd want to play with the girls when he was young,' Katerina would reply, defending him as always. 'I told you he was going to grow out of it.'

All the same, Adonis was far more comfortable in the company of females than of his male contemporaries. He thanked his friendship with his sisters for that; he seemed instinctively to understand girls, he liked their way of thinking and their warmth. He loved being around them. But girls *loved* him more.

Whereas other boys had to work hard at getting a girlfriend, Adonis always had the prettiest girl in town on his arm and seemed to exchange one for another with an enviable regularity.

Eleni and Marianna, both a little younger than him, hadn't yet reached the age for dating and would quiz him with curiosity.

'What do you do when you're alone with a girl?' they'd ask.

'Do you kiss each other?' they both wanted to know.

'Do you do the mouth-kissing thing?' Eleni would ask, giggling. 'You know, tongues and all that?'

'Stop it, you two!' Adonis would scold them and laugh. 'I'm a respectful kind of boy!' But the truth was that Adonis didn't feel inclined to do any of that with any girl, no matter how pretty she was. He put it down to his religious beliefs.

Tall and athletic, with a mass of black hair, olive-green eyes, strong chin and a Roman nose, he looked like one those Greco-Roman statues in the Cyprus Museum in Nicosia.

'Our young Adonis, true to his name,' Katerina would boast.

Good looks weren't all that Adonis possessed. He had brains, too.

Mathematics was his subject, which made him the pride and joy of Olga and Anita, but especially of Katerina, who made sure homework was done with clockwork regularity. She hadn't had the chance of a formal education herself and she was determined the children would, no matter what.

'You carry on like this and you will be a doctor or a lawyer, my boy,' she would tell him. But Adonis had his own plans; he wanted to be an architect.

'You can go to the University of Athens and then come back to Cyprus and build beautiful houses,' she'd tell him, swelling with pride, 'God alone knows how badly this island needs them now.'

Ten years on from the Turkish invasion the island was an architectural disaster. Buildings were being hurriedly thrown up everywhere unplanned in a haphazard attempt to reconstruct the towns, and the refugee camps were still evident. Although Adonis had only been a young boy during the invasion in 1974 he remembered the fear that had gripped him, and his whole family, during that time. Katerina was right; he would become an architect in order to rebuild what he remembered had been lost.

Apart from the aftermath of those weeks of fighting and the architectural carnage left behind, Adonis remembered all too well how terrified he was, and would secretly thank God in his prayers every night for being too young to be called up. So many young men and neighbours had to take arms and go and fight. The mere thought made Adonis tremble in his shoes; he wasn't one of those boys who romanticized war – on the contrary, he dreaded it. He recalled the panic that spread through the household during those hot summer months of fighting when Olga insisted they must take refuge in the cellar, and the fear, sadness and repulsion that engulfed him when injured people were sometimes brought to the house. The fighting, which lasted barely a month between July and August during the hottest months of the year, and which ended with the partition of the island, felt like a lifetime to the young children in the Linser household. They didn't really understand what was happening and why suddenly there was a war. Every child growing up on the island was aware of tensions between Greeks and Turks but it didn't really touch their lives much, nor did they imagine there could be blood spilled over it. They were just children; they only knew what the adults told them.

'It's a very complicated situation,' Olga said when Adonis insisted that someone tell him why Turkey was invading and sending parachuting soldiers at dawn to attack the island.

'Why doesn't anyone stop them?' he'd ask. 'We're only a small island – why doesn't someone help us?'

'You are too young to understand, my boy,' Olga

would try to explain. 'It goes back so many years; they've been fighting over this land for centuries . . . It's strategic, you see,' she continued, struggling to explain the complexities of Cypriot politics, 'it's geographic. Everyone has always wanted to own this island, Adonis *mou*, you know that from your history lessons.' But his grandmother's attempts to illuminate him didn't really satisfy Adonis, nor did he understand. He did of course know from school all about the many conquerors the island had endured over the millenniums: the Venetians, and the French, the Ottomans and the English, but that was a long time ago – it had nothing to do with now, with their modern lives. This was the twentieth century – no place for war, surely.

The one thing he did understand and saw all around him was the hundreds of homeless people looking for refuge. The influx of refugees from the north of the island, which had been captured by the Turkish army, was now turning their family house, and every house in town for a period of time, into dormitories until the authorities could find a way to accommodate them. People opened their doors to whoever needed help.

Whole families – parents, children, aged grandparents – fled their villages with nothing more than the clothes they stood up in. The nearest place not under siege was Larnaka, so the town was flooded with people trying to escape the hostilities.

During that time there was one particular family that passed through the Linser household and who stayed with them for several weeks. There were five of them: parents with twin baby girls and a boy called Stavros, who was the same age as Adonis. After the fighting stopped and the family was housed in one of the refugee camps, Stavros continued to visit the Linser home to play with the children, and the two boys became staunch friends; a friendship which was to last until Adonis went to study at the university in Athens.

When he was eighteen Adonis met Sophia. The daughter of a prominent lawyer and the sister of one of his school friends, she was a perfect match. A beautiful fiery girl with hair the colour of chestnuts and eyes to match. At seventeen she was far more mature than her years and had set her sights on the best-looking boy in town, making him once again the envy of his friends and provoking endless teasing from Stavros.

'What is it about you?' he'd joked. 'Must be that name of yours that's making you into a girl magnet.' Stavros too had his share of success, but nothing like his friend. Up until the time Adonis met Sophia the two friends would date several girls at the same time, go out on double dates and compare notes.

'I don't think it would take me long to make her say yes,' Stavros would boast, always sure about his latest conquests. Unlike his friend who preferred to take things slow, he was much more ardent in matters of the flesh.

'Go on, Adonis my friend, what are you waiting for, make a move,' he'd goad him.

'I'm not like you,' Adonis would snap back, 'you have sex on the brain. I have respect.' Then Sophia came into the picture and things changed.

'She's the girl for me,' Adonis told his friend when Stavros complained that he had turned into an old man. 'This is serious. I'm going to marry her after I finish my studies.'

The couple made a striking sight, turning heads wherever they passed.

The girls Adonis had dated until then had made no sexual demands on him but Sophia was different. She longed for his physical attentions and she let him know it. Her beauty dazzled him, her carnal passion confused and overwhelmed him – as far as he was concerned sex came after marriage, and as he was sure the two of them would marry at some point, sex had to wait till then.

The moment of clarity and change came to Adonis while he was sitting on a bench in the sun talking to Socrates, a fellow architectural student from Thessaloniki. Adonis had been in Athens for about six weeks for the first semester of his architectural degree, and he and Katerina had travelled together so that she could help him settle in. Anita was having one of her anxiety attacks and wouldn't get out of bed; in any case he much preferred to be with Katerina. They found a little apartment through some people his grandmother knew in Kifissia, the leafy area of Athens and close to the Metro. She stayed with him for a week before going back to Cyprus, and now he was living alone for the first time ever, enjoying the student life.

Sophia had been inconsolable when he was leaving. 'How will I manage without you?' she told him through her tears. 'You'll probably meet another girl and forget me.'

'Don't be silly!' he replied, stroking her hair. 'I'll be coming back every holiday, and you will come and visit me . . . it'll all be fine, you'll see!'

'But you'll be gone for months at a time!'

Somehow that didn't seem to be a problem for Adonis. He knew that he loved Sophia but he also couldn't wait to leave, and that perplexed him.

But sitting on that bench in the sun in Athens with Socrates, everything changed all at once for him. Everything fell into place and for the first time in his life Adonis understood – or perhaps, he later thought, he *acknowledged*. They were talking about something, he no longer remembered what it was, but at one point Socrates reached across and touched Adonis's arm in order to emphasize his point. It was at exactly that moment that he recognized with absolute certainty the electric current, the piercing longing of desire, go through his body, and travel to his loins. No girl, no matter how much beauty she possessed, had ever made him feel that way.

Later, when he returned to Cyprus for the summer, tormented about facing Sophia and the prospect of breaking her heart, it was to Katerina that he turned for guidance and it was Katerina who first sensed the change in him.

'I can't do it, Tante, how can I?' he agonized, 'I can't go through with it for my own selfish reasons. I could still marry her and pretend nothing has changed.'

'If you did that, you would ruin your life and hers,' she told him. 'We cannot deny who we are, Adonis *mou*, we are not able to choose. So long as you are sure this is what you want, you must be true to yourself.'

'Is this what defines me, then? My sexuality? Is it not a sin? Am I not a hypocrite after all these years believing in the sanctity of marriage?'

'You have love and goodness in your heart, my boy,' she told him. 'But we must love ourselves too. You can only do that by accepting who you are. Denying your nature would only cause harm to you and others.' Katerina reached across and took him in her arms. 'God is merciful, Adonis *mou*. He forgives, and you have done nothing that needs forgiveness – you are only being honest.'

His friend Stavros, it seemed, was the only one who did not forgive or accept Adonis's honesty. The decision to come out and explain to his childhood friend about his nature was met with such contempt and rejection that it was to haunt Adonis for the rest of his life.

It was a particularly hot day in August and Adonis was home for the summer break from Athens. He had been procrastinating and agonizing about speaking to Stavros, feeling nervous about how to approach his confession. By then Stavros had met a girl he was going steady with, even if he still kept a roaming eye on what else was available; Adonis knew that his friend would always be a committed philanderer and an incorrigible womanizer. But their friendship went back a long time, he loved him and considered him as his closest friend; he didn't want to pretend any longer. He asked to meet at the beach – a café would have been too busy with prying ears and the house was stifling hot; at the beach, they could walk and talk in peace.

Adonis was expecting that Stavros would react to what he had to tell him, but he had no way of knowing exactly how. Homosexuality in the 1980s was a taboo subject, especially in their small community where a man's worth was measured by his sexual prowess and virility, yet nothing could have prepared Adonis for his friend's reaction and for the look Stavros gave him that day. It was a look that screamed disgust, disdain and betrayal. It pierced his heart like a flick knife.

'How could you?' was the only thing that Stavros said, and when Adonis reached for his arm he pulled it away forcefully and, turning his back, walked away from him. That was the last time they spoke, and whenever Adonis remembered that look the pain in his heart returned.

ANITA

'Now it is *my* turn to talk about Katerina, and not only her.' Anita looked around at the three faces streaked with tears. 'Our family history is long and complicated and my friendship with Katerina goes back a lifetime.' Her voice faltered with emotion. 'I have lived with this woman since I was eight years old and she was like an older sister to me, our lives tightly linked; we knew everything about each other. You, my children, know what she allowed you to see. She gave you her love, it's true, and guidance, but there was so much more to Katerina.'

Anita reached for her glass of wine. 'Life without her is unimaginable and I have feared this moment more times than I can admit, but now the time has come.' She brought the glass to her lips and drank, hoping the alcohol's effect would loosen her tongue further and release her repressed emotions.

After decades of silence, now it was time to reveal to them the past that had been hidden.

3

Cyprus, 1943

Olga Linser, Anita's mother, a sophisticate divorcee with two young daughters, an elderly mother, and a textile business to run, took on Katerina as a maid in the winter of 1943.

On the day she went to collect the girl from her family, snow had been falling all night over the hills, and the journey to Katerina's village in the Troodos Mountains was treacherous.

Olga left Larnaka on that December Sunday morning in her dashing red Triumph Gloria, in blazing sunshine, the roof opened to the blue sky and her hair left to the mercy of the winter breeze. A woman behind the wheel was a rare sight in Cyprus in those days and Olga caused many a tongue to wag with her outlandish cosmopolitan ways.

'I just love you, *chérie*,' Christian, Olga's French lover said as he manoeuvred himself into the low passenger seat. She'd asked him along for company but also because she knew that she might need help as the drive could prove to be rather challenging.

'You are the woman for me, madame,' Christian said and kissed her on the lips. '*Je t'adore!*'

'Like you adore all your women,' she laughed and kissed him back.

'Yes . . . but you, my raven-haired beauty, are one of a kind!'

Olga was indeed one hell of a woman. A beautiful, strong matriarch who had learned early in life that men are good for a romantic encounter and not much else, especially when it came to being reliable. Her own marital experience had been disastrous. She always maintained that apart from introducing her to the wonders of sexual pleasure, Ivan, her husband, had been pretty useless. She did give him credit for being partly responsible for creating her two daughters, but there it stopped.

Christian Lamont, the cultural attaché to the French consulate, was her latest beau. She enjoyed his company, for as long as it lasted, as well as his intellect and his lovemaking. He was a good match for the sophisticated, educated and thoroughly modern Olga.

'Shall we stop for lunch on the way?' Christian asked, as she put the car into gear.

'There is a picnic hamper in the boot,' she replied. 'We'll stop before we start the climb. We'll find a field and sit under an olive tree. It's glorious this time of year, everything is so fresh and green!'

But by lunchtime, the dark clouds had started to gather and rain looked imminent. Stopping the car by the side of the road near a meadow, they pulled the roof over their heads and had their picnic in the front seat under a warm blanket.

'This is more romantic than sitting in a field,' Christian said, as Olga poured him a steaming cup of coffee with a dash of brandy from a silver flask. Predicting that the weather could suddenly change, Olga had come prepared. She knew of the island's sharp fluctuations in temperature during the winter. Within its 3,500 square miles, dramatic landscape variations from sea and flat plains to mountains nearly 2,000 metres high caused sudden fluxes.

A keen swimmer, even in winter, Olga was often seen plunging into the cold waters of the Larnaka seashore and then jumping into her car with a crowd of friends and driving to the snow.

'Oh, how I wish we could ski,' she would complain. 'There's plenty of snow up here but civilization hasn't reached us yet.'

Born on Cyprus, Olga adored the island and its landscape, but in comparison to metropolitan Western Europe it was still primitive. Her early years were pampered and spoilt, the only child of an Austrian father and an Italian mother, she travelled to both countries from an early age.

Olga's Viennese grandparents were both scientists who had made Cyprus their home at the end of the nineteenth century in order to study the rare flora of the island. Europe was as familiar to Olga as the wild mountains of Cyprus and she was at home in both of them.

She was doted upon by her rich daddy, and Olga adored him back. The connection was less strong with her mother, whose strict Catholicism clashed with her daughter's hedonism. Olga wanted to enjoy life, live it to the full and not be troubled by her mother's ethics about guilt and sinfulness. This was the twentieth century! In Europe, the flapper girls were all the rage and luckily for her, her father was on her side.

The drive through the Alpine forest up to the village, with its hairpin bends and sheer drops, was hair-raising even for an experienced driver like Olga. Although she had made the trip often it was usually in better weather, and she made sure she had a man with her willing to take the wheel if the going became too demanding. Christian was always a keen travel companion.

Luckily it had long stopped snowing and visibility was good; the landscape looked like a winter fairyland. It thrilled Olga to see the snow-covered trees; she adored the forest, which reminded her of the Austrian Alps where she had gone many times with her papa.

'Can you take over now, *chéri*?' she asked Christian,

coming to a halt after a particularly harrowing bend. 'If I carry on driving I'll probably kill us both,' she joked and pulled hard on the handbrake. 'Driving and looking out of the window are incompatible.' She laughingly settled into the passenger seat to spend the rest of the journey feasting her eyes and inhaling the cold, fragrant air.

The village, when they reached it, was deserted and covered in clean, crisp snow; an eerie silence prevailed. No man or animal was in sight. The snow must have been falling for a long time and the only sign of life was smoke billowing from every chimney. They pulled up in the square outside the village *kafeneon*, the car tyres slashing through the virgin snow.

Behind the steamed-up windows they could see half a dozen incredulous faces peering out at them. Visitors rarely ventured so high up and almost never in the winter. The car alone was a rare sight to the inhabitants and the vision of Olga in a full-length white fur coat and hat caused a sharp intake of breath as she walked into the smoked-filled coffee shop. Abandoning their card game and backgammon the men sat back and stared at the intruders. In no time at all the news of their arrival had spread like a forest fire through the village.

'Xeni . . .' Foreigners, they whispered to each other and started gathering, men inside and women outside, to look with a mixture of curiosity and suspicion.

'We are looking for the Costandi family,' Olga addressed the proprietor, a stocky man sporting a lavish moustache. She pulled up a chair by the roaring log fire, removed her gloves and hat and shook her hair loose, ignoring the men staring at her.

'Can you tell us where they live?' Christian asked this time, in perfect Greek with his French accent, causing a burst of mocking laughter from the men.

'They are over there by the church,' the man replied, pointing across the street with his chin.

They found the house behind the village church, if you could call the two miserable rooms where seven people lived a house. Olga and Christian parked the car in the churchyard and walked round the back to knock on the door. A surly-looking man with unruly hair, wild eyes and an equally wild moustache opened the door to them.

'*Ne?*' Yes? he asked abruptly with a voice as surly as his expression.

'Are you Yianni Costandi?' Olga asked, wrapping her coat tight around her.

'*Ne!*' he barked again at them and opened the door wider. 'Are you that town woman who's come for Katerina?'

'I am!' Olga replied. 'Can we come in, please? It's very cold out here.'

The room they stepped into was apparently a bedroom, as well as a kitchen, sitting room and dining room. It smelled of damp. A woman was bent over a wood stove, feeding it with logs from a wicker basket. A small child whimpered at her feet while a girl in her early teens holding a baby stood next to her.

'*Kalosorisate*, welcome,' the girl said politely. 'I am Katerina; this is my father and mother,' she gestured with her head to the woman and man. Again the girl broke the silence. 'Please sit,' she said shyly, pointing to two wooden chairs, while the two adults stood mutely watching them. 'We have been expecting you,' she said again and walked to one of the beds lining the walls to put the baby down. Looking around, Olga counted four beds and a small cot in the room plus a table and chairs, a stone sink, a food locker hanging from the ceiling, a crockery cupboard, the wood stove used for cooking and warmth, and several sacks containing mostly grains and pulses.

Olga could feel the bitter cold biting her feet. Despite the fire, the room was freezing. Shivering, she wrapped her coat more tightly around her body. She looked at Christian standing motionless by the door.

'I will make coffee,' she heard the girl say as the baby on the floor started to cry. Glancing down at the child, Olga realized that the floor beneath her feet was bare trodden earth. Nothing covered the ground. No rug, or wood, or tiles, just naked brown hard undulating earth.

Later, she also discovered that the latrine was a hole in the earth in the back yard.

'As we have agreed,' Olga began, wanting to speed up the process and leave as soon as possible, 'I have come to take Katerina to Larnaka to live with my family and work as our maid.' She looked at the man, waiting for his response.

'Yes, I agree,' he finally spoke. 'You will pay me ten pounds now and you will also pay Katerina 7 shillings a month which she will send to me.'

'I will pay you what we have agreed,' Olga said firmly, opening her handbag and taking out the money, 'but what Katerina does with her own money is her business.' She looked across at the girl who stood rooted to the spot, staring wide-eyed at her. Olga saw a flicker in her eyes. She wasn't sure what it meant; it looked like a mixture of gratitude and fear. She got the strongest of feelings that Katerina was as desperate to get out of there as she herself was.

4

Yianni Costandi was a tyrant and a bully, and Katerina lived in constant fear of him. Her mother, a weak and feeble human being, had no power over her husband. The many beatings she had suffered at his hands broke any spirit she might have previously possessed, making her incapable of protecting her children.

Katerina felt pity for her mother, but mostly she felt anger and resentment.

Terrified as the girl was, she, unlike her mother, refused to yield to Yianni, thus infuriating him further with her fighting spirit.

'I'll teach the little mare to respect her father,' he would hiss, spitting on the ground and unbuckling his belt. Katerina, unflinching, stood strong and took what he gave her. The reasons for the beatings were usually arbitrary.

'I told you to fetch three pitchers of water from the well, not two,' he had shouted at her the day Olga and Christian were due to arrive.

'The snow is deep,' she replied, standing tall in front of him, 'and my hands were freezing. I couldn't carry the three.' He raised his hand to strike her and then he remembered the visitors and thought better of it. It wouldn't do to be spoiling the goods; Katerina was now a commodity. When the message had come via an old relative that a rich town woman was looking for a girl as a maid, Yianni jumped at the chance.

'These town bitches pay handsomely,' he'd told his wife, 'and I'll have one less useless mouth to feed when she is gone.'

So what Olga saw in Katerina's eyes the day she went to fetch her was nothing less than a plea for mercy, a wish to be released from her miserable existence. To her dying day, Katerina never ceased to feel grateful for the chance Olga gave her for a better life.

Living in the Linser household, run by women, with no man ruling and abusing them, was like a dream for the young maid. Life in a wealthy city house, with kind people, food and shelter, was more than she had hoped or wished for. It was another world, far from her poverty-stricken home and brutal father, pitiful mother and five young siblings to take care of. Katerina knew everything about looking after children and was willing to take on whatever duties were required of her. She was no stranger to hard work.

As head of the house Olga was strong but fair-minded and she was grateful to have Katerina's help. She had a demanding textile business to manage alone, a house to run and two young daughters, and even with her mother's support, and the assistance of Kyria Despo, who came daily to clean and cook, the task was difficult. The girls, Sonia and Anita, aged six and eight, were not much younger than Katerina, but the hardships she had endured had propelled her into a maturity much greater than her years; the two girls took to her like an older sister.

'This is your home now,' Olga said when she brought her back to the house and opened the door into a room that would become Katerina's own for many years to come. 'I'm sure we will all get along very well.'

The room, like the entire house, was beyond anything the girl had ever imagined. A window opened on to the back garden, framing a lemon tree laden with lemons that would soon be ready for picking. At first glance it could have been mistaken for a painting. Larnaka by the coast in December was as mild and sunny as an early summer's day in her village. The winter sun flooded in through the window and she nearly stepped on Oscar, the family cat curled up in a pool of light on the Turkish rug spread on the floor. After the harsh, bitterly cold mountain village that she had left behind, the room felt like a warm embrace.

A bed with a crocheted cream bedspread stood in one corner of the room, a chair and table with an electric side lamp on it in another corner – she was used to smoking oil lamps. A double-fronted carved oak wardrobe with a full-length mirror stood against the wall. Dropping her small bag containing her few belongings, she stared in disbelief. The room was almost as big as the entire miserable house she had called home until then. The realization that she would have a bed all to herself brought tears to the young girl's eyes.

'*Eucharisto, kyria mou*, thank you, my lady,' she whispered, unable to say more lest she break down in tears.

That day when she first set foot in the Linser house, Katerina thought she had entered a palace, and Olga was the queen.

During the elementary years, Sonia and Anita were being educated largely at home with a tutor so Olga decided to include Katerina in some of the basic lessons, such as sums and reading.

'She is a bright spark, this little peasant girl, and such a hard worker,' Olga said to her mother Ernestina, taking an interest in expanding the girl's horizons. 'If she is to live with us it wouldn't hurt to teach her a few things.'

Katerina's appearance was an immediate priority to Olga, who discarded her threadbare jumper and skirt, and her shoes with flapping soles, and replaced them with a brand new wardrobe. Appearances were important to her and she was not one to keep the girl looking like a servant, with an apron and a uniform, as was customary in so many bourgeois households of the time.

'She's a pretty thing underneath it all,' Olga told her mother, 'and with a little help we can turn her into a human being.'

It didn't take long for Katerina's cheeks to turn rosy, her matted hair to become a glossy chestnut mane, and a smile to brighten her face. In just a few months her metamorphosis was complete, from a dirt-poor peasant girl to a young woman fit to live amongst the sophisticated Linsers.

'She might be our maid but she is not our slave. If she is happy then my girls are happy, and I am content and free to get on with my work,' Olga had told her mother. 'Everyone has a right to a good life,' she continued. 'I despise these people who think otherwise!'

Thirsty for knowledge and eager to learn, Katerina was absorbing everything that was on offer. The two women helped her with the art of cooking. Over the years Katerina's culinary skills developed to match those of her mistresses, incorporating a sophisticated European cuisine as taught to her by Olga and Ernestina. Of course the peasant Cypriot dishes, which mainly involved pulses, learned from her own mother and now expanded by Kyria Despo, were not forgotten either, making her an excellent cook. The old cleaner was tutoring Katerina well in the art of housekeeping, knowing that one day she'd be taking over from her.

For her part, the Linsers' new maid threw herself into her work, treasuring her new life. Sometimes she thought wistfully of her brothers and sisters and her poor mother, but even if she felt pangs of guilt for her good fortune she thanked God every day for her escape. On Sundays she would set off for the Greek Orthodox church of St Lazarus for the Sunday service to give thanks and pray. The Linsers, on the other hand, would make their way to the Catholic church of Our Lady of the Graces.

Olga's parents' and grandparents' Catholic persuasion, as opposed to the Greek Orthodox religion which was prevalent for Christians on the island, followed their family tradition. The main language spoken at home was Greek, but both of Olga's young daughters also had a good grasp of German and Italian, taught to them by their mother and grandmother. Much to Katerina's dismay they would often punctuate sentences with the other two languages, but being determined not to be left out, she too began to pick up words and phrases in German and Italian. *Darned if I'm not going to know what they're all talking about*, she told herself.

In those days in Cyprus, those who entered a household in service often did so for life. A young woman could happily dedicate her life to someone else's family, renouncing prospects of marriage and a family of her own. If the family was kind and generous, the advantages were great. She'd have her board and lodgings, a small salary, and if she was extremely lucky she might meet someone to marry. But for most girls coming from a very poor family with no dowry or prospects, the chances were extremely slim.

By the time the girls were grown up, Katerina was an established fixture in Olga's home; an important and valuable member of the household and family with no desire to leave, ready to take on the next generation. The Villa Linser and its occupants were her home, her family, her destiny.

The family house had been built in 1910 by Josef Linser, Olga's grandfather. Like most houses for the affluent at that time it was made out of the local sandstone. It was an enormous imposing building, big enough to accommodate four families by modern standards. Its style was a cross between an Italian villa and an Ottoman mansion and it stood in the centre of town, surrounded by a large garden and only a stone's throw away from the seafront. Marble steps led to an imposing front door flagged by two tall palm trees on either side.

The front door opened into a large, sun-filled hall, its floor a tapestry of colourful mosaic tiles. On entering the house, you were faced with a sweeping staircase leading up to two more floors.

The first floor housed the *saloni* – the best room of the

house, with a main purpose of receiving guests and hosting parties. This was filled with heavily carved rosewood furniture, opulently covered velvet sofas and armchairs, and a grand piano. A dining-room table and chairs stood at one end of the room, along with sideboards and glass cabinets filled with crystal and silver.

On the same level, another room served as a family room; its floor-to-ceiling French windows opened on to a veranda overlooking the back garden, while the top level housed several bedrooms and two bathrooms. The kitchen, along with a small study and a library, were situated on the ground floor, with French windows opening straight out into the fragrant garden.

Olga was born there, her father Franz grew up there and as her grandfather had hoped when he built it, many generations of Linsers to come would also be making it their home. Communal living was the way of the times. No family expected to be separated. In wealth or in poverty, people stayed together. By the time Katerina entered the Linser house, only women were left living there. Olga's father had died and she had long divorced her husband.

'Papa was the only man I have ever been able to depend on,' she'd tell her mother when her marriage fell apart.

'Women are a superior species,' she'd tell Katerina, a feminist in advance of the concept. 'We are stronger, perhaps not physically but certainly emotionally and mentally, and much more capable.' Katerina was a good pupil and Olga was her mentor.

Larnaka, 2010

Anita looked around the room at the three pairs of eyes staring at her with a mixture of surprise, sadness and fatigue. Dinner had long finished, yet they continued to sit around the table allowing the old woman to transport them to a past they had little knowledge of. Adonis's jet lag was getting the better of him but there was no question of going to bed; they were all far too intrigued to hear more.

'Why didn't Katerina ever say anything to us about her life?' Eleni was the first to speak.

'She was a very proud woman and felt deeply ashamed of her father,' Anita replied. 'But you know, Eleni *mou*, even though she hated him, she continued to send money until her mother's death. Then she severed any connection with him. After that she never mentioned his name again.'

'I can understand why she couldn't talk of these things to us when we were children, but later when we were adults – why not then?' Adonis added and reached for the bottle of wine to fill their glasses. 'We were always so close . . .'

'She had her reasons,' his mother replied.

'She was so very kind to me,' they heard Marianna say. 'I owe everything to her,' she whispered and wiped her eyes with the napkin lying on her lap.

'*You*, my girl,' Anita said, 'were her alter ego. She had a mission to save you as *she* had been saved.'

Anita reached for her glass of wine again and sat back in her chair to continue with her story, fatigue and emotion etched on her face. This was not easy for her.

'So, I suppose you are all beginning to piece together a different picture of our beloved Katerina,' she told them. 'I know you thought of her as a wise old woman of the world, but as you are finding out now, her origins were far from the woman she became, which makes her even more remarkable.'

'She knew so much,' Eleni said.

'She had your grandmother to thank for that,' Anita replied, 'and later on our family priest, Father Bernardino, he also taught her a lot. My mother treated Katerina like she treated us, like a daughter and also as a friend too. For us she was our second sister.'

'We never thought of her as anything but family,' Eleni said again and Adonis nodded in agreement.

5

Franz Linser, great-grandfather of Eleni and Adonis, was the only son of Austrian botanist Josef Linser who arrived in Cyprus in the spring of 1890 with his wife Eva and baby son on a scientific mission to record the flora of the island for the Natural History Museum of Vienna. The assignment was to be for a maximum duration of five years but the Linsers fell in love with Aphrodite's birthplace and decided to stay on the island for good, making Larnaka their home.

'This island is paradise,' Josef told his wife on their arrival. 'I can feel the presence of the gods here.' Eva was less convinced of its celestial qualities – she had left a central European capital for what she initially perceived as a primitive, Middle Eastern backwater far to the east of the Mediterranean. But her husband's enthusiasm and the obvious natural unspoiled beauty of Cyprus, rich with rare flower species, were infectious and the island soon won her over too.

'Look, Eva, look how much beauty grows on this land,' Josef would enthuse, showing her all the rare plants he had collected. 'This surely was Demeter's playground.' Eva's mind conjured up images of Persephone and her mother tiptoeing playfully through a crocus field.

They initially set up home in a typical Ottoman-style house on two floors. All rooms, plus the gallery balcony on the first floor, looked inwards over a courtyard garden, which accommodated the lavatory and a small bathhouse. But the two trees that stood in the middle of the yard, a lemon and a pomegranate tree in full bloom, made up for any early reservations she might have harboured.

'There is nothing more fragrant than lemon blossom,' she told Josef, 'and nothing more vibrant than the crimson of the pomegranate flower.'

Eva was a talented botanic illustrator, and husband and wife worked as a team. While she stayed at home and took care of their son, Josef roamed the wild country and mountainsides for rare island species of orchids, cyclamen, anemones and a multitude of seasonal plants. After he returned home at the end of the day, laden with samples, the two would record the findings in a series of exquisitely detailed botanical drawings, together with copious notes, which were then dispatched to the museum. It was not long before the couple made Larnaka, with its natural beauty and rich history, their home.

'How much history can a place claim?' Josef told his wife. 'Cyprus, my dearest Eva, is the birthplace of Aphrodite and also of the great philosopher Zeno of Citium, the founder of Stoicism who believed in the divine nature of the universe. He also claimed that in order for us to achieve true happiness we should live according to nature!'

'Then how wonderfully appropriate, Josef dear,' Eva replied, smiling broadly at her husband. 'Zeno would be most pleased since we are living by his rules.'

'And you know something else, Eva?' he continued fervently. 'Zeno was born just here where we are, in this insignificant little town of Larnaka – imagine that! Of course he travelled to Athens too and worked with the great philosophers of his time, but he was very patriotic and when they offered to make him a citizen of Athens he refused, for fear that he would appear unfaithful to his native land.'

'Well, my dear husband,' Eva replied, amused by his infectious enthusiasm, 'if Larnaka was good enough for Zeno of Citium, then it's good enough for us!'

Josef Linser was a happy man indeed; so long as he explored the hills and valleys, the mountains and plains of Cyprus, he was entirely content and asked for little else.

Once she had taken to their life on the island, Eva would only occasionally travel back to Vienna to visit her old mother. The journey was long and tedious and although she took young Franz with her, she missed Josef too much to stay away for long. After her mother died she no longer returned to her home city, unless it was with her husband and son. She, like Josef, was content to live on Aphrodite's island.

At first the Linsers were something of a curiosity to the local Greek and Turkish population of the town. But the island, which for centuries had been under the rule of the now waning Ottoman Empire, had recently changed hands from the Turks to the British, bringing a more multi-ethnic, multi-lingual population to Larnaka. The town's position as a port had always encouraged trade and move-ment; now it was becoming a cultural centre too and it was to Larnaka rather than to Nicosia, the capital, that the consuls of European countries were posted.

Eva's work and her young son kept her busy, but when the time came for Franz to attend the local elementary school she was left with more time than she knew what to do with. Conversing and forming friendships with the local women was not easy as Eva's Greek and Turkish were still in their infancy, but gradually, encouraged by Josef, she was introduced to other wives of European origin who spoke French and German like herself. One of these women was the wife of the newly appointed Bel-gian consul Hans Peeters.

Martha Peeters was a gregarious woman who, like Eva, found herself away from her native land and was thirsty for company. They met at an evening reception given by the Peeterses at the Belgian consulate to which the Linsers, along with other European residents and visitors, were invited.

'This is a perfect opportunity for you to meet some like-minded ladies,' Josef had said to Eva as they were getting ready for the occasion.

'I'm not so sure *how* like-minded they'll be,' she replied, slipping into her corset and offering him her back to be laced up. 'Exactly how many ladies do you think are going to be interested in the art of botanic illustration, Josef?'

'You never can tell, dearest,' he said and kissed her gently on the back of her neck. 'Perhaps you'll find you can communicate better with them than with Kyria Marika, the baker's wife?'

'Perhaps . . .' she replied, unconvinced. 'In any case I like Kyria Marika and the other women I've met here. For one, I'm learning Greek and Turkish from them,' she added, as she stepped into her evening dress, which had been kept wrapped up in tissue paper in the travelling trunk since their arrival. 'I have no idea why I'm taking this with me,' she'd told Josef when they were packing for Cyprus. 'I can't imagine I'll ever wear it but it's so pretty I'd just like to take it along anyhow.' Made of French lace in pale canary yellow, long enough to sweep the floor as she walked, the dress pinched tight at her waist with a small bustle at the back showing off her slender figure and ample bosom; now she was more than glad she had not parted with it.

'The local ladies are perfectly agreeable, Josef,' she continued while she adjusted her waistband, 'and at least they don't have airs and graces.' Eva intensely disliked what she considered the superficiality and snobbery of society gatherings, but she also recognized that of late all the spare time she had on her own had tipped into loneliness and she was in need of company.

'We shall see, shan't we?' she said finally, pulling on a pair of long satin gloves.

As it turned out Martha did have much in common with Eva, not least that she was down to earth, half Viennese, and a keen artist. The two women were soon to become good friends.

That evening Josef and Eva were picked up by a horse and carriage and were driven to the consulate residence situated in Larnaka's main street, overlooking the sea. Along with other streets in the town, this had recently been renamed by the British governor, who on his arrival proceeded to change many of the Greek names to English ones, and was now called 'The Strand'. Josef and Eva were irritated to see a rash of freshly painted street signs posted throughout the town, announcing such inappropriate names, in their opinion, as 'Victoria Street' or 'Disraeli Street'.

'Why do they have to go messing with the island's

heritage?' Josef had complained to Eva. '"Aphrodite" and "Zinon Street" are marvellous names and fitting for this place.'

Although The Strand was no distance from the Linsers' house and a journey that the couple would have gladly made by foot they decided for the occasion to indulge and take a cab. It was a warm spring night with a full moon hovering over the bay. From a distance the consulate, illuminated from every window, looked almost as if it was on fire. As the horse-drawn carriage drew closer, a string quartet by Mozart could be heard over the lapping of the waves on the shore and the buzz of conversation reached them, carried by the evening breeze.

As they entered the building, Martha, standing next to her husband to receive their guests, hastened to greet them.

'Welcome, Herr *und* Frau Linser,' she said, beaming as she shook their hands. 'I have heard about both of you and your work. Please, come in!'

'What charming people!' Josef told Eva at the end of the evening as they made their way home, on foot this time.

'Indeed they are!' Eva agreed. 'I do believe Martha Peeters and I could be friends,' she added, taking her husband's arm as they returned home along the promenade under the full moon.

*

'How much of the island have you seen?' Martha asked Eva one early summer's day as they sat drinking tea together in the salon of the consulate. The breeze from the open window smelled of the sea and Martha's Greek maid was busy laying out on the low ottoman coffee table some dishes of local pastries and sweets. Martha, a keen watercolourist, was interested in Eva's work and the two women had begun to meet regularly, either at Martha's elegant home or to stroll together along the promenade under the shade of their parasols. Even in late February the winter sun was strong enough to burn their pale northern European complexions.

'I've seen quite a bit,' Eva replied, reaching for her china teacup, 'though mainly in the open country when I sometimes accompanied Josef on his quest for plants. Apart from shepherds grazing their flocks, no one goes there. There are so many spectacular unspoiled places here that seem to be quite untouched.'

'You are very lucky to have been able to explore the land. I hear the mountains are very fertile, with many vineyards and olive groves. I should like to do some exploring myself and make some sketches of the country-side, but getting there is difficult. How did you travel?'

'Usually by mules and donkeys. It's quite fun if you don't mind the long trek and young Franz loved the donkey rides,' Eva enthused. 'We must take the children one day.'

'That would be marvellous, Eva. I shall talk to Hans and organize it,' Martha decided, sure that her two young sons would be delighted by the adventure.

'There are many stories and legends that would amuse the children,' Eva continued. 'We came across a place once, called *Cape de Gatto*. Apparently its name came from a breed of wildcats which still inhabit the area. They're said to be descendants of cats imported by the monks of the Monastery of St Nikola in order to kill the poisonous snakes that infested the island in the Middle Ages. What do you think of that?'

'How wonderful!' Martha applauded the story. 'Hans tells me there are still poisonous snakes on the island,' she added, 'but one just has to be careful . . .'

Martha, like Eva, had an adventurous spirit and was determined that her stay on the island was not going to be spent sitting in her drawing room hosting ladies' tea parties.

'I have heard of a village called Lefkara,' Martha told Eva conspiratorially as she leaned across to offer her friend one more *loukumi*, a Greek variation on Turkish delight, before helping herself to another. Filled with almonds and saturated with the essence of rose water and sugar they were, like so many other local delicacies, irresistible; they were her weakness and downfall though she was aware of the effect on her silhouette. Unlike tall and slender Eva, Martha was short and full-bodied and a woman who enjoyed the pleasures of life.

'I have been told that the village of Lefkara is a marvel of artistry!' she continued. 'The local women make the most splendid embroideries and lace, and the men are master silversmiths.'

'Where is it?' Eva asked, her curiosity aroused.

'It's up in the hills,' Martha replied eagerly, 'and I gather it has a long history of craftsmanship. According to legend, Leonardo da Vinci himself visited the village during the Venetian occupation of Cyprus, and he took back with him a lace cloth for the main altar of the Duomo di Milano. They say it's still on display there today . . . I think this place deserves a visit, don't you agree?'

No sooner had they discussed it than the two women started to plan their trip. Of course it would have to be made over several days, as the journey alone would take an entire day. Eva and Martha organized their trip to the last detail, deciding to take the children with them because, as they explained to their surprised menfolk, 'it will be very educational'. With them also came an interpreter, two servants and, on the insistence of Hans, a consulate employee.

The journey towards the hills, which started at dawn, was long and dusty but also picturesque. The wild rocky terrain, which at times dropped into deep ravines, was covered in shrubs and bushes such as sage – which the locals called mountain tea – thyme and capers, all perfect for the goats they saw, grazing precariously on the edge of the hills, much to the children's amusement. The women also noticed how the rather barren flatland they were leaving behind was changing with the climb, and observed that wherever there was moisture, the ground produced a profusion of vegetation with mimosa, verbena and oleander lining much of the way.

It was dusk by the time the party arrived and the surrounding mountains were already cloaked with the purple of the setting sun. Entering the village, they found the inhabitants, women, children and men, having been previously informed of the party's visit, lining up by the side of the road to see them. They stood under fig trees and olive trees, watching silently as the procession of six *xeni* on mules, donkeys and horses passed noisily in a cloud of dust. The villagers followed the procession to the square, which was decorated for the occasion with the Austrian and Belgian flags. They were ceremonially met by the *mouktar*, the mayor, and a selection of distinguished villagers both Greek and Turkish, who then escorted the party to the inn where they would be staying for the duration. It soon became apparent that a feast had been prepared in their honour, and although they were exhausted from their journey they felt obliged to accept for fear of giving offence.

'On no account should we insult them by refusing this honour,' Martha said quietly to Eva, while they were being shown to their rooms by the *mouktar*'s wife and daughter. 'Let's make sure the children are taken care of, and then we can join them.'

The truth was that while Martha was ready for a feast after their long journey with only short stops for refreshments on the way, Eva was longing for her bed.

She agreed reluctantly – 'Everyone is being so kind' – and despite her fatigue she washed her face, brushed off the dust and joined the assembled company, soon to be revived by a glass of *Commandaria*, the local fortified sweet wine.

'Apparently,' the interpreter explained, 'this wine was originally made on the island by the Knights of St John during the time of the Crusaders, and is now world famous.'

'Well, I have rarely tasted anything so delicious,' Martha exclaimed, raising her glass for a toast. 'I don't think its fame has reached Belgium yet but I will make sure it soon does!'

They were seated at a long table covered with an exquisite cream linen tablecloth made by the local women in the tradition of the lace-making of Lefkara. The embroidered motif, as the interpreter explained, was the celebrated 'Leonardo Cross', which da Vinci himself designed and gifted to the village during his legendary visit. The cross became one of the most renowned motifs and continued to be used by the local women. On either side of the ladies sat the Greek chief of police and the Turkish *mouktar*, both dressed in the traditional attire, while the interpreter sat opposite them with the rest of the party on either side of him. No other women were present. They, as custom required, were all in the kitchen cooking and serving the food, which arrived at the table at intervals, several dishes at a time, allowing the guests to savour them at their ease.

Although most of the food Martha and Eva were served was to their liking, they hesitated when a platter arrived at the table displaying the bodies of a dozen or so tiny birds. At the sight of them the interpreter's eyes lit up with pleasure as he explained enthusiastically that in Greek the dish was called *ambelopoulia*, literarily translated as 'vine-birds', also known to foreigners as *beccafico*, which were considered one of the island's great gastronomic treats. The little birds, he continued, were only found on the island at a certain time of the year during their migration.

'As soon as they are captured,' he told them, 'these delicious little fat morsels are preserved in vinegar or in wine, to protect their delicate taste and be enjoyed all the year round.'

Served whole on her plate, the bird, no larger than a small egg, appalled Eva, who was a tender-hearted nature lover. Martha, on the other hand, was willing to try them.

'They are quite delicious, dear,' she told her friend, after she was shown the correct way to eat them. She had been trying to dissect the bird delicately with her knife and fork, until she was instructed amid much laughter and joviality that the bird should be eaten in a single mouthful. But even Martha found crunching on the bird's little bones somewhat unsavoury.

The rest of the trip was as smooth and calm as the Cypriot seashores, with daily visits to the village silversmiths and the lace-makers, while the children were kept entertained by local boys and girls.

The women of the village carried out their work in their homes and there was no household without at least one member working with the lace. As it was explained to Eva and Martha, the craft was passed down from mother to daughter and the same was true with the silversmiths, from father to son. Everyone did their best to explain and demonstrate their craft, and for years to come, the people of Lefkara talked about the nice foreign ladies who showed so much interest in their village.

For their part, Eva and Martha left Lefkara with their heads full of ideas and schemes. Martha vowed to set up a little studio in the consulate building where she would continue her watercolours. Meanwhile Eva, having purchased quantities of linen and silk thread, had made up her mind to begin embroidering the minute she returned to Larnaka.

'I fancy that some of my botanic illustrations could easily be transferred to cloth with needlework,' she told Martha when the idea first came to her.

'What an excellent idea, Eva dear,' Martha replied. 'I look forward to seeing your handiwork.'

Tentatively at first, Eva started to transfer some of her drawings onto linen, then to embroider them for cushions and pillowcases, practising her stitching and techniques. The first piece she made, once she considered herself skilled enough, was a gift for Martha. She embroidered a cover for a footrest, which she had mounted onto a little stool made of rosewood by a local carpenter. She took weeks to decide on the design, anxious to give her friend something special, something of meaning, something that, when their stay at the consulate was over and Martha and her family left Cyprus, would remind her of the island and their time together.

She picked the motif with care, concluding that the most appropriate flower for the purpose was the violet. She had illustrated violets on many occasions, both in Austria and Cyprus, but on her arrival in Larnaka Eva had learned that the violet was considered by the towns-people as their emblem, growing as it did in abundance both in gardens and in the wild. Eva also learned that each of the four main towns on the island had a flower allocated to it. These, it was explained to her, were chosen according to the climatic conditions of each town. The rose was the symbol of Nicosia, the jasmine was Famagusta's, for Kyrinia it was the geranium, and Pafos the *fouli*, which she found out was an aromatic white flower much resembling a gardenia.

For the footstool, Eva chose to show the violets in little posies surrounded by their rich green leaves, which intensified the colour of the flower in a horizontal repeat pattern.

'What I love about violets,' she told Josef, 'is that they are such a humble and discreet flower. They go unnoticed unless you look down to the ground for them.'

'You are so right, my dear,' he agreed. 'You usually only know they are there by their heady aroma, which announces their presence before you've even seen them.'

A few days after Eva presented her friend with the footstool, Martha came to pay her a visit accompanied by two of her male servants holding a large horizontal painting wrapped in a cotton sheet.

'We must have had the same thought,' Martha told her as the men placed the painting carefully against the wall. 'I too wanted you to have a memento from our marvellous trip to Lefkara,' she said, unveiling it.

The painting Martha presented to Eva was a humorous representation of the banquet the village had hosted for them on their first night. The two ladies sitting in the centre were flanked by the village dignitaries, while the table covered in splendid Lefkara lace was full of delicious morsels including the small vine-birds.

The cherished picture hung in the Linser dining room for generations.

The trip to Lefkara fired up both women's appetite for exploration. They had heard much about the numerous monasteries and Byzantine churches dotted around the island, which contained fine frescoes and exquisite icons. However, most of these were situated deep in the Troodos Mountains, far too remote and difficult to access.

But one such monastery was situated in the capital, Nicosia. The great Kykkos Monastery, they were informed, which was buried deep in the Troodos forests, also maintained an annex in Nicosia, which the Holy Abbot used as his residence. Martha also learned from her husband that part of the monastery was now being occupied by the British administration as its temporary headquarters, and that if they so wished, their party would be accommodated as guests by the colonel during their stay. Since Nicosia was relatively accessible from Larnaka it was decided that that would be the destination for their next expedition, but without the children this time.

'I gather that apart from the monastery, Nicosia offers much to be seen including other churches and a decent bazaar,' Martha told Eva.

The prospect of exploring a larger city *and* a bazaar, with the possibility of finding exotic treasures to buy, was thrilling.

'We could do some shopping while we're there, since the children won't be with us,' Martha enthused. 'I have been in search of a Turkish carpet since I arrived. I'm always looking for fine things to take back to Belgium when we leave the island.'

'Perhaps I could buy some more silk thread and fabric.' Eva clapped her hands with joy at the prospect.

The journey to Nicosia, which they made on horseback this time, with mules to carry their luggage, started early in the morning accompanied by almost the same entourage as on their previous trip.

'Surely a representative from the consulate is unnecessary this time,' Martha protested to her husband, wanting to keep their number to a minimum. 'We will be met by the British Commissioner when we arrive and I am quite sure the colonel will look after us well enough.'

Martha always had a way of convincing her husband and so on a fragrant early May morning the two friends set off with two servants, a local Greek coachman and the interpreter to explore the sights of Nicosia and surrounding area. The journey proved to be a much less dramatic or scenic affair than the ride up the hills to Lefkara a few months earlier. They had hoped to see flowers and lush vegetation as before, but the road to the capital lay mainly on the flat, crossing arid sunburnt plains between stony hills. Apart from small cornfields, some sorry-looking vineyards, and a few gardens in the villages they passed through, they saw hardly a trace of cultivation. They rode for many hours on difficult roads, sometimes encountering convoys of heavily laden camels and donkeys transporting goods. They stopped twice at village inns for refreshments before finally arriving on the outskirts of Nicosia just as dusk was falling. The city, surrounded by a high Venetian wall, gleamed in the bright moonlight.

'It looks as if it has just been built.' Eva gazed at the fort in awe. 'One can hardly believe it is hundreds of years old.'

'The legacy of the Venetians yet again, my dear,' Martha told her.

The wall had three magnificent gates as entrances into the city, but to their dismay they discovered that due to their late arrival they had all been locked up for the night.

'The Commissioner is expecting us,' Martha said, worry evident in her voice but maintaining her composure. 'Surely someone will come and open for us?'

'Perhaps we should have left earlier . . .' Eva added, unable to hide her concern.

Lucky for them it didn't take too much shouting,

pounding and banging for the Turkish night keeper to appear, lantern and keys in hand, to let the latecomers in.

Once they entered, finding their way to their destination proved to be quite a different matter – and something of an ordeal as the city appeared to be deserted on account of the late hour. The moon shone brightly over the rooftops, illuminating a confusion of architectural styles, Greek, Turkish and Venetian, as well as mud houses, minarets and churches all jumbled up together.

'Oh Martha, look how exotic it all appears under the night sky,' Eva exclaimed. 'It's quite enchanting! The night becomes this city.'

Lost in a labyrinth of narrow streets they wandered for what seemed like forever until they came upon a *kafeneon*, with an adjoining inn. The interpreter went in search of someone while the coachman blankly refused to move any further and proceeded to unharness the horses, insisting they should spend the night there to let the animals rest.

On his return the interpreter reassured them that the monastery was five minutes away and before too long they were on their way again. After an hour, they realized that perhaps he had been a little liberal with the truth about the exact distance of the location, but by then Martha and Eva were so exhausted they had no breath for complaint.

On arrival they were treated to a warm welcome by

the colonel and his officers, and promptly shown into one of the monastery cells which the officers and monks alike had gone to great lengths to prepare for their stay, complete with a jug full of freshly cut roses from the monastery's garden.

'I'm sure I have never smelled such delicious fragrance before,' Eva said as the heady aroma hit them on entering the room.

'As much as I am rather hungry,' Martha said to Eva feeling exhausted as they settled into their room, 'I am very glad there is no banquet awaiting us.'

Nevertheless a simple welcome dinner, with no local culinary surprises to deal with, had been prepared for them in the officers' mess before they all finally took to their beds.

The next morning upon waking up, Eva and Martha discovered a curious climatic phenomenon: they both woke feeling chilled to their bones despite the several blankets they had been supplied with. Apparently, in Nicosia during the night the temperature plummets to many degrees lower than what they were used to by the coast.

'I must say,' Martha told Eva, 'I haven't felt this cold since I was home in Brussels. I do hope it warms up.'

Of course by mid-morning the temperature rose and they were plunged into the usual Cypriot heatwave. The two friends couldn't decide what was worse.

'We are either burning or freezing,' Eva observed.

'I will have to ask for more blankets tonight,' Martha complained, 'or I shall come down with influenza for sure.'

After breakfast the two friends were informed that the Holy Abbot wanted to meet with them, so they strolled around the grounds of the monastery with the colonel while waiting to be received in his apartments.

'His Holiness resides partly here, and partly in the main monastery in the mountains,' the colonel explained, adding that were it not for his urgent duties and the emergency situation that seemed to prevail in the capital at this time, he would have liked to join them.

'Unfortunately there is much to do,' he went on. 'There is an epidemic of typhoid fever on the island at the moment and some of our soldiers have come down with it. It is under control but it is worrying nevertheless. What about Larnaka? What is the situation there?' he enquired.

'We haven't been aware of it,' Martha replied, looking alarmed.

'No need for concern,' the colonel reassured them, sensing their unease. 'We only have one corporal unwell here at the moment and he is being looked after in isolation.'

The truth was that the typhoid fever had been raging for a while among the British troops and not just in Nicosia. Unaccustomed to the island's climate the men were ill-equipped to deal with the extreme heat and humidity, and the lack of adequate hygiene and medication caused many of them to succumb to the illness.

'The Abbot is looking forward to meeting you both,' the Colonel said, changing the subject, not wanting to worry his guests further. 'So while you wait I suggest you take a walk in the garden until he is ready.'

As Eva had previously learned, Nicosia was truly the city of the rose and May was the month the flower colonized every garden. Roses of all types grew in abundance everywhere, their pungent aroma almost overpowering. The monks who tended the garden with care also produced great quantities of rose water from their crop, which they used in cooking and religious ceremonies, as is the custom in the Greek Orthodox Church. Bees and butterflies alike inhabited the flowerbeds where a variety of herbs, vegetables and flowers – jasmine, verbena and oleander – also waited to be pollinated.

'What a delightful garden, Martha dear,' Eva told her friend as she bent down to inhale the fragrance of yet another variety of rose. 'So much colour, so much beauty! This garden satisfies almost all my senses. Sight, smell, touch, and all these bees are music to my ears . . .'

'Surely you mean *all* our senses,' Martha said, giving her friend a broad smile. 'What about taste?'

'Of course! How could I forget all those mouth-watering desserts saturated with rose water, and I believe there is a delicious cordial too,' Eva said cheerfully as she plucked a small rose to pin on her dress.

The Abbot received the ladies in person in his private apartments. The view from his balcony to the north was spectacular, and as their eyes stretched across the city and beyond, Nicosia looked as charming as it had under the stars the night before. Domes of Greek Orthodox churches, minarets and mosques rose towards a cloudless blue sky against a backdrop of the Pentadactylon mountain range.

'The name of this rocky mountain,' the interpreter explained, 'translates as "Five Fingers". It derives from the Byzantine legend of the giant hero Digenis Akritas, who apparently gripped the mountain to get out of the sea when he came to free our island from her Saracen invaders, and by doing so left his handprint on the peak.'

'What a splendid story!' Martha exclaimed. 'This really is the land of legends!'

Through their interpreter the Abbot spoke to the two friends at length, explaining with great vigour about the history of the monastery and the Orthodox Church while some of his attendant priests entertained them with sweet Turkish coffee, ice-cold water and *rose-dessert*. The so-called 'dessert of the spoon' or *glygo*, which in Greek simply means 'sweet', was made from the most fragrant rose petals from the monastery garden. Each lady was served a portion on a tiny delicate glass dish laid onto a silver filigree teaspoon.

'*Glygo*,' the translator explained, 'is the most traditional Cypriot offering to guests, and this particular one is made by the monks when the roses are in season and then preserved in syrup to be enjoyed all year round.'

Martha and Eva knew that any number of fruits such as figs, cherries, walnuts, young apples and some citrus fruits could be preserved this way and had, on many occasions, sampled their delights. However, never before had they been served rose petals this way and it was an exotic novelty for their taste buds and a sweet revelation to them both.

After a short tour around the grounds and church, the ladies were then taken on horseback to visit the interior of the city and the bazaar. The *gynegopazaaro*, 'women's bazaar', was yet another discovery for them both. They were informed that the bazaar, which took place once a week, had only female traders and shoppers, catering exclusively to women, their homes and their families, as opposed to the men's bazaar, which traded in heavy goods and merchandise.

'This is where I leave you ladies,' the interpreter said, stopping in front of a cloister that led to the market and pointing at a coffee shop across the road. 'I shall be waiting for you there while you shop at your leisure.'

In what seemed like no time at all Martha and Eva

found themselves transported from the monastery's spiritual world to a world of earthly goods. Stalls selling all kinds of merchandise, from vegetables and fruit to spices and herbs, small livestock and poultry, to cloth, trinkets and tapestries. Exotic aromas hovered in the air and women of all ages were cooking, laughing and talking animatedly to each other in both Greek and Turkish.

Exquisite Turkish rugs were laid out on the ground to be viewed while the vendors called out to them to come and buy. At some point, Eva, lost in a sea of colour and noise, recognized a stall-holder selling lace and embroidery from Lefkara, and in the absence of their male translator she tried her best to communicate with the woman in what little Greek she possessed. No language was needed. The woman recognized Eva and with great enthusiasm gifted her a small piece of embroidery, upon which Eva returned the favour and bought several more, plus yards of cloth, and silk-thread in all shades for her own use on her return to Larnaka.

By the time the two friends arrived back at the monastery the sun was ready to set and they were both quite fatigued. Martha especially was feeling rather low, complaining of a headache, and took to her bed refusing any supper.

'I knew that last night's chill would affect me so,' she told Eva as she lay down with a cold compress on her forehead. 'I shall be fine after a good night's sleep, providing I keep myself warm.'

'We have done rather a lot for one day, dear; you might feel better after a little food, perhaps?' Eva said, worried.

'I am not in the least bit hungry,' Martha replied, letting out a big sigh and closing her eyes. Eva had never known her friend to refuse dinner and her worry deepened. She, on the other hand, felt rather exhilarated and energized by their adventure and in contrast to Martha was ready to join the colonel in the mess for a little supper.

The next morning Martha's headache seemed to have worsened and she'd also developed a mild fever, so the English doctor was sent for. Discreetly and without wanting to cause alarm, he suggested that perhaps 'if lady Martha was coming down with influenza it would be a good idea to cut their journey short and go home'.

A few days after their return to Larnaka it was established that Martha wasn't in fact suffering from influenza but had contracted what the local doctor described as a 'mild form' of typhoid. Martha's husband, feeling rather mistrustful of the diagnosis, questioned whether a person could in fact contract a 'mild form' of typhoid. He knew well enough that typhoid was a serious ailment so without delay he decided that before her condition worsened

Martha must return to Belgium, where she would be treated with the correct medications.

Martha's departure was a hard blow to Eva. She was distressed about her friend's health and worried that she might not return if she did not recover well. They had become so close and shared so many interests and they had both looked forward to more adventures together. She would miss Martha more than she could say.

'Perhaps if you get well quickly you might come back,' Eva told her as they made their farewells. 'Everyone will miss you so, not to mention myself, dear friend.'

'I must get well, and it is better to be away from everyone,' Martha replied giving Eva a weary smile. 'This wretched illness is quite contagious and I have to protect the boys. You too, my friend – please keep your distance from me.' Eva wasn't too worried, she knew that contamination occurs through poor hygiene and realized her unlucky friend had very possibly been infected through drinking water during their journey. 'As soon as I am better I will either return, or send for the children,' she explained.

Martha's husband and sons were to remain on the island until she recovered, which they all believed would not take too long with the right medical care in Belgium.

One of the items that Martha requested to be shipped back with her when she left was the footstool that Eva had made for her.

'I would like to have it with me,' she told her friend, 'and while I convalesce I shall rest my feet on it and remember you and our time together in Cyprus.'

Although Martha eventually regained her health, her recovery was slow, and left her very weak, by which time her husband decided to leave his post at the consulate and return to Belgium with their boys in order to be with her.

Without Martha's friendship Eva once again found herself lonely; not only had she lost her companion, but also any hope of further joint adventures. Apart from her work with Josef in the evenings, she decided to occupy her time with embroidery and once in a while took tea with some of the circles she had been introduced to by Martha. Invariably one or other guest who admired her needlework would ask if Eva could make something for her and soon she found that the footstool she had made for her friend was the first of many embroideries she went on to make during that time. Her needlework had become the topic of conversation in many elegant salons; before long the word spread and commissions came in from households unknown to her, not only from Larnaka but from Nicosia and Limassol too, and they paid handsomely for one of her creations.

Eva realized that if she was to continue accepting so many commissions, creating bedspreads, pillowcases and cushions, she had to change the way she worked. Laborious needlework was not the way to continue. She had to find another method of transferring her botanic illustrations onto fabric.

What had started as a hobby gradually progressed to silkscreens and prints and eventually into a successful textile business, which held something of a monopoly on the island. Before long no elegant home was complete without some kind of printed 'Linser Textiles' piece. Eva's pleasant pastime had turned into a profit-making concern.

Once Josef realized how passionate his wife was about her new venture he proved to be a great help, and together they started to put their extensive knowledge of the island's flora to a different use. The couple was now discovering that some of the local vegetation, which they had identified over the years, could also be used to extract natural fabric dyes.

'I love textile printing as much as I love doing my botanic illustrations,' Eva told her husband once she started printing from a makeshift shed in their back yard, 'because it combines both activities – drawing and working with cloth.'

There had been moments of hilarity for her husband and young son when Eva embarked on her experiment with printing textiles. Mixing dyes and making woodcuts for the purpose proved to be a far messier business than embroidery. But Eva came from a scientific background and a little mess would not deter her.

'I have placed a large bucket in the latrine,' she announced one day to Josef, as he was setting off on one of his expeditions. 'When you are in the house, I would like you and Franz to make sure you urinate in it please,' she continued in a matter-of-fact tone.

'And exactly for what purpose would you like us to do this, Eva dear?' he asked, his face a picture of amusement and disbelief.

'Believe me, Josef, I have thought about it and it's the only way to do it—' she started to explain.

'And *what* exactly is this "it"?' Josef interrupted, unable to contain his laughter.

'If you would let me speak, please, I can explain,' she said with irritation. 'You might not know this, Josef, but I have discovered that urine is an essential part of the print-making process because natural dyes like the ones I am using will leak out of the cloth if they're not fixed with an astringent first.' She blurted this out in one long sentence, trying to ignore his mocking expression.

'Are you sure you've got the facts correctly, dear?' Josef replied, hardly concealing his mirth, yet not wanting to offend his already vexed wife.

'As you know,' Eva continued, ignoring Josef's question, 'the most natural way to obtain astringent is from urine, and apparently men's urine is the most effective for this purpose, so will you two help me out please?'

The Linsers' commission from the Natural History Museum of Vienna would soon come to an end, and the couple had to make some serious decisions about whether to remain on the island or to set sail for home.

'I have grown to love Cyprus more than I ever imagined. If you feel the same, dearest, why don't we stay?' Josef mused to Eva during one of their discussions about the future. 'I can help you with the textiles and make our permanent home here.'

And that is how Eva and Josef Linser came to adopt Cyprus as their own land; to build a fine family house that would accommodate the coming generations, and to establish the Linser Textiles company whose name became synonymous with elegance, lasting more than half a century.

6

First as a child, and then as a young adult, Eva's son Franz took a keen interest in his mother's burgeoning business. When he was old enough to take an active part in the family enterprise he travelled to Egypt, Italy and France in order to buy cottons, silks and dyes. It was on one of those trips to Sicily just before the outbreak of the First World War that he met Ernestina, a pious young woman, the daughter of a silk merchant, and fell in love.

Franz brought his sweetheart to Cyprus with her father's blessing and married her in Larnaka one autumn day in 1915 when the chrysanthemums were in bloom and the pomegranates were ripe for picking. The ceremony was held at the Catholic church and Europeans, Greeks and Turks alike were invited. The celebrations lasted three days and three nights in the customary tradition of the island. The newly built family home was ablaze with music, food and dancing and everyone talked for years to come about the feast that Josef Linser gave for his only son in the style of a Cypriot *panegyri*, a fiesta.

When a year later Ernestina gave birth to Olga, a

green-eyed, raven-haired baby girl, the Linser clan knew that the gods had truly blessed them.

By the time his daughter Olga was born Franz had taken over from his mother and father and was running a small textile factory on the outskirts of town.

Josef by then had loosened his ties with the textiles enterprise and left Eva and Franz to run the family business, allowing him to indulge in his favourite pastimes of archaeology and spending time with his precious granddaughter.

During those years of combing the wild hillsides for plants he had come across numerous apparently insignificant remnants of unexplored antiquity. He would often arrive home with broken fragments of ancient pottery, sometimes even entire terracotta vases and pots, their colours and decorations still intact.

'This is exquisite,' Eva said thoughtfully, examining yet another of Josef's finds; this time a small terracotta bowl almost intact, painted with dancing figures of young maidens with floral garlands. 'Surely these need to be reported to the authorities,' she said anxiously. 'They belong to a museum, not in our home . . .'

Her husband shrugged and spread his hands. 'I entirely agree. But who does one report it to when there appears to be no organized body and no one seems to care?'

The couple had arrived on the island during a time of political and cultural change after a long period of administrative inertia. The ancient treasures lay ignored, buried beneath the earth and of no concern to anyone. The newly established British rule had not yet involved itself with the prohibition of unauthorized excavations and findings. Anyone inclined to do so was free to dig and keep whatever antiquities they found, either for themselves or for trade, no permission required.

When Josef's interest in these ancient artefacts was aroused, as he explored the countryside he used the same methods as he did for his botanical finds, recording and categorizing the antiquities he came across in much the same way as he did for the plants.

'There might come a time when these treasures can be exhibited in a museum for all to see,' he told Eva half apologetically. He was aware that what he was doing was a form of looting. A large number of tombs had already been opened in the past by local people hunting for precious materials, and later on by Europeans living and visiting the island who would sell the antiquities to overseas collectors.

'You are a true custodian,' Eva would comfort him, sensing his guilt. 'You are not like others; you are doing this not for gain but for conservation.'

'If you think so, dear,' Josef replied, stroking little Olga's hair as she sat on his knee. 'It seems that when Franz was born I was never present,' he told Eva regretfully.

'You were always busy, dear,' she replied. 'You had to earn a living for the three of us then.'

'Yes, but at what cost? The years have flown by in the sea breeze and our son is now a man.'

'Yes, but look what he has given us!' Eva smiled lovingly as Josef bounced his granddaughter on his knees.

From a very young age Olga could tell the difference between poplin and linen, cotton and silk, or which plants were most suitable to produce the most vibrant fabric dyes. She was raised in a hothouse of flowers and textiles. Plants were brought into the house in profusion in order to be illustrated by her grandmother and father, and then transferred in pattern form onto cloth.

Eva had raised two generations of Linsers with flowers and textiles in their blood.

Olga was partly educated at home by her mother and grandparents, and partly by the Catholic nuns of the Terra Santa School. She was a bright, spirited child, encouraged by her father to develop her interests and use her talents and taught, above all, that she was equal to any boy.

'Never let anyone hold you back, my girl,' he told her. 'This is the twentieth century and when the time comes you can run this business as well as any man!' Her mother had a different opinion. Religion was her motivating force and she wished for nothing more than for her child to be as devoted as she was to the Virgin Mary. However, Olga was her father's daughter and she was determined that the world was hers to explore and conquer. When she was deemed old enough, around the age of eighteen, she started to accompany her father on his business trips to learn the ways of the textile industry. Franz believed that together, they would take Linser Textiles to new heights and then when he could no longer continue, she would take over from him.

'Who is going to marry her if she behaves like a man?' Ernestina protested to her husband. 'She is a daughter, not a son, Franz – business is not for her. Your daughter would do better to learn about being a wife and running a home.'

'She is as capable as any son, and cleverer than most men,' Franz argued.

'We are a good family and she has a good dowry and it would be better if you found her a suitable match instead of filling her head with ideas of business.' Ernestina never stopped complaining.

But Olga didn't need, or *want* anyone to find her a husband. She was determined she would find him herself and marry for love. Her mother might have been a God-fearing conformist but her papa had the metropolitan modern ways in his upbringing; his parents had infused his childhood with the spirit of adventure and he in turn had passed it on to his daughter.

*

Olga met Ivan, a dashing Hungarian violinist, during a masquerade ball at the Italian consulate on a chilly March night during the carnival celebrations. She was dressed as Mata Hari, and he as the Count of Monte Cristo.

She was immediately captivated. Tall, broad-shouldered, with a mass of dark hair, he looked to her the embodiment of manliness. His eyes flashed through his black eye-mask and his even teeth gleamed as he smiled at her.

He was equally spellbound and made his advance the minute he spotted her across the room, sweeping her onto the dance floor, certain that he'd never seen a more exotic creature than this Mata Hari.

Holding her in his arms, his tight grip pulling her closer, he spun her dizzily to the strains of a waltz before sweeping her out to the cool air of the veranda. His breath on her neck burned with an intensity that made her head swirl, and when he bent down to kiss her, she gave her full lips willingly. Olga had been waiting impatiently for the thrill of sexual desire to visit her. That night she knew it had finally arrived: Aphrodite's precocious love child had aimed his arrow well, piercing her with ease straight through the heart.

The courtship was short, and before the month was out, Ivan asked Olga to marry him.

'I am in love, Papa,' she told her father once she had made up her mind to accept.

'I just want you to be sure he is the man for you,' he

said with caution at the speed of the romance. 'How much do we know about him, Olga *mou*?'

'I feel as if I've known him all my life, Papa,' she replied in all her youthful passion.

As much as it pleased Franz that his daughter had made her own marriage choice, he would have preferred a more solvent son-in-law.

Ivan had come to Larnaka a few years earlier with the visiting Hungarian National Orchestra to perform at the consulate, and as so many others had done before him, he found the island so agreeable he settled there. He joined the local orchestra and scratched a living by teaching music to the children of rich Europeans and Greeks.

'I am sure he is the one, Papa,' Olga told her father. 'I know he's not rich but he is an artist, and he makes me laugh – I feel so alive when I'm with him!'

Franz could deny nothing to the 'flower of his life', as he referred to his daughter, and once again the Linser house was to hold a wedding celebration that would linger in local memory for years to come.

Ivan was welcomed into the family home and as her mother and father had done before her, Olga continued living there with her new husband. Grandfather Josef lived long enough to see his dream come true: three generations under the same roof of the house he had built with so much love.

A few months after Olga's marriage, Josef insisted on

a visit to the Temple of Apollo and the ancient city of Kourion in the south-west of the island. It had not long been excavated and was attracting much attention from scholars and amateur archaeologists like himself. Although by now automobiles had been introduced to the island, such a journey had to be made on a mule or horseback and would be long and hazardous for him to undertake at his age. The ancient city, built on top of a rocky outcrop some hundred metres high, had tombs cut out of it, with others honeycombing the surrounding hills. The journey from Larnaka would take several days and even though, by then, Josef had engaged a Cypriot companion for help on his expeditions, Eva was extremely anxious.

'You are an old man, Josef – you can't behave as if you're still in your prime,' she scolded him.

'You don't understand, my dear. This is no ordinary trip for me – this is a pilgrimage. As you know I am not a religious man, and this will be the closest I will get to a holy shrine. It is something I need to do before I die.'

And so that is what Josef Linser did. He ended his days high up on a hill that rose out of the sea to brood dramatically over a bay, surrounded by ancient ruins and tombs, a stone's throw away from the birthplace of the goddess of love, Aphrodite.

Josef died as he had lived, in the open air on his beloved Cyprus, an island chosen by the gods, straddling the easternmost waters of the Mediterranean. He stood at the summit of the acropolis of Kourion, and feasted his eyes as the ancients had done millennia before on a vista that literally took his breath away. He thanked the gods for his good fortune at having lived and worked in this marvellous land, took a deep breath and perished.

His death was a hard blow to them all, not least to Eva, who had imagined her husband was going to live forever, or at least outlive her, and could not imagine life without him.

They buried him in the Catholic cemetery in Larnaka; on his tombstone was a quote by Zeno of Citium, Josef's favourite philosopher, who according to legend had died much the same way, by holding his breath. The inscription read: *'Man conquers the world by conquering himself.'*

Not long afterwards, Eva followed her husband and died peacefully in her sleep.

Olga loved being married. Sensual and free-spirited, she relished the fact that now she could be made love to whenever she desired. Her previous flirtations with young men had been so furtive, so cautious. She had always wanted more but she had to play by the rules, had to be the chaste young woman. *Why can I not kiss a boy if I want to?* she asked herself, having no one else to ask. As an only child with no sister to discuss these matters with, and knowing that any girl with whom she was friendly wouldn't entertain the idea of talking about such things, Olga had to rely on her own conclusions. Society didn't tolerate strong-minded women and the injustice of the patriarchal world infuriated her. Now, as a married woman, she was finally sexually liberated and empowered.

Ivan could hardly believe his good fortune. The union with Olga and the Linser family surpassed all his expectations. He had married into one of the wealthiest and most elegant families in Larnaka, and had a beautiful, clever and sensual wife. Yet there were times, Ivan thought, that perhaps Olga was too clever, too physical, too strong, too beautiful.

The birth of their first daughter was an early obstacle in their marriage. Anita was born prematurely after a particularly difficult pregnancy. Olga insisted on working through most of it, even if her father was determined to keep her at bay.

'You have a duty to take care of yourself and the baby, my girl,' her mother had complained. 'You have a father *and* a husband to help you . . . *not that your husband is much use,*' she'd muttered under her breath.

Olga's pregnant body repelled Ivan. She was no longer his. He couldn't bear the sight of her swollen belly, or to touch her. She was bereft. Gone were the sensual kisses, the caresses and nights of passion. After the first heady months of marriage, when their intellectual differences had become more apparent it was their physical attraction that kept their union alive.

'You are insatiable, darling,' Ivan had laughed, making light of his irritation with her demands. 'A man can only muster so much sexual energy – we need to have a rest sometimes!'

'But you are no ordinary man, darling, you're a tiger,' she'd purr and kiss him full on the mouth, as they'd kissed when newly wed, hoping to entice him.

Once the baby was born and Olga's body resumed its former beauty, Ivan's attentions towards her increased and some of their old attraction for each other was restored.

However, the final decline in their marriage came with Olga's second pregnancy. Ivan was increasingly absent from the home and the family and indisposed to spending time with Olga, and would return from his nocturnal adventures once the household was asleep.

After Olga gave birth to Sonia, her second baby girl, and had once again regained her figure – which childbirth seemed to enhance, making it more ripe, more womanly than the young body of their courtship – Ivan was nowhere to be seen. He was glad to reap the many benefits of marriage into the Linser clan – money, family and status – while contributing nothing in return.

It wasn't long before Olga reacted. His increasing absences, blatant lies and excuses of visits to his bridge club, which she knew were really visits to the cabarets and gambling dives of town, were becoming intolerable.

'Where does he go every night?' her mother would ask Franz. 'He is a family man, not a bachelor, he has responsibilities; how can she put up with it? You should speak to him,' Ernestina complained. 'And what's more, you should never have let our daughter marry him. He was never worthy of her!' Of course Franz wouldn't dream of doing any such thing without Olga's permission. He knew his daughter would deal with it in her own way and for her sake he tried hard to conceal his disappointment in his son-in-law.

Olga was furious but said nothing. She knew of the gossip and whispering around town but she kept her dignity and waited for the right moment.

Ivan had now virtually given up his former work, and was spending his time and wife's family fortune recklessly gambling and drinking.

'I highly recommend marrying into money,' he bragged to his drinking buddies, stuffing a handful of notes into a belly dancer's cleavage while she shook her bejewelled breasts in his face.

One of Ivan's favourite dives was a newly opened cabaret/brothel reputed to have the most scantily dressed dancing girls on the island, and a secret room where men could smoke a hashish-infused *nargile*.

One of those half-naked women was a dancer called Sotiria, whose eyes fell on Ivan the minute she saw him.

That dive soon became his second home, and he spent night after night in the company of Sotiria.

'You are my master and I'm your slave,' she would whisper in his ear, topping up his *nargile* with hashish as he lay in a stupor on the Turkish divan smoking and caressing her naked body next to his. What Ivan couldn't do with his beautiful clever wife, he was now more than willing and able to do with a whore who saw him as the way out of her miserable life.

When after a few months Sotiria told Ivan that she was with child, he laughed in her face.

'Away with you, woman!' he shouted, pushing her off him. 'You think I'm foolish enough to believe this is anything to do with me?'

'I know it's yours, but even if it isn't, it doesn't matter,' she spat back at him. 'If you don't agree to marry me or at least look after me, I'll tell your wife everything.'

That night Ivan, in a panic at the prospect of being exposed and losing all he had, arrived home earlier than usual, and crept into bed beside Olga. She lay motionless ignoring his advances. He reeked of cheap perfume, tobacco and alcohol.

She'd been building up to throwing him out for a while, and now the time had come. He had to go. She was far too proud to be humiliated this way; she didn't need him, or any man for that matter.

The next day she had a meeting with her parents. They

summoned the locksmith and changed all the locks, then packed an old suitcase with what clothes Ivan had arrived with three years earlier and put it outside the front door. Neither his begging for forgiveness nor his threats for revenge had any effect. The Linser family was far too powerful to be compromised.

From then on, whatever Ivan got up to was of no concern to Olga, or her family; he was now penniless and Sotiria's blackmail no longer held any threat or currency to anyone. They never spoke to him again.

Larnaka, 2010

Anita paused at last. Her words had been spilling out, sometimes hesitantly, sometimes deliberately, sometimes in a rush of emotion, for what seemed like hours. In the room silence fell like an empty space. This time it was Marianna who broke it.

'Are you saying . . . is it possible . . . ?' she started, visibly shaken, her voice barely audible as if she was talking to herself. 'Could it be . . . ?' she said, louder now, looking around the room at her friends, who were as dazed as she was by the revelations.

Anita breathed in, then sighed deeply. She reached for the young woman's hand.

'Yes, Marianna *mou*, that is what I am saying.' The old

woman looked at each of them and continued: 'You see, we had no way of knowing for sure, but it became quite clear that your grandmother Sotiria was Ivan's . . . my father's lover and she had a child by him. It is almost certain that your mother was my half-sister. Katerina and my mother were quite convinced of it and after a while so was I.'

The day Katerina went to find Marianna's grandmother was the day she found out Marianna's identity. Old Sotiria was more than happy to be rid of the girl and relieved to have her off her hands, but not before she made her claim known.

'It's about time your mistress's clan with all their money and airs and graces took her husband's bastard grandchild off me,' she hissed at Katerina, not even bothering to get up from her knees as she scrubbed the floor. 'They got away with it the first time around so I suppose this is something. Funny, though . . .' she laughed unpleasantly, 'a fine man your la-di-da mistress married. Maybe we were not so different after all, she and I – he left us both in the lurch, didn't he?'

Not long after Olga threw Ivan out, he disappeared and it was rumoured that he had returned to Hungary. No one saw or heard from him again, not least Sotiria, who conveniently found someone else to blame for her pregnancy. She claimed the father was the brothel's owner, who didn't really care if the baby was his or not: it gave him a good reason to keep Sotiria working for nothing in return for a roof over her head. Once the child turned fourteen she was put to work too, until she in turn gave birth to Marianna who was also destined for the same fate until Katerina and Olga rescued her.

'That child has been a burden from the moment she was born.' Sotiria continued scrubbing while she spoke to Katerina. 'It was bad enough bringing up my own kid, but this little bastard is good for nothing. At least her mother had some talent and worked for her keep. This one, all she ever wants to do is read.' Katerina couldn't bear to hear any more of the old woman's poison. It released buried memories of her own miserable childhood. She had to get Marianna away from her.

'I'm not that surprised,' Olga had said when Katerina returned with the news. 'I wonder how many more children are out there that I don't know about as a result of that man. It's not the poor child's fault to have been born into that misery. I have a duty to help Marianna.'

'God bless you, Olga,' Katerina replied and reached for her hand. 'What would have become of me if you hadn't helped me? Not a day goes by that I don't feel grateful to you for rescuing me.'

'The sins of the parents and grandparents should not be passed on to the children,' Olga said decisively. 'Now it's time for you and me to help this child, Katerina *mou* – and who knows,' she went on, 'perhaps it's true, perhaps some of the same blood as that of my own girls runs in her veins too.'

'I do believe it's true,' Katerina said with conviction. 'I always felt Marianna has a strong resemblance to Sonia, did you ever notice it? Or perhaps it's my wishful thinking . . .'

'It is more than possible,' Olga replied, letting out a long sigh. 'The man I fell in love with and married was a tramp. I chose badly, Katerina *mou*. Ivan was a cad and I was a foolish girl.'

'You were so young, you weren't to know,' Katerina replied. 'Everyone makes mistakes in their lives. Love is not a sin, Olga – you were the one who taught us that. No one can pass judgement, only God can do that.'

'If it's true about Marianna, then it's a blessing that the girl found us now; but even if it's not, we will treat her as one of us.'

Eleni, Adonis and Marianna sat motionless while Anita time-travelled them once again into a past about which they had known nothing.

Adonis was the first to react. 'This is wonderful news!' he shouted, interrupting his mother's flow as he rushed to envelop Marianna in his arms.

Eleni jumped up too to join them in a group hug. 'I always knew we were blood sisters,' she said, tears streaking her face.

'My mother considered you as her third grandchild,

Marianna,' Anita continued, 'and when I go, this house will belong to all three of you equally.'

'We must hope you won't be going anywhere for a long time,' Adonis told Anita and kissed the top of her head in a sudden surge of warmth towards her. Anita might not have been a very engaged mother, her limitations were many, but she wasn't a bad person either. What she lacked in maternal instinct had been compensated for by Katerina. It was not so much that Anita had made no effort – she had been sweet and kind with the children, but that was all that she could manage. Later, in New York, when he was older and with Robert's help, Adonis started to see that his mother's weaknesses had been the result of her own unhappy life. Like her own mother she too had been unlucky in her choice of husband.

He knew some of it, but not much. He was told little about his father, only that he had died and that he had been from the same mould as his grandfather, 'Ivan the terrible', as he was referred to on the rare occasions he was mentioned. The Linser women had a habit of not talking about the men who failed to thrive when they passed through the family.

If once in a while Olga, matriarch that she was, chose to impose her authority around the house, Katerina could be heard to whisper under her breath, *'No wonder a man never lasted in this house – her "lordship" saw to that.'* But the irritation that flared up at times between the women rarely lasted long; the respect and love they all shared always won out over the disputes, and besides, Katerina tended to agree with Olga. Except for Padre Bernardino and her beloved Adonis, most males did seem unworthy of admiration. The padre, who was a regular visitor to the home and a source of comfort and support especially when the children were young, was loved by all in the Linser household.

'I imagine there are some decent and reliable men out there,' Olga would lament, 'but apart from my father and grandfather I never came across any.'

The day Franz Linser died was the saddest day of Olga's life.

After Olga had thrown Ivan out, Franz found himself once again the head of the household. Although still involved in the family business he had hoped the time had come for Olga to take over. He had never considered himself as a patriarch and always encouraged his daughter to be as active in business as himself, or any man.

'One day I'll be gone,' he would tell her, 'and you, flower of my life, will be running everything.'

'You are still young, Papa,' Olga insisted, refusing to contemplate the possibility that her father might ever leave them. 'We still have years ahead of working together.'

'I am getting old, Olga *mou*, there is no denying it.'

'You are as fit as you always were,' she told him. 'Besides, the girls are still young, Papa, they need me around – and they also need you, so you'd better make sure you stay with us until they are grown up at least.'

Olga was the first to notice that Franz's coughing had got worse. A lifelong enthusiastic smoker he coughed most of his life, so everyone was used to his raspy voice and throaty laughter, which more often than not ended in a coughing fit. But she was worried, insisting he saw the doctor. 'I've had this cough all my life,' he told her. 'It's got worse these days because of the change in the weather. It will pass.' But he knew that this was different. The first time he spat blood he ignored it. *It's nothing, it's the strain of coughing too hard,* he told himself. When the blood continued he quietly took himself off to their family doctor who confirmed the severity of his condition. Still he chose to say nothing to his wife and daughter but instead threw himself into coaching Olga in the ways of their business.

'You are the new generation, Olga, you will bring new blood, new ideas to Linser Textiles. I am getting tired and old, it is *your* turn now and then you can pass it down to your own girls.'

Franz managed to hang on till he felt Olga was ready to take on the business, before he finally let go. Olga was inconsolable. She blamed herself. She knew how stubborn he was – she should have insisted he see the doctor earlier. His loss hit her hard, but she was her father's daughter and she threw herself into work the way he would have wanted her to.

7

Larnaka, 1954

By the time they were in their teens, like most other young girls, Anita and Sonia dreamed of little else but their wedding day, much to their mother's disappointment. Olga was trying to bring up her daughters to be cultured, multi-lingual and open-minded with European values as she had been raised, so the girls' conventional view towards marriage was something of a blow.

'Why are you in such a hurry?' she cautioned them. 'Live a little first, have some fun, my girls! I was in a big rush and look how that turned out . . .'

'You didn't do too badly,' they chimed. 'You got the two of us out of it, and you didn't stop having fun either!' Olga never hid her love affairs; on the contrary she wanted her daughters to know that women had as much right as any man to live the way they chose.

Her mother, on the other hand, held the opposite view. She prayed for her daughter's sins, as she referred to Olga's liaisons, and begged the Holy Mother to guide and protect her granddaughters. Regular visits to the Catholic church and conversations with Padre Bernardino also provided her with support.

'Times are changing,' the priest would advise Ernestina. For a Catholic priest the padre seemed to know a lot about life and its perils. He divulged little about himself other than that he came from Spain and had left his politically turbulent homeland to run the Catholic Church of Our Lady of the Graces in Larnaka.

'Gone are the days when girls were kept under lock and key,' he'd continue, 'but so long as they still have their faith they will be fine.'

'If it was down to me I would keep them under lock and key,' Ernestina would reply, 'but then again if I can't control my own daughter what chance do I have with my granddaughters?'

Olga had grown up in a Larnaka where liberal values and a cosmopolitan atmosphere prevailed, influenced by the port's international trade and its various consulates. With her father's encouragement and approval Olga had grown up to think for herself and act accordingly. Now, she was trying to instil the same values in her daughters. But by the time the girls were coming of age the social consensus had shifted towards conformism and convention.

Both Anita and Sonia longed to be friends with their peers and fit in with them, but as hard as they tried, their mixed ancestry showed and they were thought 'different'.

This often worked in their favour, especially with boys who viewed them as foreign and exotic. Sonia especially capitalized on her otherness, Anita less so. Sonia liked to be different; she was more amenable to her mother's advice.

'I want to get married,' she told Olga when she questioned their desire for matrimony, 'but first I want to have fun.'

'That's my girl!' Olga approved.

'You behave as if we live in Paris or Berlin,' Ernestina would scold Olga when she was tutoring the girls on the ways of independence. 'What example are you giving to your girls and what do you think people say about us?'

'I am giving my daughters the only example that counts, Mother – that they are as good and free as any man!'

Anita was first to fall in love. She was a shy young woman, nervous and unsure of herself, forever in the shadow of her younger sister, who was not only beautiful but confident and headstrong like her mother.

Mario was eighteen and in his last year at the Larnaka Gymnasium. She was a year older and had already graduated from the American Academy where she and Sonia had been educated. She was now studying music with dreams of becoming a concert pianist.

He fell in love with her as she passed the small house

where he lived with his family, on her way to a piano lesson with her music teacher in the next street.

Most boys were aware of the Linser girls; he never imagined she would ever be interested in him. She was different from any girl he knew; she looked like a fragile exotic bird. She was otherworldly, her complexion as ethereal and pale as the moon, accentuated further by her dark hair. It took him almost a year to summon up the courage to approach her.

One spring afternoon just after Easter, when the temperature had started to rise and the red poppies and yellow daisies were claiming every field and every garden on the island, Mario realized he was in love.

He saw her again walking past his house with her music books under her arm as always. She was wearing a short-sleeved summer dress, a Linser print her mother had designed especially for her; the pattern of red poppies on a background of pale blue was as cheerful as spring itself, with a red sash that showed off her slender waist. Her hair was tied back with a white ribbon. He knew then that she was the girl for him and that next time she passed he had to speak to her.

Anita was used to Sonia having all the attention and adulation from boys and Mario's approach a few days later took her by surprise.

He had been sitting on the veranda for more than an

hour waiting for her to come round the corner, so the minute he saw her he leapt into action.

'*Kalispera!*' Good evening, he said, suddenly almost falling onto the street in front of her.

Instead of replying, Anita started back in shock, let out a scream and dropped her books.

'*Kalispera,*' she eventually replied, flustered as she bent down to pick up her books at the same time as Mario, with the result that they bumped their heads together.

'Sorry, sorry, sorry,' he mumbled, feeling like an awkward fool while Anita blushed down to her bare arms.

It didn't take long for romance to blossom, although Mario worried that she would think him unworthy of her.

'My parents are poor people and your family is the aristocracy here,' he told her when they first started courting.

'I don't care who your family is or how much money they have,' she replied. 'Only people count, Mario, and you are a very good person!'

Olga and Katerina were fond of young Mario too, and more than pleased to see the change in Anita; she had been a withdrawn child and a shy adolescent and it was good to see her happy at last. Ernestina, on the other hand, spent even more time in church, praying for her family's souls.

'I knew that this would happen if you didn't take control,' she complained to Olga. 'Like mother like daughter! Where will this end? I don't see a ring on the girl's finger either! Ah! Madonna!' she cried out, lifting her eyes to the heavens and making the sign of the cross. 'The younger one will be doing the same soon and what will we do then?'

Sonia at seventeen already had plenty of boys interested in her. But unlike Anita, who was truly in love, nobody had totally stolen her heart yet, so for peace of mind she preferred to keep her affairs a secret from her grandmother and play all her admirers one against the other. She was a highly popular girl, and when not at school she indulged in secret rendezvous. She knew that Olga wouldn't mind too much, but she also knew better than to upset her God-fearing grandmother.

'Sometimes I can't believe *Nonna* is Mama's mother,' she complained to Anita.

'Mama takes after grandfather, you take after Mama, and I take after *Nonna*,' Anita laughed. 'You don't care what anyone thinks, and I do – well I do when it comes to boys at least!'

'You're only young once,' Sonia quoted her mother, 'and I intend to have fun before I settle down.'

'You'll get your fingers burned and have your heart broken if you carry on like this,' Anita warned, sounding like her grandmother. But Sonia had a mind of her own.

However, there was one boy Sonia liked more than most; his name was Nicos. But still, she had no intention of committing herself yet.

Olga was both happy to see her eldest daughter in love and relieved that the couple were in no rush to be married. The boy had brought a sparkle to her girl's eyes and colour to her cheeks, yet Olga was deeply concerned, with good reason.

The political climate in Cyprus, as elsewhere in the postwar years, had become increasingly turbulent and there were clear warning signs of an imminent uprising against the British colonial rule. Olga was a well-informed woman, and news of such uprisings in Africa, Malaysia, and all over the British Empire were beginning to alarm her. Mario's clandestine involvement and activities with the underground network of freedom fighters that was spreading through the island was the source of Olga's anxieties. Involvement with the struggle could spell trouble for her family and business – her relationship with the British administration had always been congenial, and she had to keep it that way. She didn't always agree with their colonial tactics but kept her opinions private and her profile low. She had to protect her interests, and as a woman and the head of the family she knew her position was delicate.

'These are dangerous times,' she warned her daughter one day when they were having a family discussion about the political situation. 'Mario could get himself arrested or worse.'

'You don't understand, Mother,' Anita replied with youthful fervour. 'Someone has to do something! We must struggle with all our powers for the liberation of our country from the English yoke!' she zealously recited parrot-fashion the movement's mantra, which she had learned from Mario and his family. Patriotic blood, and in Anita's case also romantic love, was running through most young people's veins and their passion was infectious.

'It's true!' Katerina said, shaking her head. 'Show me a young man or woman who is *not* part of the movement! I agree with Anita that we have to do something for our country, but I worry too . . .' She let out a long sigh. 'I just wish we could do it peacefully.'

The main participants of the movement, which called itself EOKA (National Organization of Cypriot Struggle), were young Greek men, and students of both sexes, most of them in their last years of high school. The preparation for the revolution, or 'the struggle for freedom' and enosis union with the Greek motherland, as they liked to call it, involved mainly the distribution of anti-British leaflets and other literature, and slogans graffitied on walls wherever possible. The latter task fell mainly to young boys and girls, who stole out secretly at midnight or dawn to daub their messages to incite the people. The distribution of arms and ammunition was carried out by older partisans.

Archbishop Makarios, the much-loved and respected leader of the Orthodox Church, was a supporter of the struggle for independence, and his exile by the British, who deemed him an agent provocateur, inflamed the people's rebellious mood further. Most people were swept along one way or another by the growing impetus of the movement and supported it, if not actively, then certainly in spirit. Olga's worry was that Mario would influence Anita and his links with the patriotic movement would bring risk to the rest of the family. At the same time, she had her own views about the imminent struggle. Anxious though she was about the implications of such a shake-up, and reluctant to voice them to anyone, she was convinced that the time had come to put an end to the imperial rule.

'It's time for change,' she told her mother in the privacy of their home, 'but I'm not so sure that union with Greece is the answer. Independence should mean independence!'

The young people branded as terrorists by the British proudly called themselves freedom fighters. Most families like Mario's included someone who was involved with the struggle and secretly condoned or supported it. A brilliant student with good writing skills, Mario was assigned the job of helping to write and distribute propaganda literature.

'We have to throw out these colonial oppressors and be reunited with our motherland Greece,' he told Anita passionately, holding tightly onto her hand. 'This is the twentieth century and there is no room for imperialism any longer! We must attract the attention of the world!'

Anita wholeheartedly agreed, despite her mother's concerns. 'Cyprus would do well to stay independent,' Olga would insist whenever there was a discussion in the home, but it seemed that most people disagreed with her.

'We will have a delivery of pamphlets in a few days,' Mario told Anita one afternoon as they walked along the promenade. 'We will need a safe place to store them until distribution. Do you think your mother would agree to hide them for us?'

'I'll ask,' Anita replied, knowing that the person she would ask would be Katerina. Though Olga sympathized with the struggle, she was also relieved to be outside the British radar of suspicion. This was largely due to the family's elite status, foreign name and Olga's excellent command of the English language. She was a businesswoman and the head of her household and her responsibilities weighed heavy on her shoulders, so as much as Olga disapproved of the British colonial rule, she went along with the neutrality game.

'They think they are masters of the universe,' she

might tell her mother once in a while behind closed doors. 'They finally gave up India, and now it's time for the rest of their colonies.' But Olga preferred to keep her opinions within the confines of her home. She didn't want trouble or to attract attention.

The banging on the door was harsh, loud and insistent. A dog nearby started barking, setting off others in the distance. The noise echoed in the still of the night, rudely awakening everyone.

'Open up!' came the forceful order in English, along with more hammering at the door.

'SEARCH! Open up!'

Katerina was the first to grab her dressing gown and she hurried to unbolt the front door, followed by Olga.

'Open up NOW!' the voice persisted. Olga peered out into the night through the half-open door at the soldier standing on the front step. He pushed past her followed by four others.

'Search!' he said again to the terrified women who had all gathered in the hall in their nightclothes.

'What seems to be the problem, officer?' Olga asked in her best English.

'Search!' the command came again loud and clear from the soldier in charge, while the others stood in the hall gripping their rifles.

'On what grounds?' Olga demanded, standing tall and proudly throwing her head back in defiance.

'We have information that you are harbouring a terrorist,' he said and gave the order to start the search.

Anita felt her knees give way as she clung tighter to her sister.

'You will find no such person here!' Olga snapped at the soldiers as they spread around the house. Katerina darted a look at Anita, fear rising in her throat. Mario might not have been there but the leaflets she had agreed to hide were all tucked away in a concealed compartment in her closet. Olga was unaware of this, as the two women had decided to act without her consent.

'I will help you because I believe in the struggle,' Katerina had told the couple when they came to her for help, 'but I know it would be against Olga's wishes and that is killing me . . . I just hope to God she never finds out.'

Katerina waited and trembled; her senses were on edge and she was feeling wretched twice over. If they found the literature Mario would be doomed . . . and Olga? How could she ever look her in the eyes if she knew that she had betrayed her. They had taken good care with Mario to hide the bundle. They removed a plank of wood that created a false floor at the bottom of her wardrobe, hiding a secret storage place. In went the package and they then replaced the plank with meticulous care, covering it with shoes and clothes.

Clutching at the silver crucifix round her neck Katerina silently prayed.

The search continued for what seemed like hours as the soldiers went through the house room by room, opening and shutting doors, overturning possessions with brutal urgency and talking to each other. Katerina held her breath and waited.

At some point a shout came from one of the soldiers.

'OVER HERE!' he called, beckoning the others. The women also followed. They saw the soldier standing inside their little storeroom holding up a violin case: at his feet boxes and suitcases had been turned upside down, their contents – old shoes, clothes and broken toys – scattered all over the floor. Olga hadn't seen that violin case for years; it belonged to Ivan and it was the only thing she hadn't put out onto the street when she threw him out. Her respect for music and the beauty of the instrument prevented her from destroying it. She had also hoped that one of her girls might pick it up and learn. But Anita preferred the piano and Sonia the cello. Olga always maintained that the girls' musical talent was the only gift they inherited from their father.

The soldier stood holding the case waiting for orders.

'Open it!' the one who was in charge commanded. Everyone stood watching as the soldier ripped the case open to discover the amber-coloured instrument innocently resting in its rightful place.

'A violin!' the soldier exclaimed, deflated, disappointment evident in his voice. A machine gun would have been so much more exciting . . . Many of these soldiers were young English boys no older than Anita and Mario, seeing out their national service and unlucky enough to find themselves in the middle of a small war they understood very little about. If Olga hadn't been so furious she would have felt amused, almost sorry for this young man.

Hiding arms in a violin case! she thought to herself. *Who do they take us for, Al Capone?*

Although nothing was found during the night search, the incident was not without repercussions. The Linser household was now, as Olga had feared, under scrutiny. Anita's relationship with Mario, who as a fully fledged member of EOKA was very much under British surveillance, was having an impact on the family.

'Tomorrow at midnight we will be going out to write slogans on walls,' he told Anita one day as they sat in his mother's kitchen drinking sweet Turkish coffee. 'Tomorrow is the perfect night as there's no moon; we will dress in black so we will be almost invisible.'

'I want to come with you,' she begged, and not for the first time.

'No, Anita *mou*, I don't want you to. It's dangerous, and as much as I'd like you by my side, it's best you stay at home.'

'But you are taking all the risks, I want to do my share,' she carried on protesting.

'You are! You are doing what you can, and I think we've given your mother enough trouble . . . we have to be sensible for her sake.'

'I don't feel as if I'm doing enough to help,' she said again, reaching for his hand. 'Please, Mario, let me come?'

'You have helped plenty; both you and Katerina are doing your bit for the struggle. Just pray for us tomorrow and we'll be fine.'

Anita's heart was bursting with love for her boy and she trembled with fear lest something happen to him.

'I think if you get caught I want to be caught with you,' she said, holding tight onto his hand.

'And I think that if I get caught I want you to be safe at home,' Mario replied and gave her a kiss.

Was it bad luck or an informer? No one ever found out. They caught them before they had even dipped their brushes in paint. All four were arrested and kept in custody till dawn. After that night, Mario and the rest of the boys had to report every single day without fail to the British headquarters before sundown, or be arrested and imprisoned. The daily reporting was a safety measure to ensure that none of them took to the mountains as some partisans were now apparently doing in preparation for battle.

Under close supervision their activities were restricted and any midnight excursions reduced, although Mario continued to write literature and attend secret meetings with comrades. After all, he had taken the oath of an EOKA member swearing by the name of the Holy Trinity to struggle with all his youthful powers, in his case his pen, for the liberation of Cyprus, and not to abandon the struggle under any pretext.

April is the most beautiful month on the island. The wild orchids by Aphrodite's baths are at their zenith, and multi-coloured anemones covering the land surrounding the temple of Apollo demand every inch of the earth.

The sap begins to rise in the bodies of the young in that month, and spring is heralded with all its glory.

'*Golden April, fragrant May* . . .' as the song goes, and love hovers in the air. On the first of the month every April, parents fabricate little lies to tell their children, and young and old join in the fun. But no songs, fun, or lies were to be exchanged on that April Fool's Day in 1955 when Mario and Anita had been pledged to each other for less than a year. That day their world turned deadly serious. Thirty minutes after midnight a series of deafening explosions shook the towns of Nicosia, Larnaka and Limassol, announcing that 'the struggle for freedom' had officially begun. It took the British authorities and most of the population by surprise. Then the panic set in.

Anyone associated with EOKA was a prime suspect. Olga was alarmed and fearful for her family, and during the days that followed, Anita was forbidden to meet with Mario.

'We all love him, Anita *mou*, but this is dangerous,' she told her daughter, 'and we cannot afford to be implicated.'

'I am not going to abandon him, Mother!' Anita said, running out of the room in tears.

'We are five women living alone in a state of war,' Olga called sternly after her. She turned to the other women who sat silently listening to her and said gravely, 'We have no protector. We must be vigilant and take care of each other. Perhaps it would be best if I sent the girls to Vienna for safety,' she added, looking at her mother.

It was evening, around eight o'clock, five days after the bombings. The weather had been unusually warm and the windows were open to let in the evening breeze. A curfew had now been declared by the British so no one was allowed out after sundown. Anita sat in the living room, a book on her lap, trying without success to keep her mind away from worrying about Mario and the events unfolding around them.

The phone rang persistently in the hall, making her jump. It echoed loudly through the house. Pushing Sonia out of the way she ran and seized the receiver. It was Mario's mother.

'He hasn't come home yet,' the woman's worried voice told her. 'Do you know where he is, Anita *mou*? Have you heard from him?' she asked hopefully. Anita's heart started to pound. She sensed danger.

'Not since yesterday . . . I had a note from him,' she replied, trying to keep calm for Mario's mother, if not for herself.

'It's little Maria's birthday today and he was meant to pick up a cake on his way back from the headquarters . . . but there is no sign of him,' the woman continued, hope vanishing from her voice. 'It's well past curfew. He went on his bicycle . . . he's never missed his sister's birthday before.'

'What about the others?'

'I spoke to Michalis's and Elia's mothers; they have returned home as normal, but I couldn't reach Savva's mother, so I don't know about him.'

Anita gripped the phone hard, the taste of fear choking her.

He was missing for forty-eight hours before Mario's family was contacted. They were informed that Mario had been arrested as a terrorist suspect due to his involvement with EOKA. They were told that while he was held for questioning he had attempted to escape, and in the process he was shot and fatally wounded. The reason for the call was a summons for formal identification of the body by a family member. Both his parents went; his mother almost didn't recognize him. He'd been beaten up for information.

His friend Savvas was moved to a detention camp to be held prisoner indefinitely for the duration of the hostilities.

Anita was bereft. She couldn't accept that the young man she loved had been taken away from her so prematurely. 'I will never fall in love again,' she told her mother, secretly blaming her for her loss. Before loving Mario Anita thought her soul had been asleep. He had woken her from a great lethargy, which she feared would claim her again.

Olga felt wretched for preventing her daughter from seeing Mario during the days that led to his arrest. The whole family fell into deep mourning for the boy. Their only source of comfort and strength through that time was Padre Bernardino's regular visits and discussions with them.

'We must never lose sight of hope,' the padre told Anita. 'The human spirit has the ability to rise again, Anita.'

Having lived through the horrors of civil war in Spain, the padre knew what he was speaking of. But Anita was inconsolable. In the months that followed she began to sink into a great melancholy and the bouts of depression that would blight her existence began. The only person she spoke to was Katerina. She was her friend and ally and the one who understood.

'We have to continue our support for the struggle,' she would tell Katerina, who believed as passionately as Anita in the cause but whose respect and loyalty to Olga held her back. She understood her mistress's concerns for the safety of their female household. She knew they were vulnerable.

'My mother is the one who has brought us up to be as strong as any man,' Anita would argue when Katerina tried to explain. 'It's rather hypocritical of her to now change her rules.'

'It's not hypocrisy, Anita *mou*,' Katerina defended Olga. 'Your mother is a fair-minded woman and as brave as anyone. She needs to be vigilant for all of us.'

'Sometimes you have to act according to your beliefs regardless of the consequences,' Anita would argue back.

'Don't think she hasn't been aware of what you and I have been doing all this time and the consequences of that, yet she has turned a blind eye, which in itself is a contribution to the struggle.'

'To my mind it's not enough!' Anita persisted.

'Your mother is the only person who puts food on our plates! Never forget that!' Katerina continued. 'How can she provide for us if she doesn't work? The only way she can survive is to appear impartial!'

Often Katerina would discuss the unfolding events with the padre. He shared the two young women's commitment even if he didn't voice it publicly; their talks always gave her courage.

'Political oppression seems to follow me everywhere I go,' he confided to her during their talks. He sometimes arrived for a visit in the middle of the day, when the house was empty apart from Ernestina and Katerina, and he would sit with the two women in the kitchen and talk about religion and politics. Ernestina was always fearful and shared her daughter's concerns. The priest gave them enormous strength and they both looked forward to his visits.

Padre Bernardino was thirty-five years old; short in stature yet athletic in build with a dark complexion. It occurred to Katerina that if he wasn't wearing his Catholic priest's cassock he'd be well suited to wear the EOKA freedom fighters' uniform of combat camouflage trousers and jacket, with a beret on his head. His eyes, dark blue like a stormy sea, were deep-set and troubled. He held your gaze as he talked softly, unhurriedly, in perfect Greek, with only a trace of an accent. Spanish, he always claimed, had many similarities to Greek, especially the Cypriot dialect. Sometimes he spoke to Ernestina in Italian, her native tongue, which brought her joy and solace.

'We live in such turbulent times, Padre,' she'd tell him,

welcoming his comforting words, which she knew would always come.

He liked to make time for the old lady. If his mother had been alive, he believed she would now look similar to Ernestina; but she was long gone along with the rest of his family. His own survival was a miracle and often a cause of mental anguish to him. His guilt for still living while everyone he loved had perished never left him, even after all the years that had passed.

On one unusually wet and stormy morning in early January the padre came to visit the Linser home. Katerina was alone that day – the girls were out and Ernestina had gone to see a friend. A neighbour had taken to inviting some ladies to morning coffee and Olga was encouraging her mother to participate.

'It will do you good, Mother, to get some fresh sea air and be with people, instead of staying in the house all day. Come, it's raining so I'll drop you off in the car,' she said, ushering her out of the front door.

Katerina was glad to have some time alone, which up until recently had been a rare occurrence, but when the padre rang the bell she was more than pleased to relinquish her free time for him. He was always welcome. He stood at the front door under a big black umbrella, wearing his usual smile.

'*Kalimera*, Katerina,' he said as he stepped into the

front hall, leaving the wet umbrella beside the door, his black ankle-length clerical robe wet around the hem. 'Miserable weather we are having today,' he continued as he brushed some raindrops off his sleeve.

'We need the rain as much as we need the sun, Father,' Katerina replied. 'What we don't need is another drought this summer.'

'Of course you're right,' he said, following her into the kitchen. It felt warm and welcoming in there. The windows were steamed up from Katerina's cooking: on the stove a chicken was bubbling away for stock. She was going to make *soupa avgolemono* for lunch, everyone's favourite winter soup. The chicken from the village market made rich fatty stock perfect for the soup and the boiled chicken would break into succulent pieces that would make the rice, egg and lemon base even more delicious.

'Coffee, Father?' she asked as she reached for the *ibriki* – the little enamel pot for making Turkish coffee in. She knew he liked his strong and sweet.

She cherished time alone with Father Bernardino. When Ernestina was there Katerina left them together out of respect for the old lady – she knew how much she needed his attention and reassurance. On the rare occasions she happened to be alone with him, Katerina would take advantage of his knowledge and wisdom. Some days he might read passages from the Bible to her, and other times discuss the political climate of the island; she learned much from him.

That morning the priest seemed in a pensive mood. Perhaps it was the stormy weather, or the homely domestic scene in the kitchen, or simply because he and Katerina were alone. As a rule, he avoided talking about himself, much preferring to focus on others and their problems. When at times she had quizzed him about his country, he dodged her questions. She had never been further than Nicosia or Paphos, and Spain was unimaginable. She longed to know about his homeland but the most he ever told her was that it wasn't so different from Cyprus.

Too respectful to pursue it further she tried to imagine what Spain might be like. But something about him on that rainy January day seemed different. He was more talkative, more approachable, he looked more like a man and less like a priest to her. Even the way he drank his coffee was different that morning. As he crossed his legs and pushed the damp cassock to one side his dark trousers and wet leather shoes showed beneath, revealing the human being behind the priestly trappings, making Katerina almost blush.

'Today your kitchen takes me back to when I was a boy . . .' he said, glancing over his cup at her. She said nothing but looked back at him, willing him to say more. 'Something about the atmosphere in here takes me back to better times . . .' He let out a sigh, put the cup down, reached for a cigarette and sat back in his chair. 'I would often sit in the kitchen while my mother cooked. There were some good times when I was a boy . . .' his eyes clouded over, 'then sorrow came and wiped them all out . . .' Katerina held her breath and waited for more.

8

Guernica, 1937

It was market day on that April morning in 1937. Bright green leaves were beginning to show on the oak trees and the spring air smelled sweet. The town's main square was full of people. Local farmers brought their crops to sell and others came to buy or to look, or just for the outing. Market day in Guernica was considered something of a fiesta and everyone looked forward to it. Bernardino, along with his father, his mother, younger brother, older sister and his uncle the priest, Padre Javier, had all arrived early to help on the stall. At seventeen, Bernardino was already his father's right hand.

'Soon you will be able to take over, my son,' he had told the boy as they heaved sacks of grain to the stall. 'You will make a great farmer and perhaps make more of a success of it than I have.'

'Father, you know that is not my wish,' Bernardino said as he had done many times before. He knew that his father wanted nothing more than for him to become a farmer. Bernardino's dream was to follow in his uncle's footsteps to a life in the Church. His father, a socialist and a republican, was firmly opposed to his son's wishes and the principles of Catholicism.

'Religion is control, my son. You think the Church is not corrupt? Where do you think they get all their money from?' he would repeat to Bernardino, looking at his wife and hoping for support. But she was conflicted. As much as she wanted to agree with her husband, she had been brought up a Catholic and found it hard to take a firm stance against the Church.

'As you very well know there are some good priests too,' she'd remind her husband, 'and your brother Javier is one of them!'

'Yes, Father!' Bernardino would argue. 'Why didn't you discourage your brother from training for the priesthood if you are so against it?'

'He was older than me,' his father would laugh good-naturedly, outnumbered. 'He wouldn't listen to what I had to say – I was just a kid. You, on the other hand, my son – you are still young, so I hope to influence you . . .'

And so the discussions would go, without agreement.

That market day, they were doing very well and by the afternoon they had sold out of everything.

'We need more grain,' his father said, and glanced at

Bernardino. 'There are two sacks of wheat left in the cellar.'

'I'm on my way, Father,' the boy replied, eagerly grabbing his bicycle and heading for their house on the outskirts of town.

Moments after Bernardino entered the house by the back door and hurried down the steps to the deep cellar, the first wave of German bombers appeared in the skies over the town. When he emerged from the darkness, blinded by the bright light, he blinked in disbelief. Surely he was dreaming. In the distance, where he had just been, flames were reaching to the sky; the town centre was ablaze. He stood paralyzed, gazing at the rising clouds of smoke, trying to make sense of what he was witnessing and what might have happened in the time between him leaving the town and entering the cellar.

Apparently there had been a bombing raid, and now a new wave of fighter planes was approaching. Within moments they were over the town, almost skimming the tops of the trees and dropping bombs. Horrified, he looked on as the planes turned towards the outskirts of town. The sound of explosions and gunfire rang deafeningly in his ears. He dropped to his knees, sobs shaking his body. He had no alternative but to retreat to the safety of the cellar.

Trembling, he stayed underground for what he imagined to be days, not hours. Finally, he re-emerged, but this time, without a care for his safety, he rushed to the town. Sobbing, he fought his way through the streets reduced to rubble towards the square. The planes had retreated but had left behind a scene of utter carnage and devastation. The town was destroyed.

Desperately Bernardino searched for his family but to no avail. Dead bodies lay all around; some burned to death, some still alive but mutilated. The square, which only a few hours earlier had been full of life and laughter was now a bloodbath surrounded by a wall of fire; the only sounds audible were screams, moans and weeping. In the distance, staggering around amongst the bodies, was Father Ignazio, the local priest, his clothes in tatters and his face bleeding and blackened.

'What happened, Father?' the boy cried. 'Who did this? Why?'

'They dropped bombs, they shot bullets, they destroyed us.'

For hours Father Ignazio, with young Bernardino's help, tended to the wounded, giving the last rites to the dying and praying for them.

Katerina sat motionless as he spoke, her eyes full of tears. Finally, when he stopped, she leaned across and touched his hand which lay on the table clenched into a fist. His face was ashen, his eyes haunted. At her touch he relaxed and held on to her.

'I never imagined . . . I never knew . . .' she whispered. She wanted to give him comfort but no words came to her. They sat a long time without speaking; the only noise the sound of the pot gently simmering on the stove. Then he began again, his voice deep and quiet.

'You see, Katerina, my country was a very troubled place for many years; the aftermath of war is endless and the worst kind of war is a civil one; it scars our bodies, our minds and the land itself. These scars never heal. I pray to God it never happens here.'

She swallowed her tears; she wanted to ask questions, she wanted to know more, but she didn't dare lest she stopped his flow. She knew nothing of Spain or its wars. All she knew was that there had been a treacherous war involving the whole world and that Greece had suffered something similar to what the padre was describing. The Second World War had hardly affected Cyprus and besides, she had been just a girl then. But the recent events on the island were making everything she was being told all the more real and vivid.

He paused for a long while, both of them lost in contemplation. Then he began to speak again.

'I was troubled and conflicted with my faith for a long time after that, Katerina. My father's words kept coming back to me. I felt duty-bound to honour his wish, as if to punish myself for being alive while they were all dead.'

Katerina sat silently and waited.

'I rejected the Church for a long while, Katerina, but I never lost my faith. I joined the republicans to fight Franco, to try and stamp out their evil,' he hesitated a moment, 'and . . . during that time, I . . . got married.'

'Married!' Katerina whispered the word to herself as if she had never heard it before. 'Married?' she said again, out loud this time, the question hovering on her lips.

'Yes . . . I was married,' he replied, 'for just six months. Then Franco's nationalists killed her too; gone like the rest of my family. She was three months pregnant.' He looked down at his hands lying on the table. 'Carmen . . .' he said in a whisper, 'her name was Carmen.' He spoke the name so gently, so sweetly, it melted Katerina's heart. She reached for his hand again. 'After she died I knew that my destiny would now be with the Church and to help people who carried pain in their hearts as I did, and away from Spain.'

He leaned forward in his chair and looked at her for a long while.

'I have not spoken of this to anyone apart from my bishop, and in confession,' he said, searching her face.

She was deeply moved; he trusted her. He had chosen her – Katerina! – to open up to, though she was nothing compared to him, or her mistresses in the Linser family. She was a simple peasant woman, a maid, even though the household never treated her that way. How many times had she wished for him to confide in her and tell her about his life, his country, his world? Never had she imagined she would be privy to such intimacies or hear such despair. She felt honoured, and above all she valued his trust.

From that day on the relationship between the two changed. Padre Bernardino continued to visit the Linser home as he always had, but when he and Katerina were alone they would behave and talk as friends. They would speak freely, share stories, and he encouraged Katerina to speak of her past too.

'My father, unlike yours,' she told him, 'was a brute, and my mother in her weakness colluded with him. They were not killed like your family, but they were dead to me long before they died.'

It was his turn to reach for her hand, an intimate gesture that neither of them would ever make in front of others.

'You have a loving family here, Katerina,' he said, 'even if it's not your real one.'

'Olga, the girls, and grandmother Ernestina, have been my people since I was thirteen years old. They are more real and loving than my birth family ever was.'

'What about your siblings?' he asked. 'What happened to them?'

'Many are dead,' she replied, pained by the memory. 'Perished in the malaria epidemic, and some still live in the village.' She sensed his unease. 'You must think me harsh . . .' she said, feeling the guilt she fought so hard to banish return. 'The remorse I felt for abandoning them to their miserable fate has never left me, even if I have never stopped sending them money. But, I always ask myself, was that enough?'

'I don't judge you, Katerina . . .' he said and reached for her hand again. 'You had a hard start in life. You did what you could; you are a good person. Your father sold you like a sack of wheat, you owed him nothing.'

'I owe everything to Olga,' she replied. 'She has been like a mother *and* a father to me and as good as any friend.'

'But forgiveness is always good for the soul; maybe one day?'

'I have forgiven my mother, it's true. She too was a victim. But I cannot forgive him, not yet anyway. My mother and father might have given me life, but Olga gave me love, hope *and* a life!'

9

Olga was seriously concerned about Anita's activities and feared for both of her daughters. As time passed, political agitation against the island's colonial status was worsening; the independence movement was entrenched and persisting with new tactics all the time. Sporadic violence had escalated into full-blown guerrilla warfare; explosions, raids and random ambushes were part of everyday life. Greek Cypriot EOKA members had taken refuge in the mountains, fighting the British occupying troops, while in the towns, curfews, searches and house arrests by the English army were becoming the norm. Everyone lived with the dread of implication and Olga knew that her daughter's associations with activists made them a target for suspicion; she feared for the safety of everyone in her household.

'I want to send the two of you to Vienna for a period of time till all this is resolved,' she told them one day, at a loss to know how to protect her family. She knew that Anita was dedicated to the cause, although after Mario's death she too had accepted that she had to be careful, if only for the sake of her family.

'A little time away will do you both good,' said Olga, trying to persuade her eldest daughter – she had no problem with the younger one. 'Besides, you both want to study music and where else better than the birthplace of Mozart?'

Anita would have none of it.

'I am perfectly happy studying with Kyria Magda,' she told her mother defiantly. 'I do not need to go to Vienna!' Olga knew there was nothing she could do or say to make her change her mind, but she was determined that she would keep at least one of her girls safe.

Sonia, who had been given cello lessons from the age of nine, was now ready to start full time at the music academy. She shared neither her sister's reluctance for travel nor Anita's passion for the struggle for freedom; as far as she was concerned it got in the way of her own liberty. She had inherited her mother's free spirit, and perhaps a little recklessness from her father, and the prospect of travelling to Vienna thrilled her; she couldn't wait to get away,

Olga knew there was no time to lose; Sonia had to go, and go soon. She turned for help to some members of the Linser family still living in Vienna, with whom she had kept in touch over the years. Arrangements were made swiftly. Sonia was enrolled in the Vienna Academy of

Music and it was agreed she would stay with Great-aunt Heidi, who lived in an old apartment close to the centre of town.

The young woman was overjoyed: freedom at last! No more bombs, curfews and tears from Anita – all to be left behind. She would be free to laugh, dance and be happy again. All that political unease on the island was getting in the way of her having any kind of fun. She was setting off for Europe, the magical place she had longed to visit since childhood. She was well acquainted with Olga's stories of travels with her father, and her mother and grandmother had often talked about sending the two girls to study there. Even though she had hoped to make the journey with her sister and would miss her company in Vienna, going alone was fine too – Anita was far too serious these days. The thrill of the new was finally in sight for her.

'What about Nicos?' Anita asked her sister, knowing of Sonia's ongoing romance with the boy.

'He'll have to wait, won't he?' came her reply. 'First things first . . .'

'You are very fickle, my sister,' Anita sighed.

Nicos, Sonia's official suitor, was considered something of a hell-raiser in the town, as much of a pleasure-seeker as she was, and neither cared too much about politics. The two had known each other since elementary school and had pledged to marry eventually, but until then they were content to allow each other a degree of freedom. They were temperamentally and physically suited; both were athletic in physique: he, a keen footballer, she, the best gymnast at her school. They made a handsome couple, heads turned wherever they passed, but they were in no rush to settle down.

'So long as you don't fall in love with a German boy and stay there,' Nicos had said to her when she first told him of her departure. They were sitting on a pebbly beach on the outskirts of town discussing their future, smoking cigarettes and drinking whisky from a silver flask that Nicos carried around with him.

'I don't like German boys,' she said, laughing, and picked up a stone to throw into the surf.

'And how many German boys have you met recently, Miss Sonia, in order to know that?' he retorted, pulling her towards him for a kiss.

'Greek boys are much more to my liking,' she said, kissing him back, 'and . . . well, perhaps the odd English soldier?' she teased him.

'I know you! A good-looking boy always turns your head, so just be careful!' He took a swig of whisky and passed the flask to her.

'I can't help it if I have good taste in men!' She wriggled out of his arms still laughing and stood up.

'You can have your fun,' he said, pulling her down beside him again, 'and I will do the same, but when you return we will marry.'

'So long as you don't fall in love and marry someone else before I come back,' she replied, landing a kiss on the tip of his nose.

'I promise! You are the girl for me . . .' he said lightly, knowing better than to seem too earnest with Sonia, as they rolled on the pebbly beach in each other's arms.

During Sonia's absence Anita turned to Katerina for even more support; their dedication to the political cause united them further and they continued to be active in any way possible. Katerina's loyalty to Olga was great but so was her loyalty to her country and she was not prepared to renounce the latter altogether. Literature was still being secretly written and distributed and the two women often joined the group of young sympathizers who met at Mario's mother's house. Olga contrived to look the other way to avoid hearing any incriminating information.

Costas was a newcomer; no one knew much about him. He had arrived in Larnaka from Nicosia a few months back. Apparently he had been employed as a clerk in a government office but, as he explained, given the deteriorating political situation he had quit the British bureaucracy and was looking for another job.

'I'd rather find a job as a labourer,' he said, 'than be paid by the English.' He and Anita struck up a friendship.

'He is a true comrade,' she told Katerina when they

first met. 'His dedication and passion reminds me some-how of Mario.'

Katerina did not agree; from their first meeting she felt an intense mistrust towards this stranger.

She had sharp instincts and a keen intuition, and they were both troubling her.

Since meeting Costas, Anita had started to emerge from her melancholy, and Katerina was loath to damage this newfound recovery by voicing her reservations. The only person with whom she could discuss the matter was the padre.

'There is something about this man that doesn't ring true to me,' she told him. 'His sincerity seems false. Of course I have nothing to go on apart from my gut feeling, and that is not enough. Perhaps,' she continued, 'it's my loyalty to Mario that makes me feel hostile.'

'She does seem to be much brighter, more alive these days,' the padre told her. 'Perhaps it's best not to say anything, better to wait and see . . .'

So Katerina decided to keep her thoughts to herself and wait.

Sonia had been gone nearly a year and winter was once again on its way. The sun was still warm in the cloudless early-morning November sky and a fresh breeze was blowing into the kitchen through the open window as the women in the Linser household prepared their breakfast.

Katerina had laid out freshly baked bread, butter, honey and black olives while Anita was making coffee for everyone; always a time-consuming task since each of them liked to take it a different way. Turkish coffee has to be heated with the water on the stove, and each cup has to be prepared individually according to the quantity of sugar a person desires. Ernestina liked hers *glygo*, sweet, Olga preferred it *metrio*, medium, while Anita and Katerina took theirs *sketo*, no sugar at all.

'I think we should all compromise and take our coffee the same way, it would save so much time!' Anita joked and poured the first cup for her grandmother.

'That will never happen!' Olga retorted, cutting the bread into thick slices for toast. She had decided to enjoy a leisurely breakfast with her family that morning, and go to the factory a little later than usual. The last two weeks had been relatively peaceful in the streets and the atmosphere in the house was cheerful. Strains of a piano playing Chopin drifted into the kitchen from the wireless in the library, soothing troubled nerves.

'How long has it been since I heard that polonaise?' Ernestina asked, looking at her daughter. 'Anita hardly plays the piano any more . . . it feels like old times today. A moment of peace for once.'

'I know, Mother,' Olga replied. 'We need some respite, we have all been living on our nerves.'

No sooner had Olga spoken than the music on the

wireless was abruptly interrupted by the serious voice of a presenter making an emergency announcement. The women's good humour was instantly shattered. Orders had been announced by the authorities, they were being informed over the airwaves, for each and every occupant to line up outside their homes to be picked up by army trucks and taken to an unnamed location for questioning. Once again fear gripped their hearts. What did this mean, where would they be taken? The same message was now also being broadcast through loudspeakers out in the street.

The four women exchanged fearful glances, their appetite instantly gone. With trembling hands Anita put her cup on the table and walked to the window. Two British army lorries were already parked outside.

No one had any idea what this meant, yet in less than an hour the Linser women together with their neighbours had assembled in the street and were being loaded up on the trucks like cattle. Women and children, young and old sat huddled together in the back of the truck guarded by armed soldiers acting on orders. They waited.

The men were to be transported in the other army vehicle. Nobody understood what was happening or why. Later they discovered it was the men who were under suspicion and were being questioned, the women and children were just being detained for no apparent reason but to keep everyone together.

On the truck, next to Olga, a baby in his mother's arms started to cry and was immediately joined by some of the younger children. Fear was setting in. One little girl, terrified and screaming, tried to climb out of the truck only to be pushed back by a soldier. A Turkish woman, a neighbour, ran to the child's aid.

'Please leave her with me,' the Turkish woman pleaded with the soldier in broken English. 'She just a child, I am Turk, leave her with me.'

Turks were exempt from any interrogation or persecution by the British throughout the uprising, since it was the Greek population that was in revolt against the colonial rule; so too the Linser family should have been, but Anita's association with Mario made them a target.

'Yes, yes!' begged the little girl's mother, handing her daughter to Katerina sitting at the back of the truck, who in turn was about to pass her down to the Turkish friend on the street. The young soldier was adamant.

'STOP!' he called, holding his rifle at the ready. 'Everyone must remain! Orders!'

All at once the truck full of women erupted in ear-piercing shrieks.

'English devils! Murderers!' the women screamed in one voice in Greek. At a loss to know what to do the soldier pointed his rifle at them.

'Please, officer!' Olga raised her voice over the chaos, trying to appease him. She was the only one who spoke

English. 'We don't mean anything by this, it's just fear. What harm can it do to leave the child behind?'

'Orders, ma'am,' the soldier repeated loudly over the noise, lowering his rifle, his eyes avoiding her gaze. 'Everyone must be collected regardless of age,' and with that he gave the signal to the driver to move on.

They drove through the town methodically picking up women and children from other neighbourhoods. Once the truck was overflowing it made its way through the narrow streets towards the town's main school. On arrival they were unloaded and ushered into the assembly hall, which was already packed with earlier arrivals. In the playground the men were being lined up in single file. Amongst them Olga could see several of her workmen and numerous friends and neighbours.

On entering the hall, they were greeted not only by the sheer volume of noise of children howling and women sobbing, but also by the unmistakable odour of humanity. In the right-hand corner of the room, lined up in a row against the wall, were several buckets, which, judging by their stench, had already been used.

'How long do you think they'll keep us here?' a horrified Ernestina asked her daughter. 'I am not sure I can endure this.'

'Your guess is as good as mine, Mother, and we have no choice but to endure it,' Olga replied, spotting a chair for Ernestina to sit on. 'What I'd like to know is why they brought us here in the first place. It's the men they are interested in – what do they want with us?' She looked around for Katerina and Anita who had made their way to an open window in search of some fresh air.

'There is no way I can *go* in one of those buckets,' Anita whispered to Katerina, her head out of the window, trying to breathe. 'I'd rather burst, or wet myself!'

'Well, we shall see what happens when you need to go . . .' Katerina replied, also hanging out of the window for air.

Scanning the yard a few feet below for friends and neighbours among the men, she noticed a black van entering the school gates. It drove past the lines of men and then came to a stop directly below the window, allowing Katerina a clear view. Sitting in the passenger seat was a man with a black hood over his head covering his entire face, save for two holes for the eyes. Leaning out further, she tried to see more. The man was dressed in dark trousers and a black short- sleeved shirt. The only visible parts of his body were his forearms and hands; *hairy as a gorilla's*, she thought. On the little finger of his right hand he was sporting a gold signet ring and a long talon like a hook, a trend of the times among some un-savoury men, and something Katerina found particularly repellent.

The van stood with its engine idling for some minutes while the driver and the passenger talked. The hooded man was conversing animatedly with the English driver, making elaborate gestures with his hands. The little finger on his right hand . . . She tried in vain to make out what they were saying. After a short while the van drove away to park in the middle of the playground.

'Did you see *that*?' Katerina asked Anita who had turned away to talk to a woman standing close.

'What was it?' She turned and looked out of the window again at the van.

'A rat!' Katerina spat out in disgust. 'An informer!'

Everyone knew what that meant. He was almost certainly a Greek; a compatriot and a traitor! A spy who was willing to be bribed into giving information against his own people. Everyone gathered at the windows to look, and soon, like a chorus of hissing snakes, the word *traitor* filled the room, the sound picking up momentum, getting louder and louder, spilling out of every window and door, until a soldier burst in and, pointing his rifle at the women, silenced them.

Voiceless now, they stood by the windows and watched as their men passed one by one in front of the hooded man sitting in the van. All it took was a nod of his head to identify suspected EOKA activists and determine a man's fate. Katerina and Anita stood holding on to each other and thanked God that this ID parade only involved the men; they would both have had much to fear if the women had been targeted too.

The informer apparently had inside knowledge of who might be actively involved in the movement. Bought and paid for by the British! It couldn't be any worse. A fellow countryman bringing dishonour to his people for blood money.

'A son of a whore,' a woman standing next to Katerina hissed. 'A traitor is even worse than the bastard soldiers.'

'A man betraying his countrymen doesn't deserve to live,' another screamed, shaking her fist.

'I put a curse on him with every inch of my being,' a frail old woman dressed in black shouted, looking out of the window.

Everyone in that room had a father, a son, a husband or a friend who could be betrayed by an affirmative nod directed at him. If that happened, then the consequences were grave. He would be taken away for sure, possibly tortured like Mario, and undoubtedly be put into one of the detention camps that had been erected on the island since the troubles had begun.

'Maybe he is a filthy Turk,' another woman's shrill voice echoed around the room.

'That's more likely,' someone else shouted.

'I hope someone takes a knife to him,' a voice echoed in the room.

Olga looked at her mother; she had known this was coming. 'What did I tell you?' she whispered to Ernestina, shifting closer to her. 'The hatred will not stop here, mark my words.'

Olga had grown up with both Greek and Turkish Cypriots living fairly harmoniously side by side. The only thing that set them apart was their religion and the obvious disparity in their numbers. The Turkish population was much smaller than the Greek and that at times gave rise to some conflict between them, but on the whole the two communities were respectful and friendly towards each other. However, the uprising against the British by the Greek Cypriots was to mark the start of discord between the two communities and that, Olga always thought, wasn't really either community's fault.

'Divide and rule,' she had said with a hollow laugh to her mother once she realized how the Brits were handling the situation. 'It always works for them. Get people fighting among themselves . . .'

With the first rumblings of an uprising by the Greeks, the British governor had proceeded to expand the number of auxiliary police by recruiting a disproportionate number of policemen from the Turkish community. *What good is that going to do apart from turning Greek against Turk?* Olga observed, and once again found the British tactics not to her liking.

The knowledge that a traitor was among them brought fear and shame to the town. Nothing felt the same again after that. The rumour that went around town after the school incident was that the traitor was indeed a Greek, and that made everyone even more uneasy.

'Where will it all end, Father? It's been almost three years,' Ernestina asked the padre when he next came to visit. 'I know there are bad people everywhere in the world but to betray your country for money? It's the worst crime.' She shook her head. 'What kind of person does *that*?'

'A person with no conscience,' the padre said with a long sigh.

The episode left the Greek population bruised, and ill at ease with each other. Raids and arrests continued and there were several more such episodes during the months that followed, directed by information supplied by collaborators.

Suspicion spread like cholera and people preferred to keep themselves to themselves. No one went out any more, they had no way of knowing who might be spying on them; the cafes were almost empty, people preferred the safety of their homes.

It was during that period that the padre, encouraged by the Linser women, started coming to the house more frequently. His presence offered them security and stability, and in turn, they offered him a sense of belonging; a home.

'We despair at having traitors in our midst,' Katerina

said to him one day as they sat as usual at the kitchen table. 'I can only try to imagine what your people went through during the Civil War.'

'Compatriot against compatriot is the greatest evil, Katerina. At least in Cyprus you are mostly united in your struggle.'

'We are only a handful of people on this island – we need to be united . . . we can't afford to have these traitors amongst us.'

'Corruption and evil is a part of the human condition; if good exists, then so does evil,' he told her gravely. 'Since we believe in the benevolence of the almighty God, then we must also believe in Satan and the malevolence of darkness.' Lately as they sat together in the tranquillity of the kitchen, the padre had taken to reading her extracts from the Bible to illustrate some points of their discussion. That day it was a passage from chapter five, verse twenty of the Book of Isaiah.

'Woe unto them that call evil good, and good evil; that count darkness as light, and light as darkness; that put bitter for sweet, and sweet for bitter!'

Katerina loved these readings and discussions; they made her think and offered her a different perspective. If Olga had been her teacher in the early years, providing her with a social education, now the padre was giving her a spiritual and philosophical one.

She sometimes wondered if she could have had these discussions with Father Euthimios, her Greek Orthodox priest at St Lazarus, whom she respected and loved. He had been her religious mentor and confessor since she arrived as a child in Larnaka, but she had never sat in the kitchen with him, exchanging personal thoughts and drinking coffee.

She was well aware that her relationship with Padre Bernardino was unique. He was a man of God but he was also a man, and her good friend.

10

Katerina had not seen Anita so cheerful since the day she had announced that she was in love with Mario.

'So tell me,' she asked her as they sat on the veranda one jasmine-scented July evening, 'what brings the smile to your face and the colour to your cheeks?'

'I never thought I'd feel anything again, Katerina *mou*,' Anita replied, a sparkle in her eyes brightening her usually serious expression. 'I haven't said anything to Mama or *Nonna* yet – you are the first. Costas has asked me to marry him and I have accepted.'

Katerina had suspected that Anita's mood had something to do with Costas, who was her constant companion of late. Her own feelings towards him had not changed, but she put her antipathy to Costas down to her loyalty to Mario and tried to ignore it for Anita's sake. Seeing how animated Anita was, she continued to keep her thoughts to herself.

'So long as you are sure of how you feel, Anita *mou*,' Katerina said and reached for her hand, 'then I am glad for you.'

'Mario will always be the love of my life, Katerina *mou*, but he was taken away from me. Costas is a good man and he told me he loves me . . . I am grateful for that and I am as happy as I could ever be . . .'

Anita's only worry had been how Mario's family would take the news. She knew her mother and grand-mother would be pleased for her but her anxious dis-position kept her awake at night until she summoned up the courage to go and see Mario's mother.

She found her sitting at a table under the orange tree in the back yard of their house, dressed all in black, still in mourning for her dead son, cleaning and preparing *louvi*, fresh black-eye beans for lunch. The sight brought a sting to Anita's heart. She knew how much Mario had loved that dish.

'One of the reasons I like the summer,' she remembered him telling her when they first met, 'is so I can eat *louvi*! The summer foods are the best – watermelon and figs, aubergines and succulent cucumbers, I love them all, but for me *louvi* is king.' She wasn't as fond of them as he was. She found them bland; Katerina cooked them too in the summer but Anita preferred something more full-bodied, more seasoned like her grandmother's Italian dishes. She felt *louvi* was more of a salad than a meal; boiled until tender and simply served with an olive oil and lemon dressing, the dish didn't excite her. Spaghetti with a *put-tanesca* sauce was more to her liking: spicy and flavoursome.

But Mario's infectious enthusiasm for the dish would sweep her along and she would often join the family for lunch on *louvi* days.

Seeing his mother now sitting under the tree busying herself in the familiar laborious task of shelling and cleaning the bean-like pods, she welled up.

'*Kalimera*, Kyria Sophia!' she called out as she opened the garden gate.

'*Kalostin*, Anita,' Welcome! Sophia called back in the Cypriot dialect, looking up from her work. 'You are up early this morning?'

'I couldn't sleep on account of the heat,' Anita lied, walking towards her.

'Well, you've arrived just in time! Come . . . sit!' and pointing to a chair next to her she handed Anita a knife. Without hesitation Anita sat down and reached for a bowl. Cleaning the *louvi* was something of a ritual, which she always enjoyed.

'Remember, Anita *mou,* how you and Mario used to sit here and help me?' Sophia pushed a pile of beans towards her. 'He loved doing it; ever since he was a boy he used to help me.'

At the mention of Mario's name Anita could control herself no longer. She burst into tears. She'd spent a sleepless night anticipating this meeting and the tension was now getting the better of her.

'I've come to tell you . . .' she started through her tears

and then stopped to take a deep breath. 'What I mean is, Kyria Sophia,' she took another deep breath, 'is that I want you to know that I have never stopped loving Mario . . . you do know that, don't you?'

'I never doubted it, Anita *mou*,' Sophia replied, reaching for Anita's hand. 'Mario also loved you deeply, we all do. Now, what have you come to tell me, my girl?'

After drying her eyes and taking a sip of water from the glass Sophia had poured from a jug on the table, Anita started to explain the reason for her early-morning visit. When she finished, the older woman stretched across the table and cupped both of Anita's hands in hers.

'You are a good girl, Anita *mou*, and you are still young, you deserve to be happy.' Moving closer, Sophia took the young woman in her arms and held her in a tight embrace for a long while, each of them lost in the memory of the boy who had been taken away from them.

'I wanted to have Mario's children,' Anita finally said, breaking the silence, a sob caught in her throat. 'I always dreamed that we would have four.'

'Even though Mario was denied a life and a future, *you* have a right to live,' Sophia replied, her voice breaking with emotion. 'You have nothing to feel guilty about, my girl. You have my blessing to marry Costas and have as many children as you can. He seems a good boy and appears to be dedicated to our cause. I hope he makes you happy,' and with that Sophia took Anita's face in her hands and kissed her on the forehead.

Anita, who was always rather guarded when making new friendships, had been uncharacteristically receptive to Costas's attentions. No doubt his single-minded persistence to befriend her as soon as he met her had much to do with it, but perhaps the biggest contributing factor was his physical resemblance to Mario, even if Anita was apparently unaware of it.

'I don't know why,' she had told Katerina when she first met him, 'but I feel as if I have always known him.'

'That's because he reminds you of Mario,' Katerina muttered to herself under her breath. She had noticed the likeness between the young men but refused to acknowledge it to anyone; her loyalty to Mario wouldn't allow it. Besides, she thought, the similarities were tenuous. Whereas Mario, although not very tall, had been muscular and athletic, Costas, though similar in height, was rather lazily stocky. They had the same head of black curly hair and a square jaw, but Mario's big chestnut eyes had been open and warm, whereas Costas's were hooded, steely dark, and hard to look into. They both sported a moustache, but Mario's had been pencil thin and faint, whereas Costas's was bold, thick and macho. Mario had had a boyish aura about him; Costas oozed manly confidence. But then, Katerina thought, if the two young men had some physical resemblance, there it stopped. Their characters had nothing in common. Mario had been unguarded and sincere, but Costas she found cagey and disingenuous. But she seemed to be alone in her reservations – none of the others appeared to mind Anita's new suitor, and as the padre had pointed out, she had no particular reason for her antipathy towards him apart from her affection for Mario.

'I am very glad to see Costas is such a sensible young man,' Olga had said when she got to know him, 'and glad to see that he is being cautious. It's the only way to be these days.'

'He supports the struggle as much as I do, Mother,' Anita protested, even though she had distinctly sensed him withdrawing of late, missing meetings and discussions. She put it down to his new job.

'I've no doubt,' Olga replied, 'but at least he is taking care to be safe. You should be grateful for that, if you are going to marry him.'

Their courtship had started through their mutual support for independence, then progressed to friendship.

'If we don't get rid of the British, all that bloodshed will have been for nothing,' he told Anita the first time they met as they sat in Kyria Sophia's house one evening. A few comrades, young men and women, would meet secretly either in Mario's parents' house or in a small bar called

Socrates' Taverna, in the old part of town. They would gather a couple of times a month, and by way of precaution, in case of a raid, they would bring a selection of musical instruments so they could meet under the pretext of an evening of drinking and singing. Mario's father, a virtuoso *bouzouki* player, would accompany other members of the group, some on guitar or *baglama*, while in the absence of a piano Anita sang along with the women. That first evening, Anita had gone alone without Katerina to Mario's house, and after they had all finished talking, as became their habit a bottle of homemade *zivania* from the village appeared on the table, and then the music and drinking began. They sang bittersweet songs whose words told of oppression and displacement, of liberty and loss. On that first meeting Costas produced from his pocket a mouth organ, which he proceeded to play with professional expertise.

'You have the voice of an angel,' he whispered to Anita as she sang. His voice, hot in her ear, and his physical proximity disturbed her and she found herself shifting away from him. She hadn't felt anything like that since Mario kissed her for the first time, and the sensation made her feel flustered; moisture gathered on her upper lip and her heart pounded in her ears as she carried on singing. She shot a furtive look at Sophia sitting across the table and felt relief to see that she didn't seem to have noticed Anita's agitation.

Everything in that room reminded Anita of Mario. Photographs of him in his EOKA uniform and memorabilia were everywhere. In the corner of the room the little shrine to *Panayia*, the Holy Mother, with its perpetual burning candle, held yet another photograph of Mario, as if to sanctify him. Costas's presence in the room made her feel unexpectedly uncomfortable. Keeping her distance from him she continued to sing and then discreetly got up and slipped away to the kitchen. She splashed cool water from the tap on her face and tried to compose herself. *What is this that I'm feeling?* she wondered. Had Costas's attention unearthed feelings she had buried along with Mario, or was it Costas himself and his proximity to her that had moved her so?

The next time they met was in the neutral location of Socrates' Taverna, again without Katerina, and Anita realized that Costas had the power to upset the stability she had fought so hard to achieve. She had loved Mario with all her heart; he had been her soulmate, her comrade, her friend. She had pledged to love him and cherish him for always, but Costas's self-assured presence disturbed her and made her flush.

Anita and Sonia often talked about falling in love, about *erotas*, about Aphrodite's love child and the power of sexual love, but Anita had always dismissed it as myth and fantasy. She now feared that perhaps she was falling victim to the mischievous god against her will.

'I love Mario with every inch of my being but I don't feel a burning desire to do more than kiss him,' she had said to Sonia when she and Mario first started seeing each other. 'I think people use it as a justification for sex, especially men to excuse their lustful thoughts.'

'You think too much, my sister,' Sonia laughed. 'If you let yourself be free and let Mario show you . . . once you taste the ways of love you will feel differently.'

'*You* don't have any morals, my little sister,' Anita scolded her. 'There are higher things to love than sex!'

Anita liked it when Mario kissed her, but she would not allow the courtship to go further and he was a respectful boy so he did not persist; they were going to wait till they were married.

Costas's tactics were different. Bold persistence was more his style.

'You ignite a forest fire in me, my little Hungarian beauty,' he would whisper in her ear as he pulled her close to kiss her full on the mouth when they were alone.

'I am *not* Hungarian!' Anita would protest, pulling away from him. 'I am a Greek!' The sisters' paternal heritage was a sore point and a legacy that both girls had rejected with passion.

'Whatever you are, you are the girl for me,' Costas replied, and Anita, despite herself, would give in to his good looks and caresses.

The wedding ceremony in early September was a quiet

affair conducted by Padre Bernardino at his church with just a handful of people including Mario's family. Sonia came too. It was her first visit back since she'd left, so the Linser household was having a double celebration.

'I am a happy old lady to see one of my granddaughters marry at last,' Ernestina had told Olga and Katerina. 'And who knows, before I die I might see our Sonia marry too.'

Olga drove the couple to the church in her old red Triumph. Costas had invited a couple of his chums, one of whom by the name of Petros had just acquired a brand new black Morris Minor with four doors and leather upholstery, and Costas was insisting that they ride with him instead of Olga. Anita was furious that he'd even suggested such a thing, and refused on the grounds that she wouldn't be seen dead riding in an English car.

'I thought you agreed that we despise everything British,' she had said to him, reminding him how it represented the imperial rule.

'Well . . . yes . . . but . . .' he fumbled, '. . . this is a handsome car and the only one in town. We will turn heads as we ride to church. Besides, Petros is going to be my *goumbaros*.'

'In that case I suggest you ride alone with your best man,' she snapped, and walked away with a knot in her stomach. When she reappeared she was calmer but the knot was still there.

They were tightly squeezed in Olga's car but Anita was happy to be driven by her mother even if it meant her dress was crumpled on arrival. Since Mario's death she resisted pomp and ceremony even if her grandmother had wanted her to wear a traditional wedding dress with a veil.

'No, *Nonna*,' she had insisted, 'this is not that sort of wedding, and I am not that type of girl.' Instead Anita wore a simple cream linen dress with a lace collar and a satin sash around her waist. She wore orange blossom in her hair and her bouquet, which had been hand-picked from the garden that morning by Katerina, was an armful of jasmine that trailed down to just above her knees. Her shoes, made of cream satin like her sash, fastened with tiny silver buckles round her ankles and although the weather was still too warm to wear stockings everyone insisted she did, which made her feel hot and bothered as she walked down the aisle. She thought Costas in his dark navy suit looked handsome standing at the altar. She glanced at him as she took her place by his side, the tight feeling still in her stomach. Then, a question flashed through her mind which she immediately banished. *Could it be that his good looks are the only thing about Costas that I like?*

*

The night before the wedding Olga had prepared a magnificent dinner for the five women.

'This could be the last time we shall all be together like

this,' she had told them, making a list of ingredients as she consulted her famous cookery book for the banquet. 'Tonight we will celebrate Anita's marriage and Sonia's return! I will cook us a meal we won't forget!'

The girls laid out the table with the finest Lefkara linen, heirlooms from Great-grandmother Eva, and polished the best silver, china and crystal, which sparkled all night long in the candlelight.

It's like the last supper, Katerina mused to herself with a chuckle, when they took their seats around the table. Looking at their beloved faces as she so often did, she reflected on the contrast between her adopted family and the one she had come from. She felt fortunate to be one of these marvellous women who had taken her into their midst and made her their own.

As the night wore on and the eating came to an end, and the conversation was flowing as much as the wine, Olga raised her glass one more time.

'This time, I'd like to propose a toast to something that concerns us all,' she announced ceremoniously, 'but first I'd like to tell you all how blessed I feel to be surrounded by you, my beloved female family. We have lived together, five wonderful women, in harmonious sisterhood for a very long time. Always united, we have dealt with whatever life has thrown at us, good and bad.' Olga looked around the table, her voice resonating with emotion. 'But now our life is about to change,' she continued, 'and not only for Anita, but for all of us. For the first time in years we shall have a man living amongst us and although men have passed through this house, for you, my daughters, it will be for the first time, as you have hardly any memory of your father.'

They all sat listening, their glasses poised, waiting for Olga to continue. 'There will be a big *change* in our lives. That is not always bad, change can also bring good things, so what I would like to do is to propose a toast,' and with that, Olga stood up and looked at each of them in turn and lifted her glass, 'to *change!*'

'To change!' they all chimed in unison and raised their glasses.

'Mama is right,' Sonia said, hugging Anita, later on that night as the two sisters prepared for bed together for the last time in their bedroom. They preferred sleeping together regardless of the many spare rooms in the house, even if Olga was forever trying to convince them to spread out.

'What's the point of this big house if we don't use it all?' she told them, but the girls felt otherwise.

That night they had all stayed up far too late eating and drinking and now the excitement of the next day was preventing them from going to sleep.

'It's true what Mama was saying,' Sonia continued. 'A

new chapter is about to begin for us all. Nothing will ever be the same again, Anita *mou*.'

'For me nothing has been the same since Mario was murdered . . .' Anita murmured. *'But,'* she quickly added, brushing her dark thoughts away and giving her sister a broad smile, 'I'm getting married tomorrow! There are many reasons to be happy. This indeed is a new chapter in all our lives, my dearest sister.'

'I know Costas is not a substitute for Mario, Anita *mou*, but he loves you and you love him back – don't you?' Sonia asked, looking at her anxiously for confirmation.

'Yes, I do,' she replied, 'but not in the same way as I loved Mario. Costas is a very different character.' The two sisters hugged and kissed each other the way they had done as little girls, before getting into their beds.

'But please, Sonia *mou*, promise me you'll come back soon,' Anita added, slipping between the cool cotton sheets. 'I miss you so, and Nicos is waiting for you too.'

'Only one more year to go, and I'll be back before you know it!' Sonia replied cheerfully, and switched the light off.

11

1958

Life in Vienna when she first arrived had been just as Sonia had hoped it would be. She found freedom to do as she pleased, and was relieved to be missing the worst of the political situation back home. However, Anita was determined to keep her sister well informed of developments through regular correspondence.

Her letters were full of political incidents, while Sonia's were full of accounts of her life in the big city and the music academy.

'*They arrested the entire male population and interrogated them,*' Anita wrote to tell her after that particular episode. '*There is a traitor in our town, Sonia mou, and we all live in fear of betrayal . . .*'

'*Well, I'm glad I'm here, and not there,*' Sonia wrote back, '*but let me tell you, my dearest sister, what happened to me yesterday! I met the most handsome boy . . . well, when I say boy I actually mean man, as he is our new teacher! His name*

*is Hans and he is very good-looking and he thinks I have talent
. . . I think he really likes me . . .'*

Anita didn't mind Sonia's frivolous chatter – she knew
that side of her sister's character and her letters were a
welcome distraction from all that was happening at
home.

Living with Great-aunt Heidi in her apartment, a
pleasant walk away from the Academy, or a tram ride if
it was raining, suited Sonia well. Finding her way around
Vienna took no time at all, especially since during her
first week there she had had Olga to help her settle in.

Mother and daughter travelled by ship from Limassol
to Piraeus, then after a short stay in Athens they took the
train through Greece and the Balkans to Vienna. The journey, which took several days, was to mark the start of a
lifelong love of train journeys for Sonia.

'Please, Mama, can we stay in Athens for a few days?'
Sonia had asked when they were making their plans for
the journey. Both Anita and Sonia had always longed to
visit the Greek capital, not only for its classical associations, which every Greek Cypriot grew up learning in
school, but also for its perceived sophistication and glamour they saw in films. Most Saturday nights the girls and
their friends would be found in the Rex, the local cinema,
engrossed in whatever new or old film happened to be
showing. In winter it would be in the indoor theatre and
in summer in the open air. They would sit under the

night sky and feast their eyes on their favourite movie stars, cry at the tragedies, laugh at the comedies, learn the popular songs and dances and find out about the latest fashions. Athens in the 1950s, after the hardships of World War II and its aftermath, was undergoing something of a cinematic and musical boom, and to the young Cypriots the city epitomized style.

Mother and daughter stayed in a little pension in Plaka with a view of the Acropolis from its roof terrace. No sooner had they arrived and dropped their bags in their room than Sonia was ready to start exploring.

'Where to first, Mama?' she asked, eager to head out again as she splashed some cold water on her face to revive herself from the journey and the midday heat.

'The Temple of Athena awaits us!' Olga smiled at her daughter. 'But first let's rest a while.'

Sonia gave her mother precisely half an hour before coaxing her out of bed and onto the street again.

'We can sleep tonight, Mother!' she urged her. 'Time for adventure now!'

Weary as she was, Olga too was excited to revisit the city, especially the Acropolis; she hadn't been there since she was a girl on one of her trips with her father and now she was eager to show it to her daughter.

'I was as impatient as you the first time I visited Athens. I wanted to see everything,' she told Sonia while she was getting dressed. 'But that was such a long time ago now . . . I wonder how it has changed.'

The climb up to the Acropolis was as thrilling as Sonia had imagined and so different to how Olga remembered it. Climbing through the poor neighbourhood of Plaka with its narrow streets that snaked upwards towards the rock of the Acropolis, they passed doorways and windows laden with pots of basil and geraniums, women on flat roofs hanging their washing on lines and old men sitting on their doorsteps drinking coffee. It was all every inch as picturesque as Sonia had seen in the movies. As they approached the top of the hill, the labyrinth of steps and cobblestoned alleyways leading them upwards became steeper and harder under the unforgiving sun.

'Let me catch my breath for a moment,' Olga said, sitting on a bench under some olive trees once they reached the top.

'My fault,' Sonia told her mother apologetically. 'We should have waited till later when it got cool to do the climb.'

'I was as keen as you were,' Olga replied with a smile, wiping her brow, 'but then again . . . I'm not as young.'

The sight Sonia encountered as she entered the sanctuary stunned her. She stopped dead and stood mesmerized. In line with the main gate in front of them stood the Parthenon, gilded by the sun, more majestic and glorious than any postcard, photograph or film she had ever seen.

In the distance to the left, looming over the city, stood the Erechtheion, a temple that Sonia yearned to see possibly even more than the Temple of Athena. Its porch of the Maidens, supported by six massive female statues, the famous Caryatids, held a great fascination for the young Sonia. These sculpted female figures serving as pillars, taking the place of weight-bearing columns as they carry the roof of the temple on their heads, had always inflamed the young girl's imagination. She would gaze endlessly at pictures of them in her schoolbooks and imagined them coming to life at night to roam the city and defend it like some kind of mythological superheroes. Their beauty seemed immeasurable and their stature enviable. Later, when she was older she saw them as a symbol of women's strength. She stood looking in awe, undecided which of the two temples to approach first, then made her way towards the Erechtheion followed by Olga. She stood beneath the six maidens and looked up in wonder.

'Look at them, Mama,' she said, her eyes drawn upwards, 'aren't they magnificent?'

'They certainly are,' Olga replied and reached out to touch the foot of one.

'For me they have always symbolized female power and strength.'

'They remind me of us!' Sonia exclaimed, hugging her mother. 'Strong and powerful, with you as our chief Caryatid!'

'That's a funny image!' Olga burst out laughing. 'You do have a strong imagination, Sonia *mou* . . . but you're right, the five of us have managed well enough over the years, even if holding up our roof has given us some headaches along the way!'

The descent from the Acropolis was much easier. The sun was finally surrendering some of its ferocity as it began to sink in the west, giving way to a cooler evening. In one of the little alleyways at the foot of the sacred rock, the two women came upon a small family-run taverna where they decided to stop for a glass of retsina and the dish of the day cooked by the proprietor and his wife.

The first day of their trip had been as splendid as they could have hoped, and a welcome relief from the troubled island they had left behind.

Their next few days in Athens sped past all too quickly. There was much to see and do and Olga promised herself she would return to the city once the political situation on the island settled and normality was restored.

'I need to bring your sister here too,' she told Sonia as they strolled in Syntagma Square enjoying an ice cream. 'Anita needs to expand her horizons.'

'She is too involved with the struggle, she's not interested in anything else,' Sonia replied, making her way towards a bench under a tree for some respite from the early-morning sun.

'I wish I could convince her to join you in Vienna . . .

She is so young; I don't want her to be giving up on life just yet.' But Olga knew she couldn't compete with Anita's dedication to Mario's memory and her beliefs, no matter how much she wanted her daughter to be as free as she had been in her youth.

The train journey from Athens to Vienna was another revelation for Sonia. Sleeping, eating, reading, and going to the lavatory, all as the train chugged along, delighted and amused her. Speeding through different countries, crossing borders, encountering landscapes she hadn't even known existed and hearing languages she didn't understand, was more thrilling than she had ever imagined.

'It's so wonderful, Mama,' she told Olga the first night they climbed into their bunks to sleep. 'We start our journey in one place and by morning we'll be in another world.'

'We are so lucky to be living in these modern times,' Olga agreed drowsily, lulled by the hiss and rattle of the train as she drifted off to sleep.

Great-aunt Heidi was Grandfather Franz's second cousin. She had been married and divorced three times, had no children and had been living alone for a good number of years, so she gladly welcomed Sonia's arrival and the infusion of youthful zest into her previously solitary life.

'From now on I want you to treat my house as your home, *Liebling*,' she told Sonia when she arrived with her mother, and meant it. 'You must tell her, Olga dear, that when you leave I will be your substitute; anything she needs, I will be here for her.' She was a gracious and affectionate old lady, whose resemblance to Olga was striking and comforting to young Sonia. If there had been three other women living with them, she thought, then it would feel just like home.

Heidi's spacious two-bedroom apartment was close to Stephansplatz, shaded by the gloomy gothic cathedral looming over the city. Sonia had to walk past this building every day on her way to the Academy of Music and Performing Arts where Olga had enrolled her.

'This church,' she wrote to Anita when she arrived there, *'is the most depressing building I have ever seen – it's so colossal it makes you feel insignificant and diminished. Not to mention how ugly it is! Sometimes I think I should enter and light a candle but it just doesn't entice me. Perhaps if it wasn't so dirty and black it might look better. But at least there are so many other pretty churches on my way to school that they make up for this one!'*

Great-aunt Heidi's apartment on Grashofgasse was on the second floor of a block that surrounded a delightful courtyard. An apple tree stood in the centre of a little garden, which the residents took turns to cultivate. In the spring, Sonia could gaze down from her bedroom window onto multi-coloured crocuses, snowdrops and tulips, and an array of roses in the summer. By autumn the chrysanthemums would be in bloom and then, when winter came, all would be covered in a blanket of snow. Sonia took delight in every season. It was a private and safe place to live – access to the courtyard was through two large wooden gates situated on opposite sides of the square, which at nine o'clock each evening would be securely locked.

'You must make sure you are home in good time, *Liebling*,' Heidi warned her when she first arrived, 'or you will be locked out': an ominous warning which made Sonia tremble at the thought of being left outside alone in the big city. For the first year she obeyed the rule religiously, never staying out later than the permitted time, but once her confidence and friendships with both boys and girls at the Academy were firmly established, it was much harder for her to keep to the curfew. Her first request to stay overnight with a friend was met with resistance by the aunt who felt responsible for her safety, but in time, and having been introduced to the friends, the old lady succumbed to the young girl's pleas; after all, she remembered being young once.

Sonia's sparkling personality and appetite for new experiences were qualities that attracted people to her. Vienna, even if a little sombre and austere, was still, in comparison to Larnaka, a city of wonders.

'*At the turn of every corner you come across a palace,*' she wrote to Anita and Katerina after a few weeks, in awe of the architecture all over the city which she had never seen the likes of before.

'*You cannot imagine or believe what I came upon yesterday as I was walking minutes from Aunt Heidi's apartment! I came across a plaque on a wall of a house that said, ROBERT SCHU-MANN lived here! Imagine! The great composer lived just round the corner from me! And that's not all. I have seen dozens of plaques like it all over town. Believe me, Anita, this is the city of music! You, my darling sister, should be here with me!*'

The two young women would read Sonia's letters with excitement and her enthusiasm leapt off the pages to carry them to Sonia's Viennese adventure. After they had devoured the letter they'd pass it on to Olga and Ernestina, unless Sonia had written something that was for their eyes only and instructed them to keep it secret.

'*I am going to tell you something, but make sure Nonna does not see this letter . . .*' She knew that her Catholic grandmother would have an anxiety attack if she learned what Sonia was getting up to. '*After the concert the other night I went out for a drink, or maybe two . . . or three – I can't remember – with a boy called Ludvik . . .*' The girls would read Sonia's confessions, unsure if they should worry or just enjoy her perilous adventures from afar.

Living in Vienna, doing what she was born to do – the music, the flirting, the freedom – set Sonia's spirit free to express itself. Every day at the Academy, learning, prac-tising, meeting other students of her own age, was a pleasure no matter how hard she had to work. The Austrian capital was a universe away from where she had been brought up, yet somehow it also felt familiar, if not in physical terms then in spirit. The Viennese architecture, baroque, grand and opulent, was unlike anything she had encountered before, apart from photographs in the family albums, yet she felt as though she had always known it. Perhaps, she mused, it had been in some other lifetime. She was, after all, a descendant of the people living there. In a strange way it felt like a homecoming.

A place Sonia wanted to visit as soon as she arrived in Vienna was the celebrated Café Central. She had heard so much about it from Olga when she was growing up that she didn't have to ask twice to be taken there. Olga not only wanted to introduce her daughter to the most fashionable place in town but also to relive some of her own youthful memories. Anita and Sonia had been brought up on stories of the glory days of Vienna by their mother.

Memories from Olga's visits with her father were often recalled and narrated as bedtime stories for the girls. She would describe how Grandfather Franz would take her to Café Central before dinner, dressed in the latest Parisian fashions, Franz glowing with pride to be accompanied by his beautiful daughter and showing her off to the world. Olga would describe the excitement of spotting a famous artist or a legendary intellectual, and the thrill of drinking her first glass of champagne.

'I felt like a real young lady,' she'd tell her girls. 'Papa made me feel so grown up, introducing me to his friends. Life was just beginning and I felt on top of the world. When the time is right I shall take you there too, my girls!'

True to her word, on arrival in Vienna Olga took Sonia and Heidi to the Café for an aperitif and then on to a fashionable restaurant for a sumptuous dinner.

'I am too old for this sort of thing,' Heidi had said, but rushed off with great excitement to find something in her wardrobe to wear.

Through her regular correspondence with Anita, Sonia had also been kept informed about her sister's relationship with Costas – although the letter announcing her acceptance of his marriage proposal took Sonia by surprise.

'*I am really happy you are finally able to fall in love again, my sister,*' she wrote back, knowing well enough how hard Mario's death had hit Anita, '*and I can't wait to meet this Costas who has managed to steal your heart.*'

It was time for Sonia to make a return visit. She had been away long enough, and what better reason than a marriage celebration . . .

After the marriage, in Linser tradition Costas moved into the ancestral home.

'Grandfather Josef must be smiling up in heaven,' Olga told her mother, glancing at his portrait hanging above the sofa as they sat taking tea one afternoon some months after the wedding. 'He built this house with all its rooms for a big family, so let's hope our girls do him proud and fill it up with grandchildren.'

'I hope to live long enough to see them,' Ernestina replied, knowing that her waning health might prevent this from happening.

Anita's greatest wish was for a baby. Every month she waited with a trembling heart to find out if she was pregnant. It was already nine months since the wedding and each time her disappointment sent her into a melancholic state. Twice she had become pregnant and twice she lost the baby within weeks of finding out she was with child. Her one distraction was her involvement with the struggle, but this was rapidly coming to a conclusion. Four years had passed since the night of the bombings and now a resolution with the British looked imminent.

'We have all lived long enough with this uncertainty and worry,' Olga told her son-in-law over dinner one evening. Costas rarely graced them with his presence, preferring most nights to go to his club for a game of cards. He had settled into living with the five women in his own way, which was to spend as little time as possible with them.

His job as an insurance clerk wasn't very demanding and once work was over he'd come home, bathe, change his clothes and go out again. His presence in the home didn't have much of an impact, but the women preferred it that way. Katerina gave him a wide berth and Anita's main interest, after the first few months of romance and sexual dizziness, was in his ability to get her pregnant.

She didn't regret marrying Costas, but once he moved into the house and she came to know him better she recognized that apart from their initial shared interest in politics, which he now seemed to have forgotten, they had nothing in common. She became aware that his intellect was underdeveloped; he wasn't a stupid man so much as shallow and uninformed. Anita had been brought up in an atmosphere of culture and learning, but Costas's education was limited, didn't go beyond his six years at the village high school. He now seemed to have no other interests apart from cars, tailor-made suits, cigars and having fun with his friends. Olga heard alarm bells. She feared her daughter's marriage might be mirroring her own.

'So long as he doesn't start frequenting the brothels . . .' she said when Costas habitually started disappearing most evenings.

'Please, Mother,' Anita protested in his defence, trying to make the best of what she was secretly beginning to suspect was a mistake. 'Not everyone is like Father. Costas might not be the most cultured of people but he's not a bad man, and he doesn't live off us.'

'I know, I know . . .' Olga replied by way of an apology.

She knew that Costas earned a decent living and she was well aware that her prejudices had always been a source of irritation to her girls.

'Mother,' Sonia had scolded her more than once, when they were younger, 'if you carry on like this about men, neither of us will ever get married, and as you know we both intend to – whether you like it or not!' So Olga did her best to stifle her prejudice against certain kinds of men – mainly husbands. She wanted her girls to be happy, and if it meant they wanted to marry, then so be it. She'd have to curb her antipathy to matrimony.

One afternoon in late January Anita walked into the *saloni* to find her mother and grandmother drinking tea. The sun was pouring through the closed windows, heating up the room as if it was summer, and the two women were basking in its warmth. She sat quietly next to them and reached for the old woman's hand.

'*Nonna*,' she said, her voice wavering as she looked at her grandmother, then at Olga, 'I want your blessing.'

'You always have my blessing, *cara mia*,' her grandmother replied. 'You know you never have to ask.'

'I know, *Nonna*, but this is different,' Anita replied. 'You see . . . I have been keeping a secret from you both . . . and it has not been easy.'

The two women looked anxiously at each other and then at Anita.

'Please don't be upset with me,' the young woman continued hesitantly. 'It was very hard not speaking to you or Katerina about it, but Doctor Elias said I should wait . . .'

'What? Why?' Olga jumped in, interrupting Anita's flow. 'What's wrong?'

'There is nothing *wrong*, Mama,' she replied, realizing that the solemnity of her speech had caused alarm. Relaxing her face and banishing the vertical line between her brows she gave them both a smile and continued, 'I promise you both I am fine, everything's fine . . . it's just that . . . it's just that I'm pregnant again! *But*,' she blurted out, '*but*, this time,' she took a deep breath, 'Doctor Elias says I have passed the danger point and that is why I waited this long before telling you. This time,' she reached across to take her mother's hand while still holding Ernestina's in the other, 'Doctor Elias says I will keep the baby!'

Larnaka, 2010

Once again on that fateful night before Katerina's funeral, Adonis, Eleni and Marianna sat silent and transfixed as if hypnotized, listening to Anita talk of the past. Some of the facts they already knew, family history passed down from generation to generation. They had some knowledge of their Austrian ancestry, their great-great-grandfather Josef, and great-great-grandmother Eva. A few of her botanic illustrations and many of her textiles and fabrics had been preserved and cherished. Some original drawings that she kept from sending to the museum in Vienna were framed and hanging in the library where the children used to sit to do their schoolwork. Adonis had spent hours looking at them and as he was a keen artist they had been a source of fascination and inspiration to him. Also, some events had been talked about, memories shared, by the women of the house over the years. A painting by an old family friend depicting a banquet in Lefkara always held great curiosity for the children and now its origins had been brought to light by Anita's narration. However, the amount of detail the old woman was now giving them was almost too much to take in. Adonis was the first to break the silence. He was keen to know more about his father.

'I didn't realize how involved my father was in the movement for independence,' he said, relieved to learn something positive about him.

Adonis had always had his suspicions that the lack of information about the men in the family had something to do with Grandmother Olga's sense of betrayal and feelings of intense dislike for her husband, causing her to label most men as inadequate.

'That's how we met – he used to come to our meetings,' Anita replied, eager to return to her narration. 'So once Sonia heard that I was pregnant, she wanted to come back to Cyprus to see me. She had been offered a job teaching at the Academy by then and decided to remain in Vienna longer. I was missing her so much, but this was a great opportunity for her so we all encouraged her to stay.' Anita was once again in full flow with her story.

Eleni got up and made Cypriot mountain tea for everyone, good for soothing and calming the nerves, and then they all settled back in their seats to hear more.

12

Sonia was delighted with the news of her sister's pregnancy. At last Anita would have the baby she longed for, and Ernestina would have the great-grandchild she wished for. She felt a need to see her sister blooming after all she had gone through, and as Easter was approaching she took leave from the Academy and arrived back on an island on the verge of great change.

Anita had continued to send her reports of events, hoping to entice her sister back with promises of an imminent withdrawal of British troops.

'. . . perhaps now that things are calming down you might consider coming home,' Anita wrote. 'I miss you so much, Sonia mou; it's not been easy without you.'

Each time Anita miscarried it was Sonia's buoyant spirit that she longed for. Even if she had her mother, grandmother and especially Katerina to take care of her, it was Sonia she yearned to be with.

A less turbulent island was now more inviting for Sonia; besides, she admitted to herself that it was time she evaluated her relationship with Nicos.

'*We need to decide what we are both going to do with our lives,*' he'd written to her. '*I love you and I am ready now to settle down, but I need to know if you feel the same.*'

Of course she knew that Nicos was right; the time had now come to clarify their position. Nicos had joined his father's successful import business and as the only child and adored by both parents, he was expected to take over from his father. He was solvent, secure, and life on the island was looking up, plus his father was pressurizing him to settle down.

'I think it's time you took yourself seriously,' he told his son. 'If you are going to take on more responsibility in the business you need to take on more responsibility in your life. Sonia is a good girl and from a good family – it's time you married her.'

For Sonia, living in Vienna was fun, and now with her teaching post she was earning enough money not to live like a student any more. Plenty of young men had been interested in keeping her happy while in Vienna but none of these brief dalliances had amounted to much, and her infatuation with Hans, her old tutor, had long run its course. Once he became aware of Sonia's crush on him he wasted no time in seducing her, until she discovered that not only was he married, but he also had a baby on the way.

'My wife and I have an open marriage,' he told her when she questioned him about the young pregnant woman she'd seen him kissing one day outside the Academy.

'I didn't realize you were so provincial, *Liebling*,' he told her.

The news that Anita was pregnant was the motivation Sonia needed to get away and return home, see her family and decide what she and Nicos were going to do about their future.

Anita suited being pregnant. After her miscarriages, she had wilted like the pots of basil on the veranda when Katerina forgot to water them for a day or two. She had never been particularly robust – her complexion was pale and her slender body was thin like a young girl's – but pregnancy was now transforming her into a feminine earth mother.

She was nearly five months gone by the time Sonia arrived home, and her return couldn't have been better timed, coinciding as it did with Costas's job transfer to Nicosia. Petros, his *goumbaros*, best man, who worked for the same insurance company in the capital had put in a good word for his friend and ensured him a transfer and a promotion. This meant that the two men travelled daily to work in Petros's desirable car. They would leave early in the morning and arrive home late, some nights after the women had gone to bed. Petros had taken lodgings in Nicosia so Costas would often stay in the capital overnight with him. No one could say they were upset with the arrangement. Anita had got what she most wanted from him.

The five women were delighted to be united once again; it felt very much like old times. With her sister by her side Anita started to blossom. In just a couple of weeks, the lustre returned to her hair, the hollows in her cheeks filled up and her belly was growing at a steady pace.

'I feel like an oyster harbouring a precious pearl,' she told Sonia. 'My body has never felt more useful than right now.'

That year, the Easter celebrations for the Linser family were the best they had ever known. There was much to celebrate. Anita was with child, and Sonia and Nicos had finally announced their engagement.

Before lunch on Good Friday, after paying their customary respects to the epitaph at St Lazarus, the two sweethearts took themselves to their favourite beach where they had said their goodbyes the evening before Sonia left for Vienna.

Although Sonia was brought up as a Catholic she and the whole family loved to celebrate Easter the Greek Orthodox way. The evening service of the *Epitaphios* on Good Friday was Sonia's favourite Easter service. The epitaph, an intricately carved wooden structure, was positioned every Good Friday in front of the altar and then decorated with fragrant spring flowers. Whereas the

Catholic ritual of commemorating the entombing and passion of Christ was a macabre and sombre affair, the Orthodox one, even if eminently mournful, she found more reflective, more hopeful – as well as visually pleasing.

The epitaph structure consisted of four posts holding up a canopy roof above a catafalque or flat dais. An icon of Christ was placed on the dais, symbolically recreating the burial, and once the decoration was complete, the faithful gathered to kiss the icon in turn and pay their respects.

As children, both Anita and Sonia would go to St Lazarus with Katerina early in the morning with armfuls of flowers from their garden, as was required from every home in the neighbourhood, in order to help with the decoration. Each household would supply whatever flowers were in bloom in their gardens and take them to their local church, and since Easter always falls in the spring, every church in town smelled like a spring garden.

Women and children would set to work to cover the bare canopy. Freesias of all colours, lilies and roses, carnations and pinks, lemon and orange blossom, jasmine and branches of green myrtle would sit in buckets of water while the children handed the required flower to an adult who would then set about twisting and turning, tying and threading the stems until the entire structure, with not an inch of wood visible, was covered in a spectacular floral arrangement. Delicate white gypsoph-ila would invariably be used at the edges to create a lace-like effect. Rose petals and orange blossom would be scattered on the icon of Christ and finally sprinkled with rose water for added aroma. Each year something of a competition took place on Good Friday between the various churches wanting to produce the most dazzling display.

That year, neither Sonia nor Anita participated in the decorating ritual, but Katerina, as always, was at St Lazarus helping from early morning with her floral tribute.

'Let's pop in and light a candle and see how they are getting on,' Sonia had said to Nicos on their way to the beach, eager to inspect the women's handiwork before going to the evening service.

'Remember what we told each other last time we were here?' Nicos said, taking Sonia's hand as they sat on the pebbly beach looking at the perfect line of the horizon.

'We said we'd have our fun and when I returned we would be together,' she replied.

'And . . . ?' Nicos asked. 'I've had my fun, I'm ready to get serious! How about you? Do you want to come back now and marry me?'

'Yes, Nico *mou*, I do!' she replied. 'But I don't want to come back just yet. I'm new to teaching and I want to continue for a little longer.' She searched his face for a reaction. He stayed silent for a while and reached in his pocket for his cigarettes and flask of whisky. He took a sip, and handed her the flask.

'But do you want to marry me or not?' he finally asked.

'I do, but I don't want to come back . . . not yet.'

'That's fine by me,' he told her, inhaling deeply and reaching for the flask. 'Let's get married anyway and I'll come to Vienna with you.'

'What? Will your father agree?' she asked in disbelief.

'My father agrees to everything I ask him, so long as I agree with *him*,' Nicos replied with a mischievous smile and pulled her close for a kiss.

The lunchtime celebrations on Easter Sunday had continued well into the evening. Under the two orange trees in the garden a long trestle table had been laid out with all the usual festive fineries – swathes of blossom and scented roses and lilies, which Katerina had been cultivating with tender care. If the kitchen had been Katerina's and the padre's favourite place to drink coffee in the winter, then the garden with its two dozen pots of basil and a profusion of fragrant flowers was their place of choice in the spring.

Katerina had made her legendary *soupa avgolemono*, the customary first course on Easter Sunday, and Olga prepared her famous *kleftiko* lamb, which she seasoned with lemon and oregano and oven-cooked for hours in her earthenware pot. As a token of her Austrian heritage she also made her grandmother Eva's Sauerkraut dish. But Olga's roast potatoes, grown in the famed Cypriot red soil, were her pièce de résistance, and according to her two girls were the best in the world.

'I will never learn to cook potatoes like Mama,' Sonia announced, taking yet another mouthful and washing it down with red wine.

'There are no cooks that are as skilled as Mama and Katerina,' Anita added, then glanced at her grandmother apologetically. '*Nonna*, of course, is also a master cook – your *torta pasqualina*, *Nonna*, is the best!' she quickly hastened to add to avoid offence, and raised her glass at Ernestina. Old and unwell by now, her grandmother insisted on taking part in the preparations by issuing instructions from her armchair.

'The *Zuppa Inglese* has to be made to the exact recipe of my mother,' Ernestina told Olga. 'Make sure you use plenty of liqueur.' The essential ingredient, she insisted, was Alchermes, the aromatic Italian herb liqueur which she took care to have always in the drinks cabinet. If she heard of anyone about to visit Italy, that was the first thing she would request to be brought back for her.

Besides the lamb and soup of course there were *flaounes*, the traditional savoury pastry parcels filled with special Cyprus cheese, herbs and sultanas, a variety of salads and pastas and the festive dyed red eggs that had to be cracked in a competitive Easter game. Before the meal started a wicker basket full of red eggs was passed around the table so each guest could choose their egg. The egg-smashing ritual required two people: one person held their egg pointing upwards while the other person held their egg pointing down. The person pointing down then hit their competitor's egg from above, aiming at the pointy end of the egg in the hope it would crack. Of course, this didn't always work because very often the egg underneath could damage the egg above depending on its strength. In any case, whoever's egg cracked first was out of the game. The winner went on to smash the next person's intact egg until only one final victorious egg remained whose owner was then declared, among much festive bonhomie, the winner of the party.

There was a big crowd on that Easter Sunday. Apart from the immediate family, which included Padre Bernardino and Nicos's parents, Costas had also invited his *goumbaros*, Petros, whose arrival he announced at the last minute, to Katerina's irritation.

'It's fine, dear,' Olga had told her, sensing her impatience, 'it's the festive season, one more person doesn't matter.' Katerina was as hospitable as any Greek, but Costas didn't have to do a lot to irritate her and she didn't much like the types that he fraternized with. She had met this Petros at the wedding but she'd been too busy to pay any attention to him. Observing him now fleetingly over lunch Katerina found him a banal and arrogant young man who drunk copious amounts of wine and talked animatedly nonstop about nothing in particular. She found him particularly irksome.

At one point in the middle of the meal, Olga stood up – putting a rather abrupt end to Petros's pontifications – and raised her glass.

'*Christos Anesti*, everyone!' Christ has risen, she bellowed joyfully.

'*Christos Anesti*,' they chorused in return, in the customary Easter greeting, and raised their glasses to each other.

'Today, dear friends,' Olga carried on cheerfully, turning to look at Nicos's parents, 'we have many reasons to celebrate. To begin with, let us all drink to our children's union, and wish them a long and fruitful life together.'

'*Na mas zisous*,' Long life to them, everyone shouted and raised their glasses to the happy couple.

Glancing at her eldest daughter Olga raised her glass higher. '*And*,' she said smiling broadly, 'let us also wish our Anita a safe delivery of my first grandchild!'

'*Isygia!*' To health, they all shouted and the joyful clinking of glasses echoed all around the garden.

'Also,' Olga said before sitting down and looking around at everyone, 'let's not forget to drink to peace, and to our island's independence!'

'To peace,' they all chimed again and drained their glasses.

There was indeed much to be hopeful about on that Easter Sunday.

Lunch had been a lively and jovial affair; the food was more delicious than ever and the wine flowed plentifully. No one was in any rush to put an end to the day, and everyone ate, drank and chatted over each other noisily.

After the meal had finally ended, Sonia brought her guitar out into the garden and the singing and dancing commenced as the drinking continued. Greek and Italian songs were sung, Ernestina happy to hear her favourite tarantella tunes, and even Anita joined in with a little dancing. As the day progressed more food appeared on the table, this time the customary Easter desserts. Olga had prepared her grandmother's apple strudel and Ernestina's Italian *panna cotta*. Katerina had made her *baklava* and *galaktoboureko*, much to Sonia's delight.

'I can have apple strudel any time of the year in Vienna,' she said, helping herself to the other desserts.

'Bravo, Katerina, this *galaktoboureko* is good!' she heard Petros say, his mouth overflowing with custard cream, as he stood up to dive across Ernestina for more. *He's got the manners of a gorilla and the hairy arms of a chimp*, Katerina thought to herself and tried to ignore him.

Putting her irritation aside, she looked around the table and her heart filled with joy at the good fortune of being surrounded by these people. She glanced at the padre who smiled and raised his glass in a private toast to her. How fortunate she felt to have such a good and loyal friend. Then looking at Anita, with her swelling belly, she rejoiced in her friend's good fortune, despite her trying husband. Her dear Sonia had finally decided to settle down, and Katerina hoped that she would also at some point soon bring to the world a blessed child. Everything seemed well on that holy day; life was finally feeling good again.

The big cuckoo clock in the *saloni* struck midnight when Katerina finished putting the last few dishes away. It had been a long day and clearing up after the day's festivities – despite willing helpers she always liked to put the final touches to her kitchen herself – had taken her longer than she'd expected. It was way past midnight by the time she sank into bed and she stayed awake for a good while, unable to sleep, reflecting on the day's events which she decided had been full of joy.

She was in that blissful state between sleep and con-sciousness, when the body gives in to fatigue and the brain drifts into unconstructed random thought, when her bed-room door burst open, snapping her back to wakefulness.

'Katerina, wake up,' she heard Costas's brusque voice as he advanced towards her bed. 'She is bleeding all over the sheets,' he shouted in panic, 'I don't know what to do.'

Within seconds Katerina was up and running to Anita.

This time Anita's miscarriage, if it could be so called, hit the Linser women like a sudden mountain avalanche. No one had expected it. By the time Doctor Elias arrived, Anita was howling with the pain. She had gone into premature labour and for three hours she screamed in agony, her mother, sister, grandmother and Katerina by her side. Finally, she gave birth to a baby girl, beautiful as a rosebud. She was already dead on arrival. There was no hope of survival.

She was barely five months' gestation and although externally she looked perfect, she was incomplete. Her internal organs were unable to sustain life.

They gave her to Anita to hold. They laid her in her arms, wrapped in a cotton sheet, and she cradled the tiny bundle till the first sun-rays crept through the wooden shutters and onto her bed. Her delirium lasted for weeks and a fever raged for days due to an infection. The penicillin fought the infection but her mind remained in great confusion for a long while.

'They took my baby away,' she would lament in a low mournful murmur.

'Where is my baby, what have you all done with her?' she kept asking, and then she would wail and cry, begging them to bring back her baby girl. All that Olga, Ernestina, Katerina and Sonia could do was to keep vigil in turn by her side, follow Doctor Elias's orders and pray for her recovery. Costas offered little support, which surprised no one; besides, he was out of the house all day and by then he had taken lodgings in a house in Nicosia to use from time to time when his workload was heavy.

Sonia and Nicos had planned to marry during the week commencing with Easter and return to Vienna together, but of course there was no question of that under the circumstances.

'My sister is fighting for her life,' Sonia told Nicos when he suggested that perhaps they could still go ahead once Anita was out of danger.

'There has been a death in our family, we are in mourning,' Sonia replied, astonished at his suggestion. 'This is no time for celebration. Besides, when Anita is out of danger I must return to the Academy.'

'No matter, I'll come with you,' Nicos was quick to suggest. 'I can't see there would be any objection from anyone; we are engaged now.'

'You know my mother,' Sonia replied, 'she won't object, but my grandmother will. But then again, when did we ever listen to poor old *Nonna*?'

Larnaka, 2010

Eleni wiped her eyes and took a sip of mountain tea, now cold in her mug. The cuckoo clock on the wall reminded them all once again that the hour was late and a long day was awaiting them, but no one wanted to break the spell of Anita's story. Eleni looked at her cousin sitting across the room from her and was flooded with love and gratitude for his existence, not only for her poor aunt but for herself too.

She was the only one in the room able to empathize with what her aunt had gone through. Eleni too had had a miscarriage early on in her marriage, and even though she was able to go on and have two healthy pregnancies and two beautiful babies, the pain of it always lingered. She looked at Adonis again and thanked God that her aunt had managed to finally get the baby she longed for, but knew all too well that the scars of losing a child never heal.

Adonis, who for years had regarded his mother with criticism, was gradually able to start making some sense of what he considered to be Anita's inadequacies. Her bouts of depression, her inability to be fully present, had, he now realized, had much to do with the numerous misfortunes of her life.

'It took me a very long time to recover,' Anita said, looking around the room at the three faces staring expectantly at her. 'The period that followed, after losing my baby and Sonia returning to Vienna, was the time that Katerina and I became closer than ever. She was my saviour.' Anita closed her eyes, took a deep breath and let out a mournful sigh with the memory. 'No one could have asked for a more loving, caring friend. Now, she too has gone forever.'

As much as all three wanted to continue listening to Anita they could see that the old lady was beginning to fade; the late hour and emotion had taken their toll. The new day which was about to break would be a demanding one, and they needed to have a few hours' sleep before facing it.

'I don't want to go to bed, but I feel we must,' Adonis said, and walking towards his mother, took her arm and guided her to her room.

There would be plenty of time later for Anita to carry on with her story, after they had put their beloved Tante to rest.

Katerina had been a popular woman and much loved in the neighbourhood. St Lazarus was packed with people coming to pay their final respects to her. Adonis held his mother's arm as they made their way to the front of the church, while Eleni and Marianna followed behind.

The atmosphere in the church was laden with emotion, intensified further by the perfumed smoke drifting from the incense burner to hover heavily in the air. A long procession of mourners passed by the open coffin to pay their last respects. Each person stopped for a second to glance at Katerina, made the sign of the cross, kissed the crucifix on the coffin and then moved on to take their place at a pew.

They buried Katerina at the Greek Orthodox cemetery directly across the street from the Catholic graveyard where several generations of Linsers had been laid to rest and where Anita would also follow in time. The two friends would be separated by a road, but the birds which nest in the trees, the bees and butterflies that make their rounds gathering pollen from one cemetery to the other, would bring in their flight news from across the street.

Standing by the graveside Eleni, Adonis and Marianna held tightly on to each other as the burial ritual continued. Eleni had only ever been to two Orthodox funerals before, the mothers of two old school friends. The only other death in her family had been her English mother-in-law. She vividly remembered how inappropriately calm she had found that funeral, and how she'd tried to hold back her tears like everyone else. She also recalled how eventually she'd had to hide behind a pillar to cry, afraid that her display of grief might be considered out of place.

This Orthodox ritual, she decided as she stood under the dappled light coming through the cypress trees, possessed a primitive humility which allowed her tears and everyone else's to fall without shame or inhibition. Perhaps it was the familiarity of the priest and his chanting, mingled with the sound of the cicadas, or perhaps it was the unguarded sorrow of the mourners dressed in black that added to her sadness and moved her so. Whatever it was, Eleni, Adonis and Marianna let their grief show and their tears flow without restraint for the woman they considered their mother.

Anita stood all the while beside the priest, who as he neared the end of the service threw a handful of *koliva* onto the coffin. This mixture of boiled wheat, nuts and berries, symbolizing the circle of life, is a prerequisite for the completion of a burial. Anita reached for a handful as mourners started to gather by her side, each taking their turn. 'May her memory be eternal,' they chanted, casting flowers and soil into the grave.

After the burial, everybody gathered together at the house for the customary refreshments. Along with the traditional olive and haloumi bread for the visitors, they had served red wine and brandy as well as coffee and cake, and for the first time there was no Katerina to see to everything. Eleni, Adonis and Marianna all rushed around to help Anita, who was well aware that from now on she would have to manage life alone.

When the last of the mourners finally left, the three friends decided to leave Anita to rest and to take themselves to one of their favourite haunts in town.

'I will see you all after I have slept a while,' Anita told them, fatigue and emotion etched on her face. 'There is still much I need to tell you.'

The 1900 Bar was the place the three always met when

they really wanted to relax or had something important to discuss. They had known Spiros, the owner, since high school, and he always made them feel as if they were in their own home; a feeling that was enhanced by the fact that the place had been built as a family house in 1900 – hence its name – and resembled their own house in numerous ways. It had the same high ceilings, decorative cornices and sweeping staircase leading to a top floor, now a restaurant, which originally would have been the *saloni*, as it was in the Linser home.

Whenever Adonis visited from New York, alone or with Robert, he made a point of taking Katerina there for dinner, and on the occasions Anita felt like it, she would join them too. On hot summer nights they'd sit on the small balcony jutting out above the road, just big enough for a table and four chairs that competed for space with an impossibly luscious white bougainvillea, which looped and twisted itself round the railings trying to claim the entire balcony for itself. In winter months they would sit indoors under the high-ceilinged dining room, sur-rounded by art and Parisian posters from the 1930s, a log fire ablaze in one corner, enjoying Spiros's mother's home cooking. When he was feeling homesick in New York, Adonis would daydream about dinner in the 1900 Bar.

'She was a lovely lady, your Katerina,' Spiros told them when they walked in. 'May her memory be eternal,' he offered the customary condolence, and reached for his best single malt whisky. 'Let's drink to her memory,' he said and poured the amber spirit into their glasses. 'The town will miss her.'

Out in the street the sun was still high in the sky, but sitting in the cool half-light of the bar, with the colourful art adorning the walls, surrounded by memorabilia all so familiar from their youth, Adonis, Eleni and Marianna breathed out a long slow collective sigh of release.

They stayed in the 1900 Bar for a long time. They needed to 'decompress', as Adonis had put it.

'I guess I was exhausted and emotional last night,' he told the girls, picking up a newly filled glass of whisky. 'Everything Mother told us made me feel like I couldn't breathe.'

The day's tension had left them exhausted, so they sat in the easy comfort of the bar, drank whisky, ate pistachio nuts, exchanged happy memories of Katerina and then made their way home, hoping that Anita was up and ready to continue with her story.

They found her sitting in the *saloni*, drinking brandy and looking at old photographs. Over the years Olga had neatly arranged and preserved in leather-bound albums any surviving family photos, which Anita had now spread out on the coffee table and was leafing through one by one.

'Ah! There you all are,' she called out when she heard

them come in and, twisting around to look at them, picked up an album. 'Come, let me show you.' She shifted herself along the sofa to make space for Adonis while the other two perched on the arm of the divan to peer over her shoulders.

'But perhaps we should eat first,' she said again, looking up at the girls and pointing to the dining-room table, which had been laid for supper. 'I have made us some *soupa avgolemono* – I thought we could all use some nourishment before I start talking again.' She smiled, knowing that whenever there was a crisis in the family what they all always longed for was Katerina's egg, lemon and rice soup for its healing and comforting qualities.

They fetched the old soup terrine from the kitchen, placed it in the middle of the table, and taking their places they darted surprised glances at each other at the way Anita was assuming control again. The delicate lemony taste of the soup, creamy and frothy with a sprinkling of cinnamon on top, summoned up Katerina, as if she was sitting at the table with them urging them to eat, a smile on her face as she waited to hear their praise.

They ate quietly together and after clearing up the dishes they brewed a pot of coffee and Anita brought the photo albums to the table.

'When I started on this family story of ours, my children, I had no idea I would go into so much detail . . .' She took a sip of her coffee and looked around the table.

'But having begun I felt I had to go on, to give you the full picture before you could understand. We were five women, you see, living alone in a patriarchal society. But our household was different. Your grandmother was as strong as any man and united, we were even stronger.'

13

In Vienna, Sonia and Nicos stayed at first with Great-aunt Heidi on Grashofgasse. Heidi had become used to Sonia's company and was delighted to have the young couple brightening up her life further, but they longed to have a little place to themselves. When a small studio apartment became vacant on the top floor of the same block they found the opportunity too good to refuse, meanwhile promising to visit her every day. She helped them to settle in, giving them whatever she could to furnish their little apartment. Steep stairs led to a low-ceilinged cosy attic room, which gave access to a roof terrace that they soon proceeded to transform into a mini garden with pots of basil, scented geraniums and fennel, bringing a little patch of Cyprus to their city lives. There was just enough space to add a small table and chairs for their morning coffee or evening beer in the summer months. Once in a while when the weather and her arthritis permitted, Great-aunt Heidi would join them for a glass of wine.

'You, my *Liebling*, have been a godsend to me,' she told Sonia. 'You are the daughter I never had and this boy of yours completes my joy. All I want from you two now is a grandchild.'

'But we are not even married yet,' Sonia teased. 'We are living in sin – how can we have a baby?'

'Well, you should get married,' the old lady would persist. 'I will arrange everything.' But Sonia and Nicos were far too busy having fun to want to start a family. Sonia had her teaching work at the Academy and Nicos, after the first few weeks of getting to know Vienna, enrolled into a language school to learn German.

Larnaka, 2010

Like Adonis earlier, Eleni was eager to learn something more about her father. He had been such a figure of mystery in her life; now that so many family secrets were emerging, she needed to hear more.

'What was he like, *Thia*?' she asked. 'Did you like him?'

'Nicos?' Anita replied. 'Well . . . I liked him well enough, Eleni *mou*, we all did, *but* he was irresponsible and in the end he was the undoing of my sister.' Anita's eyes misted over at the memory. Eleni sat up, curious to hear more.

'It was your first Christmas, Eleni *mou*, you had just turned one, and your mama wanted you to spend it at home with all of us here in the house. The family kept quiet about it at the time, but now I can tell you that you were born before they got round to getting married . . . So we were also planning a small wedding celebration and we were all very excited. I hadn't even seen you yet, only your grandmother Olga travelled to Vienna for your birth, so the rest of us were longing to meet you.'

Once again the memories came tumbling out as Anita began to tell the story.

Adonis was a year and a half by that Christmas and Sonia wanted the two cousins to spend the festive season together, but Nicos wanted to stay in Vienna.

'It's fun here,' he argued, 'and the Germans *really* know how to celebrate Christmas.'

'*And I*,' Sonia argued back, 'want to see my family.'

They returned three days before Christmas Day to a sun-drenched island, leaving behind the icy north and the festively decorated Viennese streets which made the city look like a Christmas postcard; but Sonia didn't care – she yearned for home.

The news of their arrival caused great excitement in the Linser household, and the women set about turning the house into their own Christmas card, even if outside the temperature was unseasonably warm. Olga enlisted Andreas the gardener's help to erect a tree, the biggest she could find, and to bring down from the attic all the fine Christmas decorations so they could make the house sparkle for the little ones.

'This is the first time both children will be here for Christmas,' Olga said. 'If this isn't a cause for a special celebration, then I don't know what is!' She was busy fixing candles on the tree to be lit on Christmas Eve, an Austrian tradition she had inherited from her grandparents.

Katerina was up a ladder hanging decorations around the room. 'We must keep our wits about us with all those candles burning; the children could hurt themselves if we're not careful,' she said sternly. She disapproved of Olga's insistence on the tradition – 'Lighted candles on a tree,' she'd muttered under her breath, 'of all the ideas!' – but she knew Olga was determined, so she kept her thoughts to herself and always stood guard by the tree until it was time to extinguish them and then she made sure to pinch out each and every one herself.

Sonia arrived laden with gifts for everyone in the household. This was going to be the best Christmas they had ever spent together. Little Eleni could toddle about on the seafront with her cousin, and Sonia, basking in the warm sun, could feel the Austrian chill melt away, warming her bones. In the kitchen the seasonal aromas of spices were tantalizing as her mother and Katerina competed to produce their finest festive delicacies and treats for them.

The preparations had already been started days before

their arrival and the larder and fridge were well stocked. Olga had made a pile of *melomakarona*, Sonia's favourite. When she was a little girl she would beg her mother to make them all year round.

'They're so delicious, why do we have to wait for Christmas to eat them?' she would always complain.

'When you are grown up you can learn to make them yourself,' Olga would tell her. 'Then you can have them whenever you want.'

But it was Katerina who learned how to make them first and taught Sonia and Anita in turn. All three spent hours in the kitchen trying to perfect the art of baking *melomakarona*.

The recipe stipulated that either flour or semolina could be used as ingredients for the biscuit mix, but use of the wrong amount of either, and the project would be doomed. When the right quantities of sugar and oil were used and the correct consistency achieved, the biscuits would turn out well and there was always much rejoicing when the girls got it right. They would then set about moulding spoonfuls into small oval shapes, then line them up on baking trays ready for the oven. Once the biscuits were set and crisp they would remove them from the oven and leave them out to cool before they could be dipped, one by one, taking care not to break them, into a pot of liquid honey spiced with cinnamon and cloves bubbling on the stove. If the biscuit mixture was successful, then the result would be piles of moist yet firm biscuits arranged on a pretty cake dish and sprinkled liberally with crushed walnuts. However, if the girls got the mixture wrong for whatever reason, then the whole thing was a dismal failure.

'There was one time,' Anita recalled with a chuckle, 'when it went so disastrously and the biscuit mixture was so flaky that all the cookies crumbled into one big powdery heap! We had to eat it with a spoon.'

So it was that the Christmas when Sonia, Nicos and Eleni came home from Vienna, the Linser house was occupied for the first time in the way that Grandfather Josef had intended it to be. The children's laughter echoed around the rooms and the big table in the dining room was laid out with the best china and Linser-print tablecloths and napkins every evening.

They all went, including Katerina, to Midnight Mass at the Catholic church where Padre Bernardino officiated on Christmas Eve, and when they returned they had a light supper, lit the candles on the tree and exchanged gifts. Although Olga preferred to serve the traditional feast on Christmas Eve, they couldn't keep the little ones awake so late so she agreed to wait till the next day.

Greek, Austrian and Italian dishes were all on the menu for the Christmas Day banquet. Both Katerina and

Olga had been busy in the kitchen for days before they arrived.

After lunch Sonia, Anita and Katerina took the children for a stroll on the promenade while Nicos and Costas, who had graced them with his presence as it was Christmas, collapsed in the *saloni* in a stupor of over-eating and drinking.

The early-afternoon sun was beginning to turn chilly as the women and children walked along the seafront.

'I feel rain coming on,' Katerina told them, 'maybe even snow in the mountains.' She turned to the direction of the hills where dark clouds had gathered. 'It wouldn't do any harm to get some rain at last.'

'It can wait till we leave,' Sonia said and picked up Eleni who refused to walk any further unless she was carried.

'I think it will be sooner. Look,' Katerina replied, pointing up at the palm trees along the promenade, swaying in the wind.

'Compared to Vienna this is a light breeze,' said Sonia. 'Try walking along the Danube on a windy day!'

'I can only imagine!' Katerina replied and meant it. To her, Vienna seemed like a distant planet.

'The fine weather held today, anyway,' Sonia continued. 'It wouldn't have done those men any harm to come out with us for some fresh air, would it?' She looked at her sister.

'I don't mind,' Anita replied, shrugging her shoulders. 'I'd rather be with you two, and the children. Besides, they were both drunk!'

'I know . . .' Sonia said and hesitated a while. 'Nicos seems to drink a lot. Sometimes I worry . . .'

'Don't *all* men drink a lot?' Katerina added.

'I don't know, maybe they do,' said Sonia, 'but I don't like it.'

Welcoming the New Year was as important as the Christmas festivities for the Linser family and they always liked to celebrate it with friends and neighbours till the early hours of New Year's morning. This year Olga had invited quite a crowd, and as the custom dictated after midnight when the eating and drinking stopped, the green baize tables were set up and the card games commenced. Bottles of wine and liqueurs were passed around and the company was in good spirits. They never played for money, or if they did, it was for loose change only; it was a New Year tradition with both children and adults sitting down to play joyfully together.

This time, however, one of the guests, Costas's *goumbaros* Petros, held a different opinion on the subject of gambling.

'Whoever heard of playing cards for no money?' he announced loudly. 'The only reason for playing is to win; and I never lose.' He looked around the room. 'Lady Luck is always on my side,' he boasted. 'Anyone dare take a gamble with me?' He glanced over at Nicos and beckoned him to an empty seat for a game of poker.

Seeing that her fiancé was ready to take up the challenge, Sonia quickly tried to dissuade him. She was all too aware that his inebriated condition left him in no state for gambling.

'You'll lose every last pound you have in your pocket, and more!' she hissed at him.

'Live and let live, woman,' he told her and pushing past her, took his place at the card table opposite Petros.

'Let's see who Lady Luck is going to favour tonight,' Nicos laughed at his opponent and rolled up his sleeves.

The game was well underway when Katerina at last emerged from the kitchen, having put an end to her duties there. She pulled up a chair next to Sonia who was sitting by Nicos's side, keeping an eye on him.

She could feel her friend's anxiety, and reached for her hand to keep her company. Katerina was quite fond of Nicos but she loved Sonia more and she was irritated and disappointed to see him drunk again and fraternising with the likes of Petros whom she cordially disliked.

The two women sat silently watching as the men took turns to deal the cards. The cigarette smoke was thick around them and the bottle of whisky on the table almost empty. It was Petros's turn to deal; Katerina watched him with disdain, his shirt sleeves pulled up to his elbows, shuffling the pack of cards and then divvying them out in that overblown, exaggerated way of his.

She had never observed him at such close range before, and as she did, she felt a sense of dread rising up inside her. *I really do dislike you*, she repeated to herself, surprised at the level of her antipathy. It occurred to her that he had a vague resemblance to someone she had known; someone unpleasant from her past, but she was unable to think who. *Probably my father*, she concluded.

The two women continued sitting side by side, chatting in a desultory way to each other and watching the men becoming more agitated as time passed. The longer Katerina looked at Petros the more unsettled she felt, until a thought started to take hold. It nagged at her dimly but insistently, refusing to take a clear form, stuck in some deep recess of her brain, like a flickering light. Then suddenly as if the light was switched on she was flooded with a clarity so sharp, so powerful she felt giddy. The thought made her gasp and retch at the same time. The taste of fear and disgust rose in her throat.

'*Panayia mou*,' Mother of God, she murmured, lifting her hand to her mouth to muffle a scream. 'It's *him*!'

How had she never recognized the truth before? she asked herself. Possibly because she could never bear to stay near him long enough to study him properly – his presence repulsed her.

Now the subliminal thoughts that had been bothering

her ever since she set eyes on Petros had broken the surface. The continual animated gesturing and bravado; the arms and hands. *Especially the arms,* she thought. Now she couldn't take her eyes off them. She had observed those arms and hands from that window in the school hall for long minutes. *Those arms as thickly furred as an ape's*; the long fingernail on the little finger of his right hand and the signet ring; the memory of them was burned into her brain. She was sure now – or as sure as she could be, given that she had never seen his face. She swallowed the urge to scream and point at him, for everyone to hear and shame him. She knew she couldn't, not yet anyway. Costas was still part of this family, the family she loved and would do anything to protect. She cursed the day Anita had agreed to marry him.

'Tell me who your friends are and I will tell you who you are!' Her grandmother's words came to her lips. The old woman was the only member of her family Katerina ever thought of fondly, or had cared about, but she was long dead. After her death there had been no one to protect her until Olga rescued her.

She sat as if paralyzed while the men continued to play; she was aware of people talking around her, but she heard nothing. A voice screamed inside her head: *Traitor!*

Just as the screeching in her head couldn't get louder, and the urge to speak out became compulsive, Nicos sprang out of his chair and began yelling at Petros. The game was apparently over and Nicos had lost. A huge amount of money was at stake and now he was accusing Petros of cheating. The men's shouting rose above everything else in the room. A chair was overturned, crashing with a loud thud on the floor and a full glass of whisky fell off the table, smashing into splinters over the floorboards. All faces turned towards them.

Sonia screamed at Nicos to stop, and then Olga stepped between them just as they started to push each other around, poised for a fist-fight.

'*Stamatate!*' Stop!, Olga shouted forcefully at the two men, her eyes flashing with fury. 'You should be ashamed of yourselves!' Turning to Petros she pointed to the front door. 'Please leave!' she commanded. 'You are a guest in my home and this is not the way my guests behave.'

'Your friend is a thoroughly unpleasant man who takes liberties,' Olga told Costas after their guest had left, 'and he is not welcome in this house any longer.'

That night Sonia refused to sleep with her husband and without speaking to him took herself to Katerina's room.

'He behaved like the irresponsible spoilt brat that he is!' she said, her eyes filling up again. 'Nicos never thinks of the consequences of his actions. If I didn't love him, I swear I would leave him.'

Katerina lay silently next to Sonia, patiently hearing

her grievances; meanwhile her own mind was seething with confusion and distress. She always listened to Anita and Sonia but who would listen to her this time? And more to the point, who could she tell? All night she stayed awake, her thoughts chasing each other round her head. By morning she knew that the only person she could talk to was Padre Bernardino. He would know what should be done.

'How could you let *that man* lead you on like that?' Sonia hissed at Nicos the next morning over breakfast.

'Oh don't be like that, *agabi mou*,' he told her, trying to nuzzle his face into the back of her neck, 'it was only a little fun, it's only money!'

'You might think it's only money,' she replied, pulling herself away from him, 'but I can think of better ways to spend it than giving it to him. And it's not only about the money, Nicos – how could you have a drunken brawl in my mother's house? So humiliating for her.'

'Oh don't exaggerate, it wasn't really a brawl, just a little heated exchange,' he told her and leaned across to kiss her. 'Besides, Olga told *that man* exactly where to go. She's a regular sergeant major, that mother of yours!'

'My mother never puts up with fools,' Sonia replied, softening a little as she reached for her coffee.

Nicos always had the power to disarm her and make her laugh; she loved that about him. As much as she wanted to stay cross with him her anger never lasted long.

By the time they had finished breakfast that morning they had digressed into discussing their forthcoming wedding party, before making plans for the rest of the day.

'I've just been listening to the radio,' Olga said, walking into the dining room with Eleni in her arms. 'They said it's snowing up in the mountains.'

'Excellent news!' Nicos said, jumping up. 'That's what we'll do today, my little rose petal, we'll go for a drive to see the snow!'

'Don't we see enough snow in Vienna?' Sonia protested.

'Oh come on! Don't spoil it, this is Troodos-mountain snow, not city slush.'

Sonia looked at her mother. 'So long as you drive carefully it could be fun,' Olga told them. 'I always like it! Take my car.'

'I prefer to take my father's car, it's bigger,' Nicos replied.

'Shall we take Eleni too?' Sonia looked at her mother again.

'Perhaps you should leave Eleni with me,' said Olga, 'she is far too little. Besides, the two of you can have some time alone.'

Sonia was reluctant to leave Eleni and the family and

go off to the mountains with Nicos on a whim. But perhaps, she thought, her mother was right – they could do with some time alone, she'd been pretty harsh with him the night before.

They were ready to leave before noon. Nicos collected his father's car while Sonia and Katerina packed a picnic lunch for them; there was so much food left from the last few days it was more of a feast than a picnic. They changed into their Austrian winter clothes, which they had worn for the journey over, and set off. Nicos, cheerful behind the wheel, didn't seem to be suffering any effects from the previous night's drinking.

Along the coast the weather was bright until they started the climb into the hills; although there was no sign of snow, the clouds looked dark and ominous.

'Isn't this great?' Nicos said and leaned across to give Sonia a kiss. A faint smell of whisky lingered on his breath.

'Have you been drinking?' she asked, pulling back to look at him, alarmed at the early hour. 'Didn't you have enough last night?'

'Just a little drop for the road,' he replied laughing. 'Here, have a sip.' He reached into his pocket and fished out the silver whisky flask.

'Nico!' she yelled and pushed his hand away. 'It's not even lunchtime yet!'

'Oh stop worrying, it's fine, I won't have any more . . .

not yet anyway,' he teased and stroked her thigh. 'Isn't it great to be out on the road, just the two us, like old times?'

'Yes . . .' she replied without too much conviction and tried to sit back and enjoy the journey.

'I don't suppose we'll see snow until we get right up to Olympus peak,' he continued chatting. 'What do you say we push on now and stop and have our picnic when we arrive?'

The drive to the peak was long but relatively easy. Although snow had fallen heavily earlier, it had now stopped and visibility was good. The forest looked enchanting, a perfect Christmas wonderland, and Sonia started to enjoy it. By the time they arrived at the summit she was feeling jubilant.

They ran, and screamed, and played; they threw snowballs at each other like children until, exhausted and hungry, they decided it was time to stop. By lunchtime the snow had started to fall again and even if they could have found a picnic table without a blanket of snow over it, they had no desire to be in the cold any longer. Their only refuge was the little *kafeneon* in the square.

As they walked through the door, the heat from the roaring wood fire and the smell of fresh coffee welcomed them like an old friend. The proprietor was sitting alone in the empty room drinking coffee and listening to the radio. As soon as he saw them he stood up to greet them.

'*Kalos tous*,' Welcome both, he called with a big friendly smile. 'Come in, sit by the fire. Dust the snow off yourselves.'

'We brought a picnic,' Sonia said apologetically, pointing to the picnic basket Nicos was carrying.

'No place for a picnic out there,' the man said with a chuckle. 'You best eat it in here then.'

'Do you mind?' she asked.

'Why would I mind? Come, sit down and tell me what you need . . .'

'Do you have any whisky?' Nicos asked.

'No, but I have something better,' the man replied, and walking to the back of the kitchen produced a bottle of homemade *zivania*.

'This will warm you up like nothing else,' he told them as he filled three shot glasses to the brim and handed them round. They drank together the strong clear spirit made from grapes, which Sonia always referred to as firewater, and they felt the colour return to their cheeks and the warmth to their freezing limbs. They shared their picnic with the man, who delighted in their company and entertained them with mountain stories.

'It's quite lonely up here in the winter. I only ever see the forestry workers this time of year,' he told them as he poured another round of *zivania*. 'People only come in the summer, no one is mad enough to come up here in this weather . . . apart from you two lovebirds,' he laughed, and gave Nicos a slap on the back.

'Do you live here all year round?' Sonia asked.

'Out the back,' he said, pointing beyond the kitchen with his chin. 'I used to be a forester myself. Retired now.'

Nicos reached for the bottle and poured himself another shot, which he drank in a single gulp.

'Good *zivania*,' he said, putting the glass down. 'Where did you get it from?'

'I make my own at the village,' the man replied, refilling Nicos's glass.

'Will you sell me a bottle?' He reached for the bottle again.

'I think it's time we set off,' Sonia interrupted, before the man had time to answer back. 'While it's still light,' she added, taking the bottle out of Nicos's grasp.

'We have plenty of time before it gets dark,' he protested, 'no need to rush.'

'The lady is right,' said the man. 'If you go now you will be by the coast all in good time. It's safer.'

They set off as the pale winter sun, faintly visible through the clouds, was sinking towards the west. The sky was relatively clear when they started the car, but by the time they reached the next village the snow had begun to fall again and darkness to descend upon them. The flakes came down thick and fast, clouding their vision.

The mountain road was steep and narrow, descending in looping switchbacks past cliffs of rock, hazardous at any time; on the treacherous icy surface in poor light still more care was needed. A sober and more alert driver might have foreseen a skid and steered through it on a sudden hairpin bend. But Nicos's reactions were blurred and he lost control.

Sonia made the sign of the cross and held her breath as the car slid across the road and they plunged over the edge . . . The ravine was deep and strewn with rocks. A truck making its way to the peak missed colliding with them by seconds and the man raised the alarm by driving to the top to inform the *kafeneon* owner.

The snowstorm continued all night. Even though the search party was called they could do nothing till the next morning; there was a good deal of ground to cover and the hunt continued in relays for two days. Olga was distraught; she spent hours talking to the man at the coffee shop trying to establish what exactly had happened in the hours before the accident. She suspected Nicos had been drinking and this was confirmed by the coffee-shop owner; she knew her son-in-law well enough. After that day she never mentioned Nicos again – she never forgave him for causing the premature death of her daughter.

So that Christmas, when the two baby cousins met for the first time, was to be the first year of the rest of their lives, and neither of them had any memory of ever living apart.

Eleni let out a muffled sob. Marianna hastened to take her in her arms and Adonis sat motionless as if struck by a thunderbolt.

'So you see, Eleni *mou*,' Anita said, 'you see? That is why we didn't talk much about your father. It pained us too much. Your grandmother blamed him for the accident. Sonia of course was also to be blamed a little. She indulged him too much and he took advantage. He was selfish and above all irresponsible.'

When she was a girl Eleni had made up stories about her parents' accident, and had a favourite scenario which she would only ever share with Marianna. They'd sit on one or the other's bed, their legs tucked under them, and they would take turns to tell each other their story.

'They had to go to a winter ball,' Eleni would begin, 'it was at a glamorous hotel in the mountains. It was Christmas time, you see, so there were so many parties. Mama was wearing a long red ballgown and high heels and smelled of roses and gardenias, and Papa was in a black suit with a bow tie.' Excitement made the little girl's cheeks flush as she talked. 'I was not with them, you see, I was too little, I was left with Grandma Olga and so they had to come home to see me because they missed me. They left the party and drove in the middle of the stormy night because they were in a hurry to get home, but then the lightning came down and hit Papa's car and they fell into a deep ravine. They both died with my name on their lips.' When Eleni finished her story, she'd wipe her eyes dramatically, take on a tragic expression, and sit up and wait for Marianna to start her own tale about why her mother left her to follow her artistic career in dancing. Their stories might vary a little each time, depending on their mood, but they always involved glamorous clothes and dark stormy nights.

'Your mama will come back one day to find you,' Eleni would say mournfully once Marianna concluded her narration, 'but mine can *never* do that!'

The adult Eleni infinitely preferred her childhood fantasy about her parents' accident to the sordid act of drunken stupidity that had just been revealed to her. A wave of fury washed over her. *I became an orphan, purely because my father was a reckless drunk.*

'We loved you very much, Eleni *mou* – we all took care of you,' Anita said, reaching for her niece's hand as if she had read her mind. 'Especially Katerina, who took care of all of us. Together we were strong, and those of us who were weak were held up by those who were stronger . . .' Anita took a deep breath and exhaled in a long slow sigh. She looked across the room at her son.

'You see, Adonis *mou*, the men in this family left much

to be desired. Apart from your great-grandfathers – and you, of course – none were any good.'

How many more calamities, Eleni thought, *can a family endure?* She looked around at her cousin and Marianna. Adonis's face was ashen. He sat speechless, trying to absorb this succession of family secrets that his mother had decided to reveal to them. His uncle had been a drunk, and his own father the friend of a traitor. How many more family skeletons would be brought to light tonight? It was as if Anita had collected them all and threaded them one by one onto a chain like a rosary. All three looked at the old woman, who was now sitting with her eyes closed, trying to regain her strength in order to continue.

'Do you want to stop now?' Adonis asked, walking towards his mother with a glass of water. He wanted her to stop yet he urgently needed to know more. So many questions were swirling in his head, all fighting to be asked, but glancing at Anita he held back.

'You have been talking for too long now, Mother, perhaps you need to rest?' He handed her the glass and waited.

'I am fine, Adonis *mou*,' she replied, sitting up ready to start again. 'I can't stop now, I have much more to tell you.' She took a sip of water and sat back in her chair.

'So . . . what happened to that man . . . the traitor?' Adonis heard himself ask, unable to contain his thoughts any longer.

'Was Tante right? Did they arrest him? I hope so!' Marianna blurted out.

'What about . . . Costas? I can't bring myself to call him Father,' Adonis asked. 'He was clearly even worse than I was led to believe.'

The questions were being fired at Anita like bullets.

'I am sorry, my children . . . you see I have jumped too far ahead with my story and I must go back to before you two were born and before we lost Sonia, but I'll answer your questions first.' Anita took in a deep breath and continued. 'You see, my son, Costas was quite a pretender, really . . . he was what your grandmother called a chameleon, a man who changed his colours according to his whereabouts and what benefitted him. I worked it out in the end but it took me a while. When I first met him he was at a loose end with his life; he'd lost his job in Nicosia and so he tried his luck in Larnaka. He wasn't truly dedicated to the revolution, he was just passing his time with us until he met his hateful friend who suited him better than us. We discovered later on that Costas used to pass on information to Petros in return for favours . . . that's how Petros got him the job in Nicosia. But so many things happened before your mama was killed, Eleni *mou*, things which I must now explain. Things you *must* all know. Be patient – I will tell you everything I know.'

14

1959

After the loss of the baby, Anita's convalescence, both physical and emotional, was a long and painful process. The spark went out of her eyes and her appetite for anything apart from sleeping diminished. Months passed and she lay in bed, her desolation continuing unabated, as if by losing her baby she herself wanted to return to the shelter of the womb.

'I am so worried for her,' Olga had told Padre Bernardino, 'she is wasting away.'

Knowing that his support was now needed more than ever the Padre increased his visits to the Linser women.

'She seems indifferent even to the good things that are happening on the island,' Olga continued. 'She fought so wholeheartedly for our liberation, and now it's as if she doesn't care.'

'She lived for this moment . . .' Ernestina added, wiping her eyes. 'What are we to do, Padre?'

'Apart from praying,' he replied, 'all we can do is wait. Melancholia passes with time.'

While Anita lay in her darkened room, Cyprus was jubilant.

For days the streets were throbbing with people celebrating their liberation. Independence was at last upon them and the day for the return of the banished archbishop had arrived. The main figurehead and symbol of the revolution, Archbishop Makarios, who had been forced into exile by the British, was finally allowed to return, and the people of Cyprus were rejoicing. Crowds had been pouring into the capital since the night before by every method of transport they could find. Every street was lined with men, women and children to welcome their revolutionary hero and their new leader. Finally, the imperial rule was gone. Every house in the vicinity of the main square was crammed full of onlookers. Any balcony, roof terrace or veranda available was filled with people waving flags and holding up icons. The island was pulsating with elation.

'Get up, Anita *mou*, we are going to Nicosia,' Katerina called out as she walked into her friend's room. 'Come, *now*, get up – we have to go,' she said again and threw open the tightly shut windows that for months had been banishing life and light from the room. 'Come, Anita *mou*, get up, get dressed,' she repeated, trying to coax her out of her apathy. 'I'll help you bathe and comb your hair.

People are lining the streets to welcome *him* back. He is coming home!'

Katerina refused to give up trying to imbue Anita with some enthusiasm, some energy. 'The buses are waiting to take us to Nicosia! You and I must be there; this is our moment. Please, Anita *mou*, get up. For Mario's sake,' she urged her. But Anita's spirit had left her and she couldn't respond.

Finally, Katerina had to admit defeat and with a heavy, troubled heart went to the capital with neighbours and friends, but without her beloved Anita.

Doctor Elias kept a close eye on Anita too and visited each week but even *he* was uncertain how to treat her condition. The months went by and Anita gave no sign of recovery, much to everyone's despair.

'It will pass,' the good doctor told them, at a loss as to what else to suggest. 'Her nervous system has been affected by so many shocks following one after the other.'

As the person closest to her and the one who spent the most time with Anita, Katerina developed a theory about her friend's condition.

'I am so worried, Padre,' she said one May morning while the two of them were having coffee in the garden, sitting outside among the flowers under the shade of the lemon tree. The zinnias and dahlias were in full bloom, in all shades of gold, as if Midas had touched each and every one of them.

'You might think I am crazy,' Katerina leaned forward to speak confidentially to him, 'but I think Anita is lamenting not only the loss of her baby but the loss of something else too . . . I fear she is losing herself.'

'I think you are right,' he replied, moving his chair a little closer so his voice wouldn't carry. 'You are a very intuitive woman, Katerina, and I believe there is truth in what you say. Perhaps Anita is mourning the loss of her youthful spirit, and the loss of her first love. Mario's death was particularly brutal.'

Who would have thought that a man of the cloth could have such insight into the loss of love and youth – but then again, she thought, not many priests had experienced the kind of past that Padre Bernardino had, and she alone knew about it.

In all the years he had known the Linser women the padre had been a good counsellor to them and had stood by through all their misfortunes, but this one, the loss of this baby, saddened him deeply.

'I wonder,' Katerina went on, 'could it be that when Mario was murdered, Anita was too preoccupied with the revolution to fully acknowledge his death?'

'When you are too busy to mourn it catches up with you in different ways,' the padre replied. 'When Carmen was killed it was a double loss for me too. The baby she was carrying died along with her. It took me months, if not years, to acknowledge what effect that had on me.'

Katerina held her breath and listened, grateful that he was once again confiding in her.

'It wasn't until I found peace through my faith and prayer that I was finally able to understand the extent of my double bereavement.' He let out a sigh. 'You are right, Katerina,' he reached across to pat the back of her hand, 'it takes a long, long time to get over a death, and it needs work and prayer to achieve peace.'

'Perhaps Anita needs to go away – somewhere peaceful, somewhere healing,' she said, and decided to talk to Olga.

Katerina and the padre sat among the flowers for a long while in silence, both lost in thought, and then he reached in his pocket for his bible.

'Blessed are those who mourn, for they will be comforted,' he read, quoting Matthew chapter five, verse four.

As he read on, his voice was carried on the gentle breeze, mingling with the buzzing of the bees and the sound of birdsong.

The sanatorium in a picturesque village deep in the Troodos Mountains was the perfect place for convalescence.

After listening to Katerina's suggestion, Olga and Ernestina agreed that a month or two away from the town in the fresh sweet air and lush vegetation of the mountains surrounded by planes, pines, maples and poplar trees would be what Anita needed for her physical and mental recovery. It took all of Katerina and Olga's power of conviction to persuade Anita, but finally, with the blistering heat of the summer approaching, she agreed.

'It will do both you and your grandmother the world of good,' Olga had told her daughter, referring to Ernestina's declining health over the past few months.

The hot weather was on its way and it was perfect timing for all of them to escape the oppressive heat that would soon engulf the town.

'Are you sure you won't come with us?' Olga had asked Katerina once the arrangements had been made for their departure. This was the first time since entering the Linser household that Katerina would be left on her own for any length of time. 'Will you be all right?' she asked again anxiously. But Katerina had made up her mind to have some time alone.

'Of course I shall be fine,' she said, amused by the notion that they would be concerned since she was the one who always took care of everything.

'Besides, who is going to look after Oscar?' she added, laughing.

Oscar, the name given to any cat owned by the women, was the third of his namesake since Katerina had come to live with them.

'He's far too old to be left alone.' She smiled, knowing perfectly well that Oscar was not the real reason she would be glad to stay. Katerina had never lived alone nor had she ever had the run of a house, any house, and the prospect thrilled her. Since Costas had suggested that he would stay on in Nicosia during Anita's convalescence, this was Katerina's chance.

'You could come and visit us whenever you find the heat unbearable,' Ernestina told her.

'Oh yes please, my friend,' Anita begged. 'I shall miss you terribly.'

'Of course I would do that with pleasure,' Katerina replied. 'I could ask Kyria Maria to feed Oscar for a few days.'

Anita's recovery took three full months, and soon the summer would be giving way to early autumn, and it would be time to start thinking about heading down to the warmth of the coast. Once autumn set in in the mountains, the chilly weather would soon follow.

All summer long the three women enjoyed the fresh mountain air, gentle walks in the forest, plenty of sleep and good wholesome Cypriot food prepared by the kitchen staff in the sanatorium. With these things, and her mother and grandmother by her side, Anita was starting to regain her health and strength.

'I don't know why it took Katerina to point out to us that this is what Anita needed,' Olga told Ernestina, delighted to see the swift progress in her daughter. They were relaxing on lounging chairs one evening in the open air on the veranda of the sanatorium with a small glass of *goumandaria* while Anita had gone to the library to fetch a book. The sky above, black and dense as carob treacle, was littered with a myriad of stars. The air smelled sweet and somewhere nearby in the forest a nightingale was singing its song.

'That woman is our guardian angel,' Olga said, taking a deep breath of warm night air. 'I bless the day I made the journey to that forsaken village and took her home with us.'

'She is a treasure,' the old woman agreed, and took a sip of the sweet fortified wine in her glass just as Anita walked onto the veranda to join them.

'What are you two talking about?' she asked her mother and grandmother.

'We were just saying how marvellous Katerina is.'

'It's true!' She nodded in agreement. 'I miss her, I wish she had joined us for a few days. Do you think she might still come before we leave?'

'Why don't you write and ask her?' Ernestina reached for her granddaughter's hand. 'Of course you miss her, Anita *mou* – the two of you haven't been apart since you were girls. You three girls were inseparable when you were young. I so wish Sonia would come home, I worry about that girl.'

'Now that you are feeling stronger, how about going to visit your sister in Vienna?' Olga asked hopefully.

'I would love to come with you,' Ernestina gave a sigh, 'but I am too old for such journeys now. I just about made it up here . . .'

'Perhaps Katerina would come with me?' Anita looked at her mother and for the first time in nearly a year there was a sparkle in her eyes and spirit in her voice.

'Now that is an excellent idea, my girl!' Olga replied and lifted her glass of *goumandaria* to her lips.

Meanwhile Katerina was enjoying her time alone in Larnaka. Being the custodian of the house suited her very well, allowing her to do things her own way. Even though it was not the season, she decided to do a spring clean, taking her time over the task. Moving from room to room she washed and ironed all the curtains, polished every last bit of silver and crystal in the glass cabinets, scrubbed every skirting board and window-pane, dusted every corner and polished the parquet floors to a brilliant shine. She went to church at her leisure, she read books, and had regular visits from Padre Bernardino who on discovering that the ladies of the house were absent, took the opportunity to visit Katerina more often than usual and with less formality.

Although there were a number of Catholics who lived in the town, his parishioners were but a few and he knew most of them well. Olga and Ernestina were generous benefactors to his church, and this obliged him to behave in a somewhat deferential way towards them. Both women would have been offended if they'd known this as they were fond of the priest and considered him a good friend of the family. However, he felt that due to his position and their age, his behaviour towards them demanded a certain formality.

Katerina was different: her Orthodox faith set her apart from his congregation. She did not worship in his church and therefore she was not one of his parishioners, thus allowing him to be more relaxed towards her.

Their relationship over the months and years had blossomed into a warm friendship and he had welcomed it. God alone knew how lonely he had been for so long. It was good to have a real friend.

All through that hot and balmy summer, the two friends sat, sometimes in the cool of the kitchen with the ceiling fan on and the shutters tightly closed banishing the brutal heat, and at other times under the shade of the fig tree at the edge of the garden where there was more likely to be a little breeze. He always seemed to know when she was free and where to find her.

She took her early-morning coffee before she started her chores in the kitchen, and every day at one o'clock she stopped for lunch. Whether alone or with her mistresses, Katerina always laid the table for the midday meal, and in those summer months when she was alone she took to laying a second plate for the padre just in case he came, and he often did.

Early evenings after finishing her work she would be found on the veranda with a book, or her embroidery. She had a talent for needlework and would occupy herself with it whenever she was free. The various cushions, tablecloths and bedspreads she saw around the house created by Eva Linser had ignited her interest from an early age and Olga had encouraged and coached the young girl in the art of needlepoint.

The padre's favourite time to visit Katerina was when the day was giving way to evening. Then, both of them free, they could sit on the veranda, anticipating the cool breeze that the night would hopefully bring and talk unhurriedly for hours to the sound of the cicadas serenading them.

When Olga and Ernestina were present he varied his visits. Sometimes he would come in the day, at other times in the afternoon or evening, and would never, as he said, 'outstay his welcome', much to the protests of Ernestina, who always wanted more of him. But during that long summer, while sitting with Katerina under the moon and stars, he couldn't tear himself away.

His modest apartment by the side of his church, Our Lady of the Graces, was only a fifteen-minute walk through the middle of town. It was comfortable and pleasant enough at home, yet most evenings his feet led him towards the Linser house.

'When you are next free, you must come and see my

garden, Katerina,' he told her one evening as she appeared through the door onto the veranda carrying a tray with a jug of homemade lemonade, a bowl of juicy slices of watermelon and a plate of haloumi cheese. 'Yes, you must come, although springtime would be best,' he continued, 'when the roses are in full bloom.'

'I will,' she promised and laid the tray down on a chair serving as a table in front of them. 'I imagine most flowers perish in this heat.'

'You are right, there is very little at the moment. Some geraniums that seem to survive anything, and the pots of basil which as long as I water them reward me with a profusion of leaves that do a good job of keeping the mosquitoes at bay,' he said, referring to the common belief that the pungent aroma of the plant acted as a deterrent to the insects.

'That's why I keep so many pots of it myself,' she replied, pointing with her chin at the dozen or so pots of basil around the veranda.

Katerina leaned forward to pick up a plate and fork and handed it to the padre.

'Summer doesn't feel like summer without an evening snack of watermelon and haloumi,' she remarked, holding out the bowl of fruit to him. 'In much the same way as winter is not winter without black Russian tea and buttered toast!'

'I so agree . . . watermelon is so refreshing.' He leaned

forward to spoon a slice onto his plate. 'In my part of the world we have something similar,' he said, looking at the piece of watermelon on his fork. Katerina sat back in her chair, waiting to hear more of his past. As always she longed to hear him talk. 'You see,' he continued, 'in my country, we eat our local cheese with quince, which gives a similar effect to watermelon and haloumi.' He reached for a piece of the Cypriot cheese. 'The taste of that combination is the same as this . . . sweet *and* salty.' He bit into the melon and then took a bite of the cheese. 'Mmmm . . . delicious!' he said with his mouth full. 'My mother used to make quince jelly from the tree in our garden.'

'I remember that there were several quince trees in my village up in the mountains,' she told him. 'My grandmother used to make *glygo* and *gydonopasto*, a sweet paste for dessert. Now I buy the fruit in the market when they're in season.' She offered him another slice before continuing cheerfully, 'I will make you some *gydonopasto* sometime and then you can try it with haloumi and see if you like it.'

These familiar, inconsequential exchanges with the padre pleased Katerina as much as the deeper, more philosophical instructive conversations she had with him. These chats felt real, human, intimate. He too relished the talks between them. They made him feel less of a priest and more like his old forgotten self, allowing memories of his past life to re-emerge. Memories he had never forgotten but buried in his heart for far too long.

'Perhaps I should plant a quince tree in my garden,' he said again and leaned forward for another slice of cheese.

He was rather proud of his garden. When he'd first arrived on the island, the little yard surrounding his rooms and adjoining the church had been barren. Apart from a small lemon tree and a jasmine that had seen better days, the place had been overrun by weeds and wild daises. Gradually he set about restoring, cultivating and converting this wasteland into a fragrant, bee-loving piece of heaven. He planted mainly scented roses, with the prominent position given to his pride and joy the Rosa Damascena with its thirty deep pink petals and heavenly scent, a variety of rose that had been imported to Cyprus from Damascus for the main purpose of extracting and producing rose water. He didn't have time for this activity but enjoyed and revelled in the flowers' exquisite aroma. Some of the local ladies in neighbouring houses regularly asked the padre if they could harvest some flowers for that purpose. It was a bountiful bush and so long as they didn't strip it entirely of its blooms, he agreed. He was of course always rewarded with several bottles of rose water, which he enjoyed using in different ways. In the summer, he would splash it all over his face, a fragrant and refreshing start to the day, and sometimes add a few drops to his glass of ice-cold drinking water.

Inside his modest apartment, his rooms were pleasant enough, if a little ascetic, containing everything a man of the cloth could possibly need. In winter the living room was warm and cosy and in the summer the large ceiling fans in every room kept the place cool; yet his excuse for his frequent visits to Katerina was that it was much cooler outside on her veranda than in the oppressive heat of his rooms. The truth was that he had no need to make any excuses for these visits. Katerina was as happy in his company as he was in hers. In fact, she had never enjoyed the company of anybody as much as she was enjoying his.

In the course of those summer months he came to realize that being with Katerina was the highlight of his day. He found pleasure in her presence almost as much as he had cherished his time with Carmen in another life so many years before. He started to become aware that this young Greek Cypriot woman had a quality about her that was reminiscent of his one and only love. Perhaps not so much physically, although Katerina did possess those burning dark eyes that could penetrate into his soul as Carmen's had. But apart from their soulful eyes, the two women couldn't have looked more different. Carmen was small-boned and lightly built like a little bird; he could scoop her up and lift her with one arm and when she was pregnant no one knew about it, it hardly showed. She had the figure of a girl and the short haircut like a boy's that most of the partisan women wore then for practical reasons. Katerina, on the other hand, was curvaceous and womanly, and in height almost as tall as him. She was full-breasted, her waist tiny and her legs shapely and long. She did nothing to accentuate her figure – on the contrary she tried to hide it – but it was obvious, one couldn't help but notice. Her hair was a mass of chestnut curls that rested on her shoulders when she didn't have them tightly pulled back while working, which was most of the time.

Nevertheless, despite Katerina's obvious physical differences to Carmen, he saw the beauty in her and the same gentle kindness and spirit. Both women possessed an innocent curiosity, a passion for their country, and natural wisdom. Katerina reminded him without doubt of the young woman he had taken as his wife a lifetime ago and whom he had never stopped loving.

During the long hot summer Padre Bernardino acknowledged gradually, secretly and reluctantly that his feelings towards Katerina went much further than the pure friendship that had existed between them at first. The small spark that had been kindled during their tranquil evenings on the veranda, encouraging memories of earthy human feelings, slowly developed into a forest fire, which try as he might and must, he could not extinguish. When he was with her he felt happier than he had felt in years – free, elated. When he was alone he was troubled and fearful. When he tried to process what was happening to him it always resulted in torment, guilt and remorse for these newly awakened feelings towards a woman. Carmen was the only woman he had loved or would ever love, he had made that pledge and kept it – till now. He tried to find solace in prayer. *I am not a man, I am a priest, I have no right to these feelings, my path is chosen*, he would berate himself over and over again.

While he busied himself with his priestly duties or officiated at the ceremony of Mass he would became a priest once again, not a man; thoughts of Katerina melted away. The vows of priesthood he had taken were solemn and sacred; he had taken them knowingly and willingly and they had given him the peace and comfort he had sought since he was a boy. It was true that he had been just a man once. But that was a long time ago and the memories and feelings that he had buried deep down and were now resurfacing had to be banished and fought against. Again and again he reminded himself that he had taken vows to God, to his Church, to his faith and to chastity. They were equally as binding as each other and to break them would be a mortal sin.

But the flesh is weak and all too human. When he saw her again those emotions welled up once more. What he felt for Katerina he had to accept was love. A profound and deep love, a love he had only ever experienced once in his life before. His guilt was redoubled, for he was betraying his faith but also the memory of his wife. To begin with he told himself that what he felt for Katerina was a platonic and chaste love. But as time went on and when he was quite alone in the deep of the night, either in his bed or awake in contemplation, he had to acknowledge that this love of his was more than all of those things. The unwelcome and disturbing presence of carnal desire had captured his body and spirit and he was brought low by its torments.

Katerina had never been *in* love. Her heart was bursting *with* love for those she cared for, and she felt it deeply and sincerely, but never had she harboured a secret physical longing for a man, or felt that which Greeks called *erotas*. Aphrodite's love child had given her a wide berth and she was perfectly content and resigned to the fact that she would remain immune for the rest of her life. Both Anita and Sonia had talked to her about it when cupid's arrow had taken his aim at them, but she didn't care much for the idea. Men, as Olga had always firmly told her, were an unreliable species, their uses limited, and looking around her she decided her mistress was probably right. By then she was twenty-eight years old, and had accepted that she would never feel sexual passion run through her veins for anyone. She was more than happy with the people she loved.

When she first started to feel what she imagined must be *love* of the kind she had heard and read about in romantic novels, she was shocked and appalled – while also feeling helplessly at its mercy. It had happened so unexpectedly, was so unwelcome and, worst of all, it was aimed at the wrong person. *This can't be happening*, she insisted to herself. Surely it was delusion even to dream that what she felt could be reciprocated. She wondered perhaps if she was losing her mind. Padre Bernardino was a dear beloved friend, not an object of desire. He was like Anita and Sonia, Olga or Ernestina; that was the kind of love she knew about, those were the kind of loyal nurturing feelings she was accustomed to having towards those she dearly cared about. Feelings of tenderness and concern, not disturbing longings.

He was her friend, her mentor, her spiritual educator; there should be no place in her heart for these unsettling emotions and desires. She was normally a grounded, pious, sensible person in control of her emotions and her actions – why then this sudden state of madness? Her head was full of unanswered questions. Why on earth was she behaving like a silly adolescent girl, anticipating his arrival with trembling anxiety when in the past she had looked forward to seeing him with pleasing composure? She wasn't a vain person, so why did she start wearing her hair loose, making sure it was brushed and shining even when she was doing her chores, and taking care to look her best at all times just in case he came to visit? Why was she catching herself in secret indulgences like sneaking into Olga's room to spray Parisian perfume behind her ears and in her bosom, before his arrival? She was certainly unhinged.

She had been worried about Anita, supposing that her misfortunes had sent her a little mad – *but look who's mad now*, she kept telling herself. *This is surely the behaviour of an unstable person*. Her head swirled with guilt. Mostly she tried to block it out, not to think about it, or about anything of significance at all, because if she did, she was flooded with confusion and shame. The padre had always treated her like a cherished friend, he was honest and truthful, he had opened his heart, taken her into his confidence and spoken of personal matters that no one else knew or would ever know about him. Her infatuation, she decided, was a form of betrayal and unworthy of his trust. He had been nothing but honourable and virtuous towards her; he was a priest, a man of God. He had never given her reason to think of him otherwise. The padre, as Ernestina had told her once when Katerina had asked her to explain the difference between Orthodoxy and Catholicism, is married to the Church, and that is why he could never be married to a woman, unlike an Orthodox priest.

Katerina knew that a Greek Orthodox priest could have a wife and a family, and indeed many of them did.

The priest in her village had twelve children – she had been friendly with some of them as they were of similar ages to her and her siblings. Her grandmother used to feel sorry for his poor wife who seemed to be perpetually pregnant. But Padre Bernardino, Ernestina had told her, was a Catholic and he had taken the vows of celibacy, which could never be broken.

When she looked at herself in the mirror she didn't recognize what she saw. Who had she become? What did she want? Did she ever imagine that he would leave the Church and break his vows for her? He had had a wife once, but that was a long time ago, before he had dedicated his life to the Church and God.

She longed for composure. She needed to govern her feelings, do something to save herself from humiliation and shame, which her actions and emotions, if they ever betrayed her, would surely bring upon her.

She decided she must distance herself from him, for a time at least. Going to the mountains to visit her ladies, put space between herself and this fixation, instil order into her thoughts – that was the solution.

'I had a letter from Anita,' she told him, avoiding his gaze, when he next visited. They were about to sit down for the midday meal and she was busy bringing food to the table. 'She wrote to invite me to join them at the sanatorium.' She turned away and walked to the sink to fill the water jug from the tap.

There had been something of a heatwave during the past few days; the barometer had risen to forty degrees and Katerina had kept all the shutters closed in an attempt to keep the house as cool as possible. Padre Bernardino hadn't come to visit for several days, and she was nervous at the prospect of meeting him again. She wore her apron over a floral short-sleeved summer dress and had put a little rouge on her cheeks. Looking in the mirror that morning she was alarmed to see how pale she was. She had missed him, and her mind was full of imaginings about why he hadn't come. She reassured herself that it must have been the heat that had kept him away, or matters of the Church or perhaps he was unwell; but mostly she told herself that he must have been trying to avoid her. *Obviously my behaviour has put him off. He must think me such a fool and worse.* But Katerina couldn't have been more wrong. She had given nothing away; he thought she acted the same as always, friendly, courteous and hospitable, and it was *his* actions he had been afraid of. They were both swimming in a sea of guilt and lovesickness, each too far out of their depth to notice anything of each other's behaviour.

'How long will you be away?' he asked now, trying to hide his disappointment. 'It will be good to escape this heat,' he quickly added in an attempt to sound sincere.

She tried to avoid his question. 'Anita says it's cool up there and at night they even cover themselves with a blanket. Hard to imagine in this inferno.'

'How is Anita?' he asked awkwardly, at a loss as to what else to say.

'She is improving; it has done her good to be there.' Her reply was as stilted as his question.

'Will you stay long?' he ventured again, as casually as he could, hoping for an answer this time.

'Not long . . .' she said and the thought of being away from him made her feel sick to her stomach. 'Anita has been asking me to visit, it's time I did before they have to return.'

'When will that be?' Alarm rose in his voice. The thought of their return and a full house again distressed him.

'You have no idea how much I have missed you!' Anita said the minute she stepped out of the bus in the square. 'You'll love it up here as much as we do,' she continued excitedly. 'Come, follow me, the sanatorium is just a walk away. It's not a hospital, you know, it's like a hotel. They cook and clean and look after us and all we have to do is sleep, eat, walk and relax. I even play the piano a little . . . You will like it, you'll see, and you'll have a rest – God knows you need it too, Katerina *mou*.'

Anita was well aware of how much energy and emotional effort Katerina had put into helping her during those months she had been ill. 'Mama and *Nonna* love it here too, and like me they're so glad you decided to join us. Come, let's go, they're waiting for us.'

Anita was far too excited to stop talking; her vigour had returned along with the colour in her cheeks, which was more than Katerina could say about herself. The hours she had spent sitting on the bus had been taken up with exhausting thoughts of the padre; thoughts that filled her mind with further confusion and bewilderment. Almost for the first time since she had entered the Linser house as a girl, Katerina felt alone. Olga, the girls, even the padre had always been there to consult and support her when she was in need. This time, she realized, she was on her own. This was her problem and hers only, and no one else could help her.

Olga and Ernestina were sitting waiting for them on the veranda with a jug of lemonade and a plate of sesame *koulourakia*, which were all the more welcome to Katerina for having been prepared by someone else.

'Welcome, Katerina *mou*,' Olga said, kissing her on both cheeks. 'We have missed you.'

'Come, sit down, my girl,' Ernestina added. 'What news do you bring for us? How is the padre?'

At this mention of the very person who occupied her thoughts, Katerina's face flushed crimson and she turned away, praying to God that no one had noticed. She was in luck as Olga was busy pouring a glass of lemonade for her, Anita had walked away to drag another chair over, and Ernestina's eyesight, she knew, was rapidly failing her. Settling back in one of the deckchairs, she took in a deep breath of pine-scented air and tried to banish thoughts of the priest. Perhaps, she thought, Anita was right – a little rest would do her good and clear her thoughts.

'How is Oscar?' Anita asked cheerfully, taking a seat next to her friend.

'He is fine and sleeps all day long. What else do cats do apart from sleep and eat? He doesn't even chase mice any more,' she said and they all laughed like old times.

'He's getting old, ill and decrepit like me,' Ernestina said with a sigh and a little chuckle. Looking at these three women whom she loved most in the world, women who until now had been her whole world, Katerina was flooded with a sense of well-being and relief. As much as she had loved being alone in the house and with the padre, she had missed them. They were her family, her life, her reality and stability. She even wondered if perhaps the separation from them was the reason that she had developed such inappropriate feelings towards the priest. Sitting with them now she welcomed the calm and peace these women gave her and yearned for tranquillity instead of the turmoil and anguish that falling in love had brought her.

She shared a room with Anita, as they had sometimes

done when they were girls and the two young women talked late into the night. Anita did most of the talking and for that Katerina was grateful.

'Sometimes I forget I am married,' she confessed one night. 'Not once have I missed Costas since I came here, nor do I miss him when he stays in Nicosia; I feel more relief than anything. I often wonder why I married him.'

'You were in love with Mario, Anita *mou*,' Katerina replied, avoiding any critical comments she might have been tempted to make about Costas. 'No one could have taken his place.'

'If Mario had lived everything would be different now.'

'He was exceptional.' Katerina shook her head and sighed with the memory of him.

'*And* he was the love of my life . . .' Anita hesitated a moment. 'Sometimes I think by marrying Costas, I have betrayed Mario.' She lifted herself up on one elbow and looked at Katerina. 'Perhaps,' she said in a whisper, her eyes glistening with tears in the dark, 'I am being punished for that.'

Focusing on Anita, talking and listening to her, allowed Katerina to banish the confusing voice in her own head and pretend that what had taken place in her heart during the past few weeks was a fancy or a dream. Since her arrival, long walks in the forest, and the fresh air, had done wonders for the nervous exhaustion she had brought with her, and had contributed to her ability to relax. For the first time in many days Katerina had stopped thinking about herself and delighted in her friend's recovery.

Anita was at last emerging from her deadening melancholy and along with her physical improvement came the ability to speak about her grief.

'Nature heals,' she said one day as the two friends made their way gingerly down a steep trail which led to a small waterfall and a stream. 'Nature reminds us that we are a *part* of her, and not *apart* from her,' she said, emphasizing the words, and stopped to fill her lungs with mountain air.

'We are all God's creatures,' Katerina replied softly.

They had woken early that morning and left as dawn was breaking. They wanted to walk before the temperature rose by mid-morning as it always did. They had taken a small backpack to carry fruit, bread and olives and a flask of coffee for breakfast, which they would have once they reached the waterfall. By the time they arrived at their designated spot they were both more than ready for a rest. The ground was covered in green ferns, and pine needles provided a soft surface on which to lay their tablecloth, spread out the food, and enjoy their early-morning picnic to the sound of cascading water and birdsong.

'It's almost too cold to drink,' Anita called, crouching over the stream and scooping water into her mouth with her hand. 'This water, this forest, this waterfall, they are marvels of nature,' she enthused again, walking back to Katerina who had already laid out the tablecloth and was now biting into a juicy peach. 'We must never take the small pleasures of life for granted,' Anita added as she sat down next to her friend, tucking her legs beneath her dress.

'It is true, we have much to be grateful for,' Katerina agreed.

'I know I've had my share of misfortunes,' Anita leaned forward to break off a bunch of grapes, 'and maybe I have been unusually unlucky . . .' her voice trailed off, '. . . but of all the things that have happened to me, Katerina *mou*, my one great sorrow is that I will never be a mother.'

Katerina reached for her friend's hand and both women's eyes filled with tears. Anita held Katerina's hand tightly and neither spoke for a long while.

'I had her in my arms,' she whispered eventually, 'so still, so peaceful, so perfect, she was still warm . . . I shall never forget that tiny, tiny body against mine.'

Moving closer, Katerina pulled Anita into her arms and held her there for the longest time. She let her cry silently and mournfully until there were no more tears to be shed. At long last all the pain and sorrow she had felt for so many months that had been buried deep down in the silent reaches of her soul, poured out little by little, rising up to the surface until all was spent.

Then, gradually in the soft mountain air, they dried their eyes, poured coffee for themselves, kicked off their shoes, stretched out on the warm earth and looked up through the trees at the clear blue sky. They reached for each other's hands and for a while they lay lost in their own silent thoughts.

Katerina tried unsuccessfully to banish his face imprinted on the blackness of her closed eyes, flooding her with a bittersweet joy.

She had arrived with the intention of staying for two or three weeks and since she had arranged for Kyria Maria to feed Oscar and water the garden she had no compelling reason to return.

'Must you go?' Anita pleaded. 'Please stay longer, stay and go back with us, we only have a few weeks left.' But thoughts of the priest got the better of her, she needed to be near him.

The padre spent the entire time she was away in the church attending to duties he didn't even have. He filled his hours with work till late into the evening and then took himself to his rooms trying to banish thoughts of Katerina. Books, and prayer late every night often kept him awake till dawn. When he reached for the Bible he repeatedly found his fingers leading him to the pages of The Song Of Solomon.

'Let him kiss me with the kisses of his mouth: for thy love is

better than wine.' He read the verses compulsively. *'A bundle of myrrh is my well-beloved unto me; he shall lie all night betwixt my breasts.'* Should he take comfort or discomfort in reading these passages? Had Katerina ever read them? She was a pious woman and they often read the Bible together but could he ever read those words to her? He could not. She was *his rose and his lily of the valley, a lily among thorns,* but express his love for her? He could not.

The morning bus brought her back to Larnaka. She hardly gave herself time to drop her suitcase in the hall, unlatch the kitchen shutters and open a window to air the room, before going straight to his church to look for him. She wanted to let him know she had returned, she wasn't in the habit of telephoning, and besides she longed to see him. It was early afternoon and the sun was beating down with a ferocity that surprised her. The few days she'd spent in the freshness of the mountains lulled her into the assumption that the summer was in decline and cooler days were ahead.

The interior of the church was fresh and welcoming, flowers in the vases on the altar and under the statute of San Sebastiano exuded a delicate scent, but he was not there. She took a moment to get her breath back and regulate her heartbeat. She sat on a pew and breathed in the delicate fragrance of the lilies, gathering her courage before venturing into the churchyard in search of him.

Finally she found him in his garden watering his pots of basil. He had the watering can in one hand and a cigarette in the other. He was dressed in a pair of navy-blue trousers and a white short-sleeved shirt. She'd never seen him without his priestly robes. He looked thinner and paler than when they'd last met; yet his arms looked strong and muscular. At that moment she wasn't looking at a priest. This was a man standing before her. She stood silently watching him from a little distance, savouring the moment, a flutter of joy in her heart.

At last, sensing her gaze, he looked up.

'Katerina *mou*!' he exclaimed, a startled smile brightening up his face. 'When did you arrive home?'

'Just today,' she replied and took a few paces towards him. 'I wanted to let you know . . .'

'Is everything all right?' Concern was etched on his brow. 'Did you come back early?'

'I did,' she said and stopped, in case she said too much.

'The others?' he asked again, holding his breath in anticipation.

'They are still there. For a few weeks more.'

He exhaled, and smiled with relief.

'Would you like to come in?' He gestured towards his rooms. 'Have a glass of water, lemonade?' he continued, remembering his manners.

'No, no, thank you,' she said, rather flustered, 'I must go and see to the house, I came directly here.'

273

He put down the watering can, stubbed out his cigarette and walked towards her. 'Good to see you again, Katerina, welcome back.'

'Why don't you come by this evening if you are free?' she asked and felt herself blush with longing for him and fear of being considered too forward.

'Try to keep me away,' he replied cheerfully and picking up her hand he brought it to his lips.

All the way home she felt light as a rose petal and the back of her hand pulsated with the memory of his lips on her skin. She made a stop at old Michalis's grocery shop to buy fruit, haloumi, village bread and olives.

'*Kalosorises* – welcome, Katerina!' the grocer greeted her when she walked through the door. 'Are the ladies back too?' he asked, not letting her forget that everyone knew everyone's business in this provincial community.

'Not yet, Michalis,' she said non-committally, looking around in case she forgot something and spotting some bottles of *goumandaria* on the shelf. She had developed quite a taste for the drink up in the mountains. Each evening after dinner they had all enjoyed a glass while sitting talking on the veranda.

'Good for medicinal purposes,' Ernestina had told them. 'Helps with the circulation and full of vitamins.'

'It's especially good for enhancing one's mood,' Olga had said, laughing, as she handed them all a glass.

Katerina couldn't remember if there was a bottle at

home so she bought one just in case. She and the padre would have a celebratory drink on the veranda later on, she thought. She was about to walk out of the shop when another thought struck her; she turned around and began scanning the shelves again.

'Anything else you want, Katerina?' Michalis enquired.

'Did your wife make any *glygo gydoni* last year?' she asked hopefully.

'She did indeed and very tasty it is too!' he replied, reaching into a cupboard behind him and handing her a jar of quince pieces in syrup.

The house was as clean and tidy as she'd left it, her spring cleaning still very apparent. Nervously she prepared their modest meze. She cut and sliced the watermelon and left it in the fridge to ensure it was chilled and refreshing. She placed the jar of the quince *glygo* on the table ready to be served at the end of the evening with their coffee. The chunks of fruit plunged in syrup were not like the quince jelly or the quince paste they had talked about previously; this quince was not to be eaten with cheese but taken with their coffee as a dessert and she wanted to surprise him with it. She wanted to know how it compared with his own Spanish version, which he had described so eloquently to her. She arranged slices of haloumi and cucumber on a pretty platter and the bread in a colourful basket; everything was ready on a tray long before he came. She couldn't wait to be sitting on the veranda with him once again.

She bathed and put on her blue cotton dress with the white rose motif: a Linser print and one of Olga's signature designs. The rose had always attracted Olga as a pattern on fabric. She not only used the entire flower in all its colour variations, but also lone petals to create an abstract pattern. Katerina loved this short-sleeved summer dress and would only wear it on special occasions. She hung her gold chain and cross round her neck, a gift from her mistress on the first birthday she'd celebrated after coming to live with them. She washed and brushed her hair, and sprayed a little *Soir de Paris* from Olga's dressing table behind her ears. Then, picking up her embroidery, she made her way to the veranda. It was good to be back. This house, this town, were her home. She loved it, she cherished it, she couldn't imagine living anywhere else. She was glad to be back but she was also pleased she had made the journey to Troodos; not for herself – being away had made her suffer – but for Anita. She knew her presence had done her good. She loved her like a sister, far more than she loved any of her own siblings; she loved all the women deeply and would do anything for them. But she also knew that they would do the same for her, and they had already done plenty.

She heard him walk up the front steps before she saw him. She half expected to see him dressed as he had been earlier, but in his long clerical robe he was transformed once again into the man of God that he was.

'*Kalispera*, Katerina,' he greeted her cheerfully and handed her a little posy made of jasmine flowers. 'From my garden,' he told her. 'I have at last managed to salvage the bush.'

'Thank you,' she replied and brought the flowers to her lips. The heady aroma filled her senses and the satin feel of the petals on her lips added to the sensation. He knew how much Katerina loved these little posies, or garlands, which she gathered like most girls and women did in the summer months. Anita, Sonia and Katerina enjoyed indulging in this summertime pastime. They would pick the jasmine flowers in the early afternoon when they were still tightly closed buds. Once they had collected enough, they'd laboriously thread each bud, one at a time, using a needle and a length of cotton thread; when the thread was full they would tie the ends together in a knot to create a tiny garland. By evening the buds would burst open into their delicate white blooms and the garland could then be worn round the wrist, pinned to the hair or just held in the hand to relish the aroma emanating from it.

'You made it for me?' she asked wide-eyed as she slipped it over her hand onto her wrist, an exquisite scented floral bracelet.

'I remember you told me you had to pick the flowers

when they are closed buds so I did it this afternoon . . . did I do it right?'

'Perfectly,' she said and brought her wrist to her lips again.

'It's good to be here, Katerina,' he said as he sat down, 'but mostly it's good to see you again.'

There was no awkwardness in their behaviour this time. The relief of being together again overcame all other considerations. All the guilt and agony about their feelings seemed to melt away once they were in each other's company. They sat on the veranda like old times, they talked and laughed, she told him about her stay in the mountains and about Anita's recovery. They ate with enjoyment the dishes she had prepared for them and when Katerina fetched the bottle of *goumandaria* and two glasses he was more than happy to participate in a celebratory drink.

'I always think it tastes like Holy Communion,' she said as she poured them another glass. 'It feels blessed . . .'

She made coffee and served up the quince *glygo*, allowing him to savour it and comment without the knowledge of what he was tasting. She waited for his reaction. His delighted surprise at the first taste was all that Katerina had hoped for.

'It brings back so many memories . . .' he said, taking another bite.

'Does it taste the same?' she was curious to know.

'Oh yes – perhaps a little sweeter but just as delicious.'

The cicadas obliged with their usual serenade, and the moon, almost full, lit the veranda like a lantern, so no candle or electric light was needed that evening.

The hour was getting late. They drank more *goumandaria – more than necessary*, she thought – but Olga's words kept coming to mind about it being 'good for enhancing one's mood'. She felt light-headed and happy.

'I'll fetch some water,' she said at some point and reached for the jug. He reached for it too and their hands collided; he pulled away as if he had touched a flame. Their eyes locked for a second. She sprang out of her chair and ran into the house. He followed. As she walked into the darkness of the room she stumbled and he caught her before she fell. She was weightless, no substance, no bones, he held her tight against him. She thought she was a feather, a petal, a jasmine flower floating in the air. In the darkness he searched for her mouth and found it ready, waiting. Nothing existed, no past, no future, no present, no God. Time had stopped. Was it the flesh that seized them both, or was it the mind that led to this madness? No matter. Mind and body had mingled into one. *They* became one. How did she know what to do? How did she know how to give herself to him so completely, so unreservedly, so absolutely? It was as if she had been born for that moment of surrender. Was it just a moment? Or was it hours, days, months, an eternity?

The soft flesh, the dark mysterious velvet folds that engulfed him, touching his very soul, evoking a memory so dear, so deeply buried, his ecstasy flowed like the blood in his veins, giving him life.

Dawn found them naked, limbs entwined in Katerina's bed. She woke first. The faint light escaping through the slightly open wooden shutters betrayed the infant new day. Shadows still danced on the walls. She knew the sun must just be making its appearance over the horizon and soon its rays would be flooding the room. The room faced east and she often watched the sun rise from the sea. It was one of her pleasures to observe the amber globe appear as if by magic from the horizon, a vision that never ceased to delight her, a novelty after her early years in the mountains. Normally finding herself awake at such an early hour she would watch at the window, but now she could not leave him. She looked around the room. Their clothes were discarded on the floor and on the chair by the window. She had no memory of undressing. His robe in a pile by the bed looked incongruous, irreverent. He was fast asleep, one arm draped around her torso pinning her to the bed; the other, bent at the elbow, lay on his pillow, palm upturned, cupping his face as if in contemplation. She watched him sleep, hardly daring to breathe lest she woke him. She was sure that in that sleep of his he was fighting some kind of spiritual battle, the vertical line between his brows seeming to confirm her suspicions. She watched him, trying to guess. When he finally opened his eyes she didn't see torment or a stormy sea in them. She saw calm waters and love.

'*Kalimera*, Katerina,' he said and cupped her face with his hands and kissed her lips. The relief she felt at his gesture manifested itself in silent tears. She had feared he might wake up regretful, tormented and ashamed.

Her feelings were of intense happiness *and* sadness. He kissed her tears away and took her in his arms. He stroked her hair, and kissed her some more. She couldn't remember a time she had felt more complete. She wanted to speak but found no words. She wanted to sing but found no voice.

He held her tenderly like a precious gift. To sleep and wake up with another by his side was one more distant memory, the joy and intimacy of which he had pledged to forsake. It felt natural, it felt human and he wondered how he had ever lived without it.

For her, the amazement of lying next to *him* filled her with a primitive pleasure. How many times had she slept with another human being out of necessity? How many nights had she been kept awake by a sick or fretful younger sibling? Oh, to lie in his arms to feel cherished, to feel love. She looked into his eyes again: this time in their blue depth she believed she saw the flicker of regret.

He gave a sigh and folded his hands behind his head. For so many years his faith, his God and the Church was all the solace and comfort he'd needed. But how did any of that compare with the intensity of emotions that consumed him at that very moment? Was he now doubting the validity of his faith? Did his love for Him diminish because of his love for Katerina? No! The love for Him would never diminish, he was sure of that – he had known it since he was a boy. He turned to look at her, the room still bathed in the light of dawn. She lay still by his side, her face turned towards him, her eyes searching for clues.

'Good morning . . .' she whispered, wishing to speak yet not daring to speak his name. As if guessing her dilemma he pulled her to him again.

'Call me simply Bernardino, Katerina *mou*,' he said, eyes brightening with amusement. 'That is my name after all!'

They lay in each other's arms until light seeping through the wooden shutters flooded the room as if the sun himself was rebuking them for their happiness.

In the days and weeks that followed before the women returned from the mountains the lovers found ways to be together. They were watchful and careful, making sure to visit at times deemed acceptable, or if Bernardino stayed the night he would leave before dawn. They lied to themselves, and to each other, that what they were doing was acceptable. In the hours he was alone he tormented himself with the knowledge of his sinful actions but the pull of his love, his passion, was too powerful to resist.

'I will leave the Church and marry you if you want me to,' he told her as they lay in bed one night.

'Your faith is everything to you, I could never ask you to do that.'

'You are everything to me now; I thought I would only ever love one woman and my God.' He pulled her close and kissed her eyes.

'I thought I would never know love at all,' she replied.

'I love you as a man, Katerina, with my soul and my body. I love Him as a priest, as his servant. The two loves are so different, yet so powerful.'

'And for that I could never ask you to leave Him for me. I thank God for sending you to me. You are my gift from Him, you are my angel,' she said and kissed his hand.

'But I have fallen . . .' He went to say something else but stopped; instead he closed his eyes and brought her fingers to his lips.

In a few days the others would be returning, so they were making the most of their time alone. They were about to have lunch; Katerina had made *dolmades*, stuffed vine leaves, peppers and tomatoes, which she knew was one of his favourite dishes. She was about to fill his plate when the ringing in the hall shattered the peace. She put the pot back on the stove, looked at him with alarm in her eyes, and ran to pick up the phone.

She held the receiver with trembling hands as she heard Olga tell her that Ernestina had passed away peacefully in her sleep the night before, and that she was now making arrangements for their immediate return and would Katerina inform the padre to start preparing for the funeral. Olga, in control as always, spoke efficiently and quickly to avoid giving either of them a chance to break down. Katerina knew her mistress well. She might have sounded matter of fact but Katerina was well aware that that was Olga's way of coping. No time to waste or lose. Things had to be arranged and no one other than herself was going to see to them. There would be time for grieving later.

'What happened? Who was it?' he asked anxiously when Katerina, her face pale and her eyes red-rimmed, returned to the kitchen.

They had planned to reduce their meetings, try and resume some kind of normality in their lives in preparation for the women's return. But neither of them had expected it would happen so suddenly, so sadly, and bring their dream-like world to such an abrupt end.

They buried Ernestina in the Catholic cemetery, in the family vault next to her beloved Franz. Two generations of Linsers were buried there. *How many more would follow?*

Katerina asked herself as she held tight onto Anita's arm, her eyes wandering across the graveyard over the old marble tombstones marking the resting places of so many Catholic families who had arrived on this small island over the years as visitors and chosen to make it their home.

Half of the townspeople of Larnaka attended Ernestina's funeral. She was a popular and well-known figure in the community and even though most people attending were Orthodox, they all crowded into the Catholic church to pay their respects. The eulogy that Padre Bernardino gave to his congregation was most touching and heartfelt. Katerina had never attended a Catholic Mass before, so she watched in awe as he performed the funeral liturgy. He was dressed in the traditional black funeral vestment, looking sombre, truly sad at the loss of a dear parishioner and good friend. The ritual was not dissimilar from the Orthodox one; the wafting of incense and sprinkling of holy water on the coffin, accompanied by chanting and praying. She watched the man she loved, the man who had shared her bed days before, and realized that the figure who was now leading her employer's funeral service, standing by the altar in front of his flock, was an altogether different man. This was a *man of God*, with a calling far greater than the calling of an ordinary man, a lover or husband. She looked at the priest and at that very moment she knew. She understood that she might love him with her body and soul, and that she would love no other for as long as she lived, but she had no right to come between him and his faith, between him and his God; and moreover, that had never been her intention.

Larnaka, 2010

The stunned expressions on the three faces turned towards Anita spoke far more than words could ever convey. None of them – not Eleni, not Marianna and certainly not Adonis – could have guessed or suspected what his mother had been telling them. A tragic, doomed love story straight out of a romantic novel, and the heroine their very own beloved Katerina! How was this possible? Katerina in love! Katerina and the padre! Katerina the virginal mother of them all, their maiden *tante*!

All three had liked and respected the padre when they were children and remembered the sadness felt by the family when he left the island. None of them had ever seen Katerina cry, apart from the day the priest came to bid them all farewell. The three children had been playing one of their board games – Monopoly, Eleni recalled – and Adonis was winning when Padre Bernardino came to the house.

Grandmother Olga, Anita and Katerina were sitting in the *saloni* waiting to receive him. On the dining-room table all the best china had been laid for tea and the three-tiered cake dish was laden with all kinds of spectacular cakes and pastries. On a separate glass platter sat a huge *karidopita*, a chocolate walnut cake – Olga's speciality and Adonis's favourite. Abandoning their game, the children peeked through the door at all the mouth-watering sweets and hoped that they would be called in to join the tea party once the guest of honour arrived. They were used to seeing the padre when he called in, he loved the children and always had time for them, but this visit was different. It seemed formal and a little solemn. Katerina had been baking since the previous day and the three children were aware that she was doing it all with a heavy heart. Her usual cheerful expression when cooking had been replaced by a sadness in her eyes.

'What's wrong, Tante? Are you unhappy?' Eleni asked, offering to help with making the *koulourakia*.

'Yes, my darling, I am very sad because our good Father Bernardino is leaving us.'

'Where is he going?'

'Far away . . .' Katerina replied and looked away so that Eleni couldn't see her tears.

The tea party was indeed a solemn affair and even when the children were invited in, the atmosphere around the room was heavy. The three tucked into the cakes with relish and were incredulous to notice that none of the adults seemed to have an appetite. The padre accepted a cup of aromatic tea, flavoured with cinnamon, but to the children's amazement refused any of the treats he was offered. *All the more for us*, Adonis thought, stuffing another *melomakarona* into his mouth.

'How can we live without you, Padre?' Olga said, twisting her lace handkerchief nervously in her hands.

'The new priest, Padre Ignazio, will be a good friend to you all. He's a good man,' he told them, 'you'll see . . .' He looked at Olga. He could not meet Katerina's eyes.

Why are they all so miserable? Adonis wondered, reaching for a piece of cake and longing to return to the game he felt certain he would win.

The memory of that day came flooding back to all three. Now at last they were beginning to understand its significance. Each of them remembered feeling sad to see the padre leave; he was the one regular male presence in their home. He came to visit them before he left and gave them a bible each as a parting gift. Adonis still had his.

'How did you all find out about the affair?' Adonis was the first to break the silence which hovered expectantly in the room keeping them all on edge.

'Ah! That is another story, my children,' Anita replied and reached for a glass of water. 'Once again you must have patience and I will tell you everything. We were very close, Katerina and I . . . and over the years there was nothing about each other we didn't know or didn't tell each other; I was privileged enough, you see, for Katerina to trust me and gradually confide in me. But there is one thing you must all know: make no mistake . . . this love of theirs was *not* an "affair". What the padre and Katerina had was a great love, one that transcended all boundaries.'

Transfixed now more than ever, Anita's audience sat motionless, waiting for her to continue with the story.

15

She went looking for him. She needed to see him alone, away from the house and family. She had rehearsed what she would say; she was guided by a feeling so strong, so powerful that it almost matched the strength of her love for him.

Again, like the only other time she had paid a visit to his house, she found him in the garden watering his plants. This time he was wearing his ecclesiastical robes. Was he on his way to church, she wondered, or had he just arrived home? She stood back to watch him. Her heart ached with tenderness for him. It seeped into every cell of her body. What could possibly follow after so much love? Nothing could equal it. What she felt was even greater than the act of lovemaking, which at the time she perceived as the most powerful experience of her life. Nothing could diminish her devotion to him, not even separation; she knew that.

She watched him and waited; he did not sense her presence. He appeared to be deep in thought, a frown furrowing his brow. She moved closer and quietly spoke his name, in almost a whisper. He looked up, startled, and smiled in sheer pleasure at the sight of her.

'Katerina . . .' He hesitated on seeing her serious expression. 'What is wrong?'

'Nothing is wrong,' she replied, her face softening, her smile soothing his frown.

'Come, sit.' He pointed to the two chairs by the lemon tree.

'Can we go inside?' she asked, pointing to the door.

Padre Bernardino hadn't lived the ordinary life of a priest. He had loved, and he had sinned. But through all the perils and adversities of his life one core aspect had always remained constant: his faith and his love of God which he never lost sight of even during his darkest days of grief and temptation. He came to believe that the hardships of his earlier years had been put there in order to test him, to make him stronger and to deepen his devotion to Him. He believed he had served his God and the Church with faith, honesty and truth but like most men he was fallible, and now he found himself divided as never before between his earthly passion and his pastoral vocation. His bond with Katerina went deeper than anything he could have believed possible. In his moments of despair when alone and in prayer he realized that the two loves were equal in his heart and were tearing him apart. He found it impossible to make a choice. He kept telling himself that it wasn't just the flesh that propelled him to her, it was a love beyond the carnal, and if she asked him, he was willing to defect from the Church, marry her and make a life with her.

At first Katerina was tongue-tied. She was aware of the significance of what she needed to say but she couldn't find the words. They sat in his small living room, light pouring in through the window from the garden. She chose a chair that stood opposite his and folded her hands in her lap, silently searching for the right words. He waited, wondering what she might have come to tell him. On the one hand the young woman sitting opposite him represented all that was joyful in life, all that was human – and on the other, the symbol of his betrayal. He got up and went to sit beside her. He picked up her hand and silently held it in his. Her throat dry, she swallowed several times and looked deep into his eyes.

'Bernardino . . .' she started, but now it felt wrong to address him simply by his name. She had called him that when they were alone, ever since he'd asked her to do so; it had felt right and natural then. Whispering his name as they made love made her feel at one with him. The intimacy of it thrilled her. She loved nothing more than to hear him whisper hers in her ear. Now it felt inappropriate.

Unease washed over her; they were sitting very close, his robe touching her leg. He continued to hold her hand, waiting for her to begin. She took a deep breath and looked into his eyes, those eyes that she could never have enough of, and started to speak. Her voice in her ears sounded wavering and small.

'My love for you is unequalled, you must never doubt it, nor must you ever doubt that I will love you for as long as I live . . .' She paused for a moment before she carried on. 'Just as I am certain of and have never doubted your feelings for me.' She took another deep breath but this time she looked away. She couldn't bear to continue, she wanted to prolong the moment before she had to tell him what she'd come to say. Her eyes wandered out of the window and into the garden and rested on the jasmine bush. Slowly she turned to face him, her eyes overflowing. 'But,' she continued, 'I am also certain that this love of ours cannot be. You do not belong to me. As much as I want you for myself, as much as I love you more than life itself, you are not mine. And I have no right to steal you away from your vocation, which you have dedicated yourself to.' He tried to speak but she stopped him. 'Even if you left the Church, even if you tried to live as an ordinary man, you would not be happy; you would regret it and what's more your guilt would follow you and that would only bring us misery. And not only your own guilt, but mine too for taking you away from the calling that you are committed to.' She had rehearsed what she was going to say to him. She had planned it, she had even written it down. She had intended to say that they were not worthy, that they had both sinned, and that this was God's punishment. But she didn't. Those words remained unspoken, because deep down she didn't believe them. Her true belief was that since God was himself the spirit of love, He would not want to punish them for doing nothing more than loving each other.

If she had had the courage to speak to Olga and seek her advice she was sure her mistress would have told her the same thing. Olga believed that there is only one sin that God does not forgive, and that is the sin of deliberately inflicting harm on others.

Love does not perish when it is real, Katerina told him. They would live with the knowledge and memory of what they had shared, and it would be enough to give them strength and sustain them through the years.

When she finished talking they sat silently holding hands for a long time, a haunted look in the padre's eyes while he tried to find the strength to speak. He wanted to tell her she was wrong, that they *could* make a life together, that if she wished it he'd discard the cloth, he would leave the Church and they would marry. Part of him wanted to say all of those things, take her in his arms and reassure her, kiss her tears away. But that was the part of him that wanted to please her, it was the part of him that was a man in love and not a priest. Instead he said nothing, because he couldn't; because the other part of him, the greater part that had vowed to give his life to his faith, would not let him.

'No . . .' he finally murmured, the only word that left his lips.

But they both knew it had to be that way. Nothing else was possible for either of them. Once more, Katerina proved to him that she was wise beyond her years. They kissed for the very last time and agreed their passion would bind them together forever and what they had shared would make them stronger. Life would continue as before but with one big difference: they would have love locked in their hearts.

16

1961

It took no time for Katerina to realize that she was pregnant. For a whole week she remained in denial: *I'm under the weather, it's emotional, it's influenza*, she told herself as she lay awake fretting through the night. Eventually, she was forced to acknowledge the truth. She was three weeks overdue and she had never missed a period since she'd started menstruating at the age of eleven. She was well familiar with the signs of pregnancy, having seen them first hand in Anita several times.

The option of getting rid of the baby was inconceivable for her. She knew that in cases like hers, when a domestic servant girl became pregnant, the family might arrange for an abortion or at the very least allow her to have her baby and then give it away, but more often than not the young woman would be thrown out for bringing shame to the family.

Katerina knew that Olga didn't fall into this category of employer. She had grown up hearing Olga's liberal opinions on the subject of female equality and all she'd ever experienced from her was love and kindness. Nevertheless she had no way of knowing for certain how she might react when faced with the test of her ideals against the reality of a situation such as this. The last thing Katerina wished for was to bring shame to the family and load another heavy burden onto Olga's shoulders; she was at a total loss to know what to do or who to turn to.

Alone in her room she tried to review the paths that were open to her. She was well aware how few they were. But the love in her heart, and the new life that she was carrying in her body gave her the will and determination to go on. The only thing she was certain of was that she would keep her child, no matter what.

This baby growing inside her was a testimony of her love, the most precious thing she could ever possess. She had been prepared to live with the mere knowledge of that emotion and now like a gift from heaven she would have its personification. Since she couldn't have Bernardino she would have his child. The baby would carry his genes, carry the bloodline of the man she so passionately loved but had chosen to renounce; God, she thought, had rewarded her for her actions. She had now been granted a baby, a boy or a girl that would be the physical merging of the two of them. What more could she have wished for? Of course *he* must never know. That would destroy everything she was trying to protect him from. She would have to face this alone. The path she was about to take was full of obstacles but she was determined to find the strength to follow it, however great the problems ahead.

There were days, however, when the enormity of what she was undertaking overwhelmed her and her strength deserted her. Where would she go, and how would she manage to bring up a child on her own? She had no means of supporting herself without work. She was a fool to think she could manage this alone. In her isolation, despair took over from her determination for independence and dark thoughts would engulf her mind. And then she would start to wonder whether she should take the risk of broaching her predicament with Olga, and ask for her help as she had done so often before.

She had saved some money after her mother died since she stopped sending most of her wages to her, so perhaps she could go and live in the mountains where living was cheap, or ask Olga to help her find some work in another town. As she lay in bed at night her imagination took hold and she envisaged all manner of schemes. All that mattered was that she would be with her baby and so long as she had enough to feed them both they'd manage. *Yes*, she told herself hopefully, *Olga might help me*. She couldn't imagine that her mistress would abandon her, she was kind and good, and Katerina had heard her speak sympathetically about the predicament of a 'fallen girl'.

'Everyone makes mistakes, it's only human,' she would often lecture her daughters, 'but these mistakes happen though ignorance, and the consequences are there for life.'

Yet no matter how tolerant Olga was, when Katerina remembered whose baby she was carrying and the gravity of her own predicament, all her hopes came tumbling down and crushed any glimpse of optimism she had. What if Olga rejected her, found what she had done abhorrent? She couldn't bear that. This was her own problem, and she had made her decision. *I must face the consequences of my actions*, she thought, and continued to torment herself with uncertainty until the day the padre came to visit.

Up until the time she discovered she was pregnant Katerina had managed to keep herself composed when in company, but when she was alone she cried herself to sleep each night. During their last emotional meeting in his house, she and the padre had agreed to take some time to become accustomed to the idea of returning to the friendship they had enjoyed before they became lovers. In his absence her heart ached for him but she had been determined to maintain control of herself, keep her distance and honour her decision. He too kept his promise;

he immersed himself in his church duties, spent time with his parishioners and took solace in prayer, whilst Katerina threw herself into supporting Olga and Anita after Ernestina's death.

'I think your grandmother would have liked us to give some of her clothes to charity,' Katerina suggested to Anita, looking for small jobs around the house to keep her busy. Ernestina's sudden death had affected the young woman and there was fear she might fall back into her earlier state of melancholia. The months of retreat, of good food and exercise at the sanatorium had done wonders for her physical health, which in turn had brought about a great improvement in her state of mind, so at last she was beginning to think less about the past and more about the present and her future. To Katerina's relief Anita had concluded, while in the mountains, that marrying Costas had been a mistake and she should decide what to do about it.

'The only thing I ever wanted from him,' she admitted to Olga one night when Katerina was still with them at the sanatorium, 'was the one thing he could never give me . . . not that I'm blaming him, but I often think that if Mario had lived we would have more than one child by now.'

'Didn't he make you happy for a while at least?' her mother asked.

'Not for long. I suppose I was looking for consolation

after all I'd gone through.' Anita let out a sigh. 'I was naïve, Mother, I should have listened to my heart . . . it never belonged to Costas, it died with Mario.'

'Oh my girl,' Olga said and took Anita in her arms. 'Don't allow your heart to die. Love and happiness finds a way, and often in the most unexpected manner.'

So trying to prevent Anita from suffering a relapse was helping Katerina forget her own broken heart until the discovery of her own pregnancy, and then the roles seemed to be reversed. Anita, alarmed to see the usually robust Katerina looking pale and frail, started to fuss over her.

'You are eating like a bird these days,' she scolded her as Katerina continued to cook for them but hardly ate anything herself. 'You should follow your own advice, my friend; what is it you always tell me about food being good for the soul?'

But what Anita didn't know was that Katerina's morning sickness was getting the better of her.

Shortly after Katerina had realized that she was pregnant Padre Bernardino came to visit. Olga had invited him for tea to discuss a memorial plaque for Ernestina that she wanted to install in his church.

'We haven't seen the padre for a while,' Olga remarked to Anita and Katerina, 'and when he comes we must encourage him to continue his visits to us. We know how fond of *Nonna* he was, but we love him too, and what's more we need him more than ever now.'

'That is so true – he always knows what to say to us,' Anita agreed as she and Katerina were busy sorting out Ernestina's bedroom. She was going through some of her grandmother's clothes from the big double-fronted oak wardrobe while Katerina was sorting out a tangle of neck-laces in a jewellery box. 'I think I've only seen him once since *Nonna*'s funeral and I do miss him. He is such a comfort to us all,' she added. At the mention of the padre Katerina automatically brought her hands to her belly, letting go of the box she was holding which landed with a loud crash on the floor, spilling all its contents. She stood frozen, watching a shower of beads rolling all over the parquet. She hadn't laid eyes on him for three weeks.

He looked paler and thinner, his robe hanging loosely on his body. Katerina was in the kitchen when Olga let him in through the front door and she caught a glimpse of him in the hall. She felt faint at the sight of him; a mixture of joy and sorrow.

'He's here!' she heard Anita call from the hall, then she rushed into the kitchen to help Katerina bring the tea and cakes to the *saloni*. Katerina stood rooted to the spot as if paralyzed, holding a plate of sesame *koulourakia*.

'What's wrong?' Anita looked at an ashen Katerina.

'Nothing!' she replied quickly, putting the plate back

on the table, and she turned away to pick up the teapot, trying to steady her trembling hands. She wanted nothing more than to see him, to hear his voice, to sit by him, be near him, but the thought of it made her feel giddy and nauseous. *Calm down*, she scolded herself and, taking a deep breath, she turned to face Anita.

Wearing a smile that hid her true feelings she followed her friend into the drawing room.

Katerina wasn't given to emotional outbursts. If she shed tears they were usually in moments of sadness, grief or happiness but she soon recovered her self-control. However, the turmoil that overcame her after the padre left them was alien to her. She managed to keep her composure throughout his visit, pouring tea, serving cake, busying herself in and out of the kitchen and even briefly participating in a little conversation. But the minute he left the house, her poise departed with him and without even clearing up in the kitchen she went to her room and burst into a deluge of tears and sobbing.

The sound of crying reached Olga's ears as she passed by Katerina's bedroom. The noise was entirely unexpected. She was used to her daughters succumbing to tears but that was not Katerina's way. She eased the door open a little and peeped into the room. Katerina was sitting on the edge of the bed hunched over with her head in her hands, sobbing. For a moment Olga was at a loss as to how to react and stood silently watching. Then pushing open the door she crossed the room and sat by the young woman's side.

'What is it, Katerina *mou*?' she asked, putting an arm around the bent shoulders. 'What happened?' she repeated gently, mystified at what could possibly be wrong. Ernestina had been mourned well by all three of them; they had shed many tears since her death, and while at times they might shed a few more in her memory their grief didn't warrant this outpour that Olga was now witnessing from Katerina. She sat silently holding her and waiting patiently for her sobbing to subside, hoping for an explanation. Whatever it was that was wrong, Olga knew it must be serious. Finally, Katerina turned to face her, eyes pleading.

'I didn't mean to love him,' she said through her tears and covered her face again with both hands, 'not in that way . . . Please forgive me,' she whispered.

'Do you want to tell me about it?' Olga asked gently, stroking her hair as Katerina's sobs shook her body and her tears continued to fall. Olga waited; tears, she always said, had to be shed down to the last drop otherwise they would never dry.

When Katerina finally stopped, Olga reached across and cupped her face in her hands.

'Whatever it is, Katerina *mou*, I am here to listen. I am your friend, your mother, please talk to me . . . together we will find a way through. You know you can tell me; whatever this is.'

Once she had started to speak Katerina's secret came pouring out of her like blood from a flesh wound. As she spoke, Olga sat listening intently. What she was hearing rendered her motionless in disbelief, and silent for a long time. Finally, she spoke.

'Oh my dear girl, my dear, dear girl.' She sat back and looked at the younger woman long and hard.

Then she looked deep into Katerina's eyes. 'You have to remember one thing, Katerina *mou*: we don't have control over who we fall in love with. When the arrow strikes us we are helpless.'

Olga had lived a life against the grain of convention; she had always been a rebel and a nonconformist and prided herself at dealing with whatever life could throw at her, or her family. She was her father's daughter. This was far from the easiest problem she had ever encountered, she was well aware of that, but deal with it she was determined she would, and she was grateful, even if she felt slightly guilty to admit it, that her mother was not there to witness this real crisis and potential scandal for the community. That, she knew, *would* have created a much bigger problem for them all.

She loved Katerina like a daughter and since that day when she had rescued her from her pitiful life she had pledged to stand by her. This was not just Katerina's predicament; it concerned them all. The priest was dear to her too, she loved and respected him for his kindness, humility and wisdom; she thought him a good man, which he was – a man. Olga had faith, but she had never shared her mother's absolute religious convictions. 'Faith without doubt is dogma,' she'd argue and although she was born a Catholic, her upbringing in an Orthodox country had exposed her to a different doctrine and she welcomed the permission of marriage in priesthood. She believed that imposed celibacy was not compatible with human nature although she was also aware that if an Orthodox cleric wanted to achieve a high standard in Church then he too had to abide by the rule of celibacy. She was always one for discussion and for putting her views forward but on religious matters she had refrained from discussing too much with her mother; she knew it would distress her.

She could see that Katerina's love for the padre was unequivocal, the baby she was carrying was the proof of that love, but she accepted and understood the young woman's heartfelt plea to keep the pregnancy a secret from him. As always Olga had made up her mind that, one way or another, she would find a solution, and an idea was already starting to take shape in her mind.

17

For two whole days Olga said nothing while Katerina waited in torments of anxiety. The head of the household mulled over her idea carefully in her head, examining it from one viewpoint and then from another until finally she was satisfied. Then she summoned Anita and Katerina to join her in the *saloni* for a talk.

Still unsteady from the emotional turbulence caused by her confession, Katerina hadn't spoken to Anita yet, uncertain of what to say, and was biding her time before revealing her secret to her friend. However, unbeknown to her, Olga had decided she must speak to her daughter before the three of them met, to see if Anita considered her idea acceptable; then together they might be able to present it with conviction to Katerina. It was radical, it was daring, she was prepared to hear objections, but Olga could think of no other way to preserve Katerina's honour *and* keep the baby.

The combination of dread and morning sickness made Katerina's nausea almost unbearable. She sat motionless, her breathing shallow, her head swirling while Olga explained her proposal. A soft breeze blew in from the open window, carrying with it the sound of children playing in the street. Katerina was oblivious to all of it, focusing her mental and emotional energy on listening to Olga and trying to comprehend what she was saying to her. She waited silently until the older woman had finished talking before attempting to say something in response, but when she tried to speak she found she had no voice, or breath, to utter a word. She looked at the two women sitting on either side of her; the suggestion that had just been outlined to her was unforeseen and profound. She could never have anticipated, or imagined it. She was filled, all at once, with a mixture of shock, relief and gratitude in equal measure. These women were her entire world, and now that she needed them more than ever they were by her side again. Her heart swelled with affection for them both. Gradually regaining her voice, she asked Olga to repeat what she had just told her. She needed to hear it all again, to understand fully.

'So you see, my darling girl,' Olga concluded, unsure of what Katerina made of her plan, 'this way we keep the blessed baby with us – it will be our child, and we will love and cherish it as it deserves. No one, apart from us, will ever know or suspect that the baby is not Anita's but yours. All that matters is that *we* will know and he or she will be loved three times over!'

Katerina absorbed everything she was being told like

nourishment. She sat quietly listening, all her senses on high alert. She needed to think. She closed her eyes, trying to imagine the scenario, an internal monologue going on inside her trying to find possible loopholes.

'What about Costas?' she suddenly said, as if talking to herself. She knew that Anita hadn't shared a bed with him for over a year. 'He would know, wouldn't he?'

Olga darted a conspiratorial look at her daughter.

'Yes . . . well . . . Costas . . .' Anita began, cheeks flushed. 'There is only one way we can manage this. Whatever my feelings about him now, there is only one way and that is . . .' She hesitated for a second. 'I have to make Costas think the baby is his!'

The shock that showed on Katerina's face vividly expressed what she thought of the idea.

'Costas is a mere detail!' Olga hurried to add, seeing her reaction and intervening before the young woman had time to object. 'Without knowing it he will help us achieve our aim and I am certain he would not want to rejoin the household and become a family man. He's far too comfortable with his bachelor life in Nicosia.' She looked from Katerina to Anita and went on, 'In fact, I guarantee this will give him all the more reason to stay away!'

'Mother is right,' Anita agreed, 'he never wanted children, it was always me who insisted . . . he has no idea that the effect of my last miscarriage has left me unable to get pregnant again . . . and in any case I've made up my mind. After we have the baby I want to divorce him!'

'So you see, Katerina *mou* . . .' Olga cut in again, eager to explain the rest of the plan. 'Before your belly starts to grow,' she lowered her voice and moved closer, 'you and Anita will go to Vienna to stay with Sonia until the baby arrives. I will tell everyone that Anita has fallen pregnant again and that she will have a better chance of carrying the baby to full term in Austria under their far superior medical care. Naturally you will be going with her to help.'

There was a lot to consider, but Olga seemed to have thought of everything.

Katerina sat quietly absorbing the many aspects of this bold plan, looking for possible obstacles. Another thought struck her.

'What about Nicos?' She took a sharp intake of breath and brought her hand to her mouth. 'What will we tell *him*?'

'Nicos doesn't need to know anything that we haven't told anyone else!' Olga rushed to reply. 'He's not in Vienna, he's in Cyprus now, remember? He won't be a problem. He will know *only* what we tell him.'

With everything that was going on it had completely slipped Katerina's mind that Nicos had recently returned to Larnaka to run the family business following his father's illness, and of course Sonia would always guard their secret. It was true, Olga had indeed thought of everything.

'I'm not worried about Nicos,' the older woman went on, 'he's far too preoccupied with his own family dramas to pay attention to us. He'll be pleased that Sonia will have some company.'

The more they talked about it, the more possible it all sounded. Olga appeared to have worked her plan out well.

'I will travel to Vienna with the two of you,' she explained, 'in order to find a doctor and a hospital where you can have the baby. After the birth Sonia will look after you, and then you, Anita and the baby will travel back to Cyprus together.' Olga looked at Katerina. 'So you see?' she said and clapped her hands with satisfaction. 'Simple! Who will ever know, apart from us, that y*ou* gave birth instead of Anita?'

In a matter of a few hours Katerina's life took a turn that she could never have anticipated. All through her sleepless nights and fretful days worrying about how she was going to cope, what Olga had suggested would never have entered her mind as a possibility. She went from preparing herself to face whatever hardships life was going to throw at her alone, to the comfort of knowing she would remain in the loving fold of her adopted family to raise her baby with the help of the women she loved most in the world.

What does it matter, she told herself, *who the child calls 'Mama'? It will be a lucky baby adored by three women*. All that mattered was that her son or daughter would have a loving home and she would be there every day of her child's life watching it grow up in an environment of tenderness, security and acceptance.

18

After Anita's early pleasure in her marriage to Costas, their initial physical attraction had faded and she had only encouraged sex with him in the hopes of starting a family. Since her miscarriage and illness she had avoided physical contact with him but if they were going to carry out their plan and make it a success she had to change her approach – and make it convincing. Seduction wasn't a form of behaviour that came naturally to Anita, but she knew there was no other way. She had come to find his presence tedious and irritating and was thankful she only had to see him once in a while as he was now spending most of his time in Nicosia with his 'dubious cronies', as Olga referred to Petros and his ilk.

Anita decided the solution to her predicament must be to somehow revive those early days before she became ill; to think herself back to the time when they had lived as man and wife.

'I did have feelings for him once,' she told Olga and Katerina when they were discussing how to achieve their aim. She closed her eyes and tried to conjure up an image from the early days.

She decided the best way to see him was to take a trip to Nicosia. She would drive to the capital on the pretext of a shopping spree and request to stay the night.

'I work late,' was the only thing he found to say, surprised at her unexpected request when she telephoned.

'No matter,' she replied, undeterred, 'I'll wait for you to finish; I have plenty to do and friends to see, I have buried myself in Larnaka long enough. I need to see people I have neglected for too long, and *you*, my dear husband . . .' she said sweetly, emphasizing the words, '. . . *you* are one of them.' Taken aback further by Anita's unusually dulcet tones, he had no option but to accept. 'You can take me to dinner after you finish work,' she added, amazed at her ability to sound so casual and convincing. *Where there's a will, and a good enough reason, there's a way*, she thought with a smile as she put down the receiver.

A visit to the hairdresser, which was well overdue, restored Anita's raven locks to their former lustre, framing her heart-shaped face and accentuating her pale complexion. 'We need to bring you up to date, Anita *mou*,' Effie the hairdresser told her, inspecting her unruly curls in the mirror. 'This won't do at all! You have a great head of hair but you're doing nothing with it. You've let yourself, go my girl,' and smiling she picked up the scissors, ready to attack.

By the time Effie had finished cutting and restyling, the transformation was complete. Reflected in the mirror, Anita saw to her pleasure a new positive and attractive self, infused with energy, ready to embrace what lay ahead. She had indeed let herself go, and had allowed her spirit to be crushed. The situation they were facing felt very much like a state of emergency, reminding her of the days of the revolution. She would once more rise to the challenge. Then, she was fearless – she would be that once more! *We are all in this together*, she told herself. *Katerina's problem is also my problem.*

She felt confident that with Olga's guidance they would manage. Katerina's honour would be saved and they would have a blessed baby to love, cherish and protect. It didn't matter that she wasn't going to be giving birth herself. God only knew how hard she'd tried, but she was resigned to the fact that her body wasn't built for childbirth. She just hoped Katerina's was.

She felt a little nervous behind the wheel at the start of her journey; she hadn't driven anywhere of much consequence for a while but soon she began to relax and enjoy herself. Olga's car was always a delight to drive and given the good weather she put the roof back, tied a scarf round her newly coiffured hair and let the sun beat down on her. Anita was on a mission. There was nothing she liked better.

She hadn't been to Nicosia for at least two years and walking down Ledra Street, the main shopping artery of the city, commonly known by the locals as *Makridromos*, 'the long road' on account of its length, she felt exhilarated. The street was buzzing with life and noise. Cars beeping their horns at every opportunity, shops and cafes, newspaper kiosks, and shopkeepers calling out to her as she passed by, made her realize how isolated and low-spirited she had been for so long.

She had arranged to meet two friends, Maria and Sophia, in a little *zaharoplastio*, a patisserie just off Ledra Street called Hurricane, its name a legacy from the British occupation. The two women were already sitting at the table waiting for her.

'What took you so long to come and see us?' Maria said, jumping up to greet Anita as she walked in. They had all met in Larnaka through their activities in support of the struggle, and now both women were married and had moved to Nicosia with their husbands.

'We meet here every Saturday morning,' Sophia said, embracing her friend warmly and kissing her on both cheeks.

'We have a women's only gathering here once a week,' Maria added. 'The men of course have theirs *daily*,' she laughed.

'We drink our coffee, eat our cakes and gossip . . .' Sophia interjected.

'Not only that – we still talk politics, but not as we used to.'

'If you were living in Nicosia, Anita *mou*, you could join us.'

'Oh yes . . . we've missed you, and our talks – you should come more often . . .' The two women took turns to bombard her with words, delighted to see their friend and hardly giving Anita a chance to speak.

'I missed you too,' she finally replied, genuinely glad to see them both again.

'So, tell us, what brings you here at last?' one of them asked.

'Well, believe it or not, I came to see my husband – he is living here most of the time now . . . *and* to see you two, of course,' she added.

'Could this mean we might have the pleasure of you moving to the metropolis?' they both laughed.

'Perhaps . . .' Anita said and reached for her cup.

'Well let's hope so!' Maria replied cheerfully. 'Marriage must suit you, my friend – you are looking good on it. Any babies yet?'

'No, not yet, but I'm hoping. How about you?' she asked, smiling sweetly.

'I have a boy! Two years old next month and we're trying for a second one. There is nothing better than being a mother, my friend – wait and see!'

'Sooner rather than later, I hope,' Anita replied and reached for her glass of water.

They had arranged that she would pick Costas up from his office in her car. Walking into the building Anita could feel the eyes of his male colleagues looking approvingly at her. She had made sure she looked her best. She was classy and elegant, and her coral-coloured linen dress, which stopped above her shapely knees, the string of pearls around her neck and her high-heeled shoes confirmed it.

'You look very . . . *nice!*' Costas said, almost lost for words and clearly surprised at her appearance. Lately whenever he had seen Anita she had looked washed out and plain. Gone was her ethereal otherness that he'd found so attractive when they first met. Now she just looked pale and drab. Although he would never have admitted it in so many words, when they met he had sensed she was out of his league, her family and money set her apart from any other girl, and he felt flattered when she accepted his courtship. But all that had gone a long time ago; since her miscarriages and depression all he'd been left with, he thought, was a sad dowdy young woman, desperate for a baby.

'Thank you!' she replied, smiling, and gave him a kiss. Aware of the admiring looks she was receiving from his colleagues, Costas puffed himself up and, offering her his arm, led her out of the office into the early evening.

'So, my little wife,' he asked over dinner and after several glasses of red wine, 'what made you decide to come and see me?'

'I am a woman, and isn't a woman allowed to miss her husband and his attention?'

'Well of course, but I thought you didn't care much for my attention these days,' he replied, moving a little closer to her.

'Oh darling ... that's only because, as you know, I haven't been well,' she cooed, giving him a little look and reaching for her glass of wine. 'But look how well I am again!' She took a sip and smiling sweetly went on, 'In any case, isn't a woman allowed to change her mind?' She reached under the table and stroked his leg.

'You always did ignite a forest fire in me in the early days, my little Hungarian beauty,' he whispered and reached for her hand resting on his thigh. Her irritation rose but she checked it; any other time she would have hissed at him that she was *not* Hungarian, but instead she kept on smiling and sipped her wine.

His lovemaking was quick and unremarkable; it always was with him. Not that Anita had anything to compare it with, of course – she had never gone all the way with Mario – but she'd always thought that the sexual act ought to carry some pleasure with it. When she first married him, curiosity and the possibility that it might result in pregnancy had made it tolerable.

The next morning, she woke early. She had slept fitfully, waking up every hour in the hope it was morning and she could make her escape. He lay fast asleep snoring by her side. She couldn't wait to jump up, get dressed and run away, but she'd got this far without slipping up and she needed to play the game convincingly to the end. She waited until he opened his eyes and with the excuse that she didn't want to bump into Petros who was occupying the next room she got up, got washed, dressed and left. He didn't protest much, if at all.

Once on the open road, and well on her way, she started to breathe normally again. A cheerful little melody she'd been hearing all her life started to play in her head. Smiling, she started humming it softly, and before long the words found their way to her lips. At first she sang quietly, but soon her singing gained momentum and grew louder until finally she was shouting the song at the top of her lungs. She sang all the way back to Larnaka, repeating the refrain with joy and glee.

I don't want you, I don't want you, I don't want you any more,
I don't love you, I don't love you, I don't care any more,
If you stay or if you go you mean nothing any more

I don't want you, I don't want you, I don't love you any more.

She arrived home exhilarated, eyes shining, cheeks burning and hair rearranged by the wind; no headscarf to keep it in place this time. She felt free and liberated. She had done it! She'd managed to summon the strength and composure to do what she'd set out to do. There had been moments when she'd doubted she'd be able to carry out the plan. But she had! She'd done it for herself, for Katerina, for her mother, for the baby. Their baby!

Olga and Katerina were waiting for Anita with bated breath to find out how it had gone. They'd had their doubts about whether she would manage to go through with it, but Anita's glowing face when she walked in told them what they needed to know.

'I can't say it was easy, but I was determined to do it, and I did!' she told them, feeling thoroughly pleased with her achievement.

She went to see him. This time she found him in his church; it was early afternoon and he was preparing for evening Mass. He didn't hear her come in; he was by the altar and had his back to the door. She glided in silently and took a pew near the front and waited till he'd finished.

'Katerina *mou*!' he whispered when he turned around and saw her. This was the first time they'd been alone together since they had agreed to part. He walked up to her and kissed her tenderly on her forehead, making the blood drain from her face and her lips tremble. 'Are you well?' he asked, concern in his voice.

'Oh yes, I am well,' she replied and tried to smile. He didn't ask why she was there, but instead asked if she'd like some lemonade.

'I have some freshly made,' he said and gestured towards the house.

She sat in his garden under the lemon tree now laden with a new crop while he went inside to fetch a jug and glasses. Once again she had rehearsed what she was going to tell him a thousand times but still her hands were shaking. She was glad for the few minutes alone to try and steady her nerves.

'I can't express how glad I feel that dear Anita is with child again,' he said when she eventually told him the news, and his face looked as glad as she had ever seen it.

'I will pray to God each day when you are in Vienna that all goes well and that Anita will have the blessed baby she has longed for. Having you and her sister there will be all the support she'll need.'

'Yes . . .' she murmured, lowering her eyes lest he see her lie and the pain reflected in them.

'I will visit Kyria Olga often – I will go as soon as she returns,' he continued, 'and she will give me all your news. You could also write to me if you like, Katerina – just to let me know how you are and how Anita is doing.'

'I will,' she said, trying to stop her lips trembling.

'I shall pray every day that the pregnancy progresses well and that Anita has a healthy baby.'

'And so will I,' she said and the voice in her head cried in anguish and the ache in her heart grew intolerable.

They arrived in Vienna on a crisp and sunny November day. Sonia had come to the station to meet them. Great-aunt Heidi was waiting anxiously to greet them at the apartment. The two women had made space for their visitors and were prepared for what was to come. Olga would stay with Heidi while Anita and Katerina would stay with Sonia.

When they first arrived, Katerina's pregnancy hardly showed and she felt as healthy and robust as ever. Her energy levels were high and her excitement at finding herself in Vienna was even higher; never in her wildest dreams could she have foreseen the circumstances of this visit and was determined to experience and enjoy it to the full, while she could. Sonia took leave from the Academy to show them as much of the city as she could before Katerina began to feel too heavy.

'Once the weather turns really cold it will be harder to move around the city and by then you'll be bigger,' she explained. 'The best way to see the city is by foot and once the snow comes you'll want to stay in the warm.'

Sonia threw herself wholeheartedly into supporting Katerina and her sister. However much she loved her independence and despite having flown the nest quite early her heart still belonged with the women she had grown up with. 'We will pull through,' she declared when she first heard the news, both of the pregnancy and also of Olga's plan. 'We will always stick together,' she told her mother when she telephoned to tell her what they had decided. 'After all, Mama, we have a reputation to live up to – we are the Caryatids of Larnaka, aren't we?'

The excitement of being in Vienna overshadowed any anxiety Katerina might have had about her strange situation and she was now keen to see all the city had to offer.

'I'd like you to show us all the things you've been describing in your letters,' she told Sonia after they'd settled into the apartment,

Most of all Katerina wanted to visit the Opera. She wanted to hear the music that Anita played on the piano and the records Olga played on her gramophone. She longed, too, to visit the galleries with paintings she had only ever seen in books. This, she knew, was the chance of her life and she had to fill her eyes and ears and memory with all the cultural treasures she had been told of and had read about through her years in the Linser house with Olga as her mentor and teacher.

'Everything I see, everything I hear nourishes my soul,' she told the girls one afternoon as they sat in the fashionable Café Central for a pre-concert tea and apple strudel, 'but with my taste for Viennese cakes now I am worried it's not just my soul that is being nourished.' She laughed. 'If I am not careful I shall be the size of a house before I give birth to this baby!'

Olga remained with them in Vienna until she had secured a suitable doctor and hospital who would take care of Katerina and the birth. She had left her foreman in charge of the textile factory and she needed to return to work, but she refused to leave until she was satisfied Katerina was in good hands, by which time the prospective mother was almost five months gone and looked it.

Katerina's first visit to the doctor was a crowded affair; Olga, Anita, Sonia and Great-aunt Heidi all came with her in a show of solidarity. When the five women walked into the doctor's surgery he didn't know which one of them was the expectant mother. He guessed that Olga and Heidi weren't candidates but he gazed in surprise at the other three young women sitting in a row looking anxiously at him.

'Now which one of you young ladies am I to examine?' he said, peering over his glasses at them.

After their initial visit Doctor Schmidt announced that

Katerina was healthy and well and that there was no need to be worried or for all of them to keep coming to see him.

'Visits will be more frequent closer to delivery time,' he explained. 'Now I suggest you all relax. Unless there is a problem you have no need for concern,' he looked at Olga, realizing she was in need of reassurance more than the young woman carrying the child, 'and when it's time for the baby I will be here to take care of it, and of all of you,' he told them, glancing with amusement around the room at all five in turn.

With Sonia and Great-aunt Heidi's care the two friends settled into living in Vienna with ease. Katerina was a healthy young woman and took well to being pregnant; Anita, however, worried endlessly for both of them. She tried not to let her anxiety show too much but her own unfortunate experiences insisted on revisiting her.

The winter months came and went peacefully and Anita tried to keep her fretting to herself by lying awake at night listening to Katerina's breathing and anticipating signs of danger. When the snow fell the two women either stayed in the warmth of the apartment or made their way to Café Hawelka, which was even warmer. Cosy and welcoming, the place became a second home to them. Most mornings Katerina and Anita would walk with Sonia part of the way to the Academy and then make their way to the cafe with its comfortable shabby armchairs and sofas, hot chocolate and apple strudel, frankfurters and mustard. They'd spend the best part of their day in there reading books and newspapers, which Anita would translate to Katerina and even try to teach her some German phrases.

By early summer Katerina's belly had swelled like a hot-air balloon, and she began to feel as heavy as the pregnant donkeys she remembered up in the village. All the time the baby was growing inside Katerina so was the bond between her and Anita. Their connection grew deeper and stronger and their shared experience was to link them together for life.

Larnaka, 2010

'So you see,' Anita said, her face streaked with tears as she reached for Adonis's hand, 'Katerina and I didn't just share love and friendship. We shared a life . . . we shared *you*, my son.' Adonis opened his mouth to speak but she stopped him. 'You were her flesh and blood and she gave you to me with such grace and dignity and above all humility. I know she deserved you more, I know she was a better mother to you than I ever was. I tried, I did, but I wasn't very good at it.' Anita's voice was now breaking but she carried on regardless. 'There must have been times when she felt resentful of me – I know, I could see it in her eyes, though only at the beginning, only when we came back from Vienna and she had to hand you over . . . but I will admit I felt some resentment too, at times. Unlike her, I never had that blessed chance to give birth to a healthy child, to feel it grow inside me and then . . .' A sob rose to her throat and she stopped talking. She reached for a glass of water, took a sip, let out a long sigh and continued. 'The pain of losing my baby never went away; the sadness always lingered but the feelings of resentment either from me or from her didn't last. I want you to know that you brought much joy into my life, my son. I was lucky to have you, to share you, to love you. Both Katerina and I knew that what we did was for the best for all of us, especially for you.'

Adonis sat silently holding on to Anita's hand, letting her speak.

'Katerina was made for childbirth. During those last two months of her pregnancy, I lived in fear that she would go into labour while Sonia was at work and I wouldn't know what to do. One Sunday afternoon while we were sitting in the sun, in the famous Volksgarten, eating ice cream with Great-aunt Heidi and Sonia, Katerina looked at me and very calmly said, "I've either wet myself or my waters have just broken!"'

Katerina gave birth swiftly and easily in the apartment with both Anita and Sonia by her side. 'Everything my body did wrong, hers did right,' Anita continued. 'I can't say it didn't bother me,' she looked around the room, 'it hurt, but it didn't last long and I knew it wasn't Katerina's fault; the only thing that lingered was the melancholy. I think most of the time she and I managed our destinies well.

'After you were born, we stayed in Vienna for three months until you were strong enough for us to take you on the long journey back home. Katerina was an instinctive mother; she tried to include me, to show me, teach me, but the maternal instinct didn't come naturally to me. Then it was time to come back to Cyprus and tell the world you were mine.'

Adonis sat listening, motionless and speechless. Conflicting emotions were rising inside him. Suddenly he got up and started silently pacing the room.

'Didn't either of you think that I should have been told when she was still alive?' he said eventually, fighting to keep his composure. 'Didn't any of you think about me?'

'You were the only one she ever thought about, never doubt that – you and the padre,' Anita replied.

'Didn't she think that she had a moral duty to tell me at some point? Didn't any of you? I'm a grown man, for God's sake . . .'

'I could see how she suffered over the years that you didn't know the truth, Adonis *mou*, but she had given her word to God. She made a vow of silence, and she would never have betrayed the padre. He remained the love of her life till the end. His name and yours were on her lips when she died. He left not knowing anything. She wanted it that way; she had made up her mind she wouldn't come between him and his God and she kept her word.'

'Where did he go?' Adonis asked, unable to control his tears now.

'He was offered a position in Rome – I remember he wasn't sure if he should go.' Anita reached for his hand and looked him in the eyes. 'I expect he didn't want to leave her, or you . . . He was very fond of you – you have his eyes, you know.'

'Is he still alive?' Adonis asked, his voice barely audible now.

'I don't know. They wrote to each other regularly; she lived for those letters.'

Adonis managed to fall asleep for a few hours as the pale light of dawn started to creep through the shutters. He had stayed awake for most of the night, his head swirling with questions, his heart with emotions. He shifted from one to the other, driving himself to despair. He knew all about the five stages of grief, Robert had warned him about it when the news came about Katerina's death. Now he was apparently grieving for a host of other things too. Initially, when Anita had been speaking, disbelief as opposed to denial was his first reaction, but that had only lasted moments.

Now as he lay in his bed he started going through the rest. Anger definitely took hold of him for a while. *How could they let me go through life not knowing the most important things about myself?* He started to blame his grandmother and her cunning scheme. All sorts of alternative sequences ran through his head, tormenting him. *She always wanted to control everything*, he told himself, *she had to be the boss . . .* Then his anger shifted onto Anita and Katerina: *Why didn't they tell me earlier when she was still alive instead of letting me find out now that she's dead? What good is that?* The questions kept coming without any satisfactory answers as his head throbbed and the temperature in the room became hotter and hotter. The ceiling fan was doing nothing to cool him down and opening the window would only bring in the mosquitoes, so he lay there, unable to move in a pool of sweat, his brain pulsating with dark thoughts. He would have given anything to put his arms around her knowing she was his mother. *What's the use?* the voice in his head lamented. *It's all too late now.* A crushing sense of gloom engulfed him. *Robert!* he suddenly thought. *I need to speak to Robert.* He reached for the glass of water on the bedside table, drank it down thirstily and picked up his mobile phone and dialled Robert in New York. Three a.m. Cyprus time, he started to calculate – Robert would just be getting home from work, had probably just opened a bottle of wine and would be thinking about dinner. Thoughts of Robert started to make him feel better.

'Hey you!' his voice came trickling down the line. '*You* sound mighty sexy,' he continued, responding to Adonis's husky middle-of-the-night voice, 'but shouldn't you be asleep now?'

'That is exactly what I should be, but my brain won't let me . . .' his voice trailed off.

'What's up, honey?' Robert asked, sounding serious now, his soothing voice already having a calming effect. 'It's not surprising you can't sleep – you had an emotional day, my love.'

Adonis propped himself up on the pillow and took a deep breath.

'Yes . . .' he replied. 'I certainly have, and you don't even know the half of it.'

Finally, he got up and made his way to the kitchen; he felt closer to Katerina there. The others were still asleep. Anita was a notoriously late riser and the only one who ever got up early had been Katerina.

The conversation he had had with Robert earlier had done him good. It was healing. Robert could always make him feel better, that's why he was so good at his work. He knew the right words to say to help Adonis see things from a different angle, as Katerina had also used to do when he was younger. Those two had the ability to disperse any dark doubts hovering around him. Strange as it sounded Adonis had often thought that Katerina and

Robert were similar in many ways. Their unconditional love for him was one of them. But there were other similarities too. If Katerina had lived at a different time, in a different world with different opportunities he thought she could have been a good therapist.

He looked around the kitchen. Everything was in its place, exactly as she'd left it and how he remembered it. He reached for the Turkish coffee that Katerina always kept in an old tin, which evidently in some distant past had contained Earl Grey tea. She hadn't much cared for it – she preferred Russian tea, but Olga had been fond of it. Next to the coffee was the sugar in a glass jar and above it on a shelf the *ibriki*. She'd kept two of them in different sizes. If she was making coffee for herself or when the padre came to visit she'd use the small blue enamel one, but if it was for more people she always used the larger stainless steel one. That of course depended on whether everyone took their coffee the same way; if not she had to make each cup separately.

He picked up the blue enamel *ibriki* from the shelf and placed it on the gas stove. He liked his Turkish coffee *metrio*, a flat teaspoon of sugar to a heaped teaspoon of coffee. He opened the tin and took in a deep breath, filling his lungs and the room with the aroma. He began making it the way Katerina had taught him.

'This is how you make the best cup of Turkish coffee in Larnaka,' she told him when he was around fifteen and started wanting to drink coffee. 'Watch and learn! First, you measure your water – one cup for each person, but take care not to add too much, otherwise it will taste weak,' she instructed while going through the process and making sure he was watching. 'The sugar goes in first and then the coffee; you stir it all well for a minute or so, and then – this is important – while you are cooking your coffee you do *not* take your eyes off it because if you do it will be a disaster! Not only will the coffee be ruined if it boils over, but you will have made the biggest mess on my stove and you will have to clear it up!' Her cheery chuckle echoed around the room.

Alone in her empty kitchen, Adonis thought how improbable it was that he would never hear her laughter again. As he stood at the stove vigilantly watching over the *ibriki*, he felt sure she was standing next to him making sure he was doing it right. He lifted the *ibriki* off the flame at the perfect moment and poured the coffee into a small old-fashioned cup, one that Katerina liked to use for herself. The *kaimaki*, on top, was thick and creamy; it even had a bubble in it, which according to Katerina symbolized love. Smiling, he carried it to the table and sat down; he had made the perfect cup indeed.

'Bravo, Adonis!' he fancied he heard her praise him as he took his first sip, and then felt Eleni's arms wrap around him from behind, hugging him tightly and causing him to spill some of his coffee. 'Now you can make me one too,' she said and kissed the top of his head.

He had hoped to savour his solitude for a little longer, but he didn't mind; Eleni's company was always welcome.

'*Kalimera, agabi mou!*' he said, putting his cup down and turning around to give her a kiss.

'You see, Adonis, the way I see it . . .' she said, ignoring his greeting, and launching into what appeared to be the continuation of an existing conversation between them, 'in my opinion and if the truth be known, she's always been your mother.' She pulled up a chair and sat next to him, elbows on the table, staring into his eyes. 'It's as you said the other night: she mothered all of us one way or another, but *you* were different. *You*, Adonis *mou*, *you* were her true child, and *you* are the product of a grand passion! Isn't that wonderful to know? I thought of nothing else all night.' He nodded and started to say something back but Eleni continued with her stream of consciousness without giving him a chance.

'Looking back now, it's obvious; the bond between the two of you was different. I used to think it was because you were a boy, but now it all makes sense. I have to admit that all last night I tossed and turned, tormenting myself and thinking *why couldn't she be* my *mother!* Can you believe it? I was kind of jealous; I became six again . . .'

'I know, I know, I'm trying to take it all in, it's all too much . . .' Adonis started to say, but Eleni's flow would not be curtailed.

'This is so amazing, it's so romantic, a true love story! She must have loved him so much . . . I couldn't have done what she did. I couldn't have given him up.'

'I guess that *is* true love,' Adonis put in at last just as Marianna walked through the door still in her nightdress.

'She had a lot of love to give to us all,' she said as she pulled up a chair to join them. 'I was just a stranger and she took me in. God only knows where I'd be now if it wasn't for her.'

'I would have probably married Sophia,' said Adonis, 'had a couple of kids and made a mess of my life.' Robert's words from the night before came to mind again, softening his sense of injustice. Their talk had helped him to see the complexity of the situation. 'It will take years to understand it all fully,' he had told him, 'but we can work it out – I will help you. Those women you grew up with managed to deal with whatever life threw their way by sticking together, and so will we!'

'She was quite remarkable,' added Eleni, moving up to make space at the table for Marianna, 'especially when you think how she started her life.'

'That unreserved love of hers, for all of us . . .' Adonis's voice trailed off again, his eyes welling up.

'It's funny how life turns out,' Marianna said, putting

an arm round his shoulders. 'Eleni and I have no recollection or memories of our real mothers. Out of the three of us we thought you were the only one who knew your mother . . .'

'As it turns out none of us knew our mother, *or* our father,' added Eleni, 'but in the end Adonis is the only one who actually *knew* both of them!'

The three of them stayed talking for a long time. The cuckoo clock struck ten when Anita finally came to join them. Then Adonis got up and made more coffee and toast and they sat around the kitchen table eating a breakfast of village bread, orange-blossom honey, carob syrup with tahini, and black olives. When they finished Anita pushed her plate away and leaning forward on the table, she began her discourse again.

'I have told you a lot, my children, but I haven't quite finished all I need you to know . . . Lend me your ears for a while longer and I will continue. If Katerina is listening I hope she approves of what I've said so far. I know it will take time for you to digest everything you've learned, but I hope it will give you an even clearer picture of where you came from and who this woman that we all loved really was.'

19

1961

It was Katerina who came up with the name Adonis. Anita insisted that she should choose the baby's name.

'I know that to the world I will be known as his mother but this is your child, Katerina, and so you must choose what we call him.' She thought long and hard and decided on Adonis. 'It's a name that represents love and beauty,' she told them. 'If he had been a girl I would have liked to call her Aphrodite.'

Olga and the padre stood anxiously at the port, waiting for the women to disembark with their precious bundle. Anita walked ahead holding the baby in her arms while Katerina followed. She saw him looking up at the passengers on the gangplank, anxious and small searching for her in the crowd. The autumn sun was high in the sky and as she walked into the open air the heat engulfed her like a passionate embrace. Her love for him had not diminished one iota.

They had come in two cars. 'I will take Katerina and Anita with the baby,' the padre told Olga, 'my car will be more comfortable for them.'

The journey to Vienna was long and tiring – a boat from Limassol took them to Piraeus, with an overnight stay in Athens, before boarding the train for Austria. They arrived in Vienna on a crisp and sunny November day. Sonia had come to the station to meet them.

Whereas the passage to Vienna with Olga had been exciting and fun, this return trip was something of an ordeal and they were all thankful it had come to an end. The baby was suffering from colic and cried most of the way while Katerina, who had started to wean Adonis so that Anita could bottle-feed him, was suffering from mastitis. For Katerina the hardest thing was giving up breastfeeding her baby. She cherished those three months in Vienna when he was truly hers and she always secretly believed that their bond was sealed during those months of nursing him and sleeping with him in her bed.

On arrival they found that Olga had arranged everything. She had turned one of the rooms into a nursery for when the baby was deemed old enough to sleep alone, but had also put a cradle next to Anita's bed. For the first few months Katerina took to sleeping with Anita so they could both attend to him in the night. Olga's plan was working out perfectly. Costas, as she had predicted, on hearing the news that Anita was pregnant, had made himself scarcer than ever, continuing to live in Nicosia and rarely visiting Larnaka.

Anita was determined to separate from him eventually but for the sake of town gossip she thought it wiser to wait a while longer. Besides, it made little difference if she was still married to him or not, she saw him so infrequently he had no impact on their lives, but putting off the divorce would keep wagging tongues at bay. She knew that the right time would come.

It was just over six months after Sonia and Nicos's fatal accident and the Linser household was still in deep mourning when Costas came to visit.

Anita was battling unsuccessfully to keep herself from reverting into a state of depression while Katerina and Olga were doing their best to keep going for the sake of the children. During that period Adonis at the age of two and Eleni not far behind were the two bright rays of happiness illuminating the house, and Father Bernardino with his regular visits gave the women the hope and support they badly needed. Katerina's heart never ceased to ache at the sight of him but she thanked the *Panayia* that he was still there and in their lives. She knew he loved her, she could see it in his eyes, and the pleasure she derived when she saw him with Adonis was immeasurable. Every Sunday at St Lazarus she would stay on after the service to pray in front of the icon of the Holy Mother. She would cross herself, light a candle and silently speak to her.

'*Merciful Mother of God, Holy of all Holies, every day I am alive I will thank you for granting me this child. You are a mother like me so you know my joy and my pain and I beg you to always watch over him.*' She would cross herself three times, kiss the icon with devout devotion and leave.

It was one such Sunday when Katerina returned home from church that she found Costas had unexpectedly called round. He had restricted his visits to mainly religious holidays, Christmas and Easter, but apparently he wanted to speak to Anita about something important. The last time she'd seen him had been at Nicos's and Sonia's funeral. Since the New Year incident with his *goumbaros*, aware of everyone's disapproval – especially his mother-in-law's – he had kept his distance. He found Anita alone; Olga had taken the children for a walk to the beach.

When Katerina returned from the church the house was unusually quiet. The little ones were taking a nap so she went straight to the kitchen to make some tea, thinking that if Olga had been out with the children she'd probably be needing one too.

Startled, Katerina heard the hushed voices drift into the kitchen from the *saloni*; Costas had apparently been and gone and Anita was now relaying their conversation to her mother.

*

'It's been a while since I came to see you,' he had told her, sitting awkwardly at the edge of an armchair, 'and there is something I want to discuss with you.' He looked nervous.

'Yes?' Anita replied. 'What is it?'

'Well . . .' he started; she could smell tobacco and alcohol on his breath. 'Well, you see,' he continued, clearing his throat, 'Petros has been offered a passage to England with a possibility of a job and he thinks there might be a position for me too in the same firm. It's a good opportunity.'

'England . . .' Anita said, trying to sound indifferent while feeling a rush of blood rise to her head as fury overtook her. Her anti-colonial feelings were still latent; independence from the British was still in its infancy, it was barely two years since the island had got its independence, and it would take time for rebel blood to cool down. Nonetheless she said nothing. She nodded, bit her tongue, wore a frozen smile on her face and pretended she was taking an interest in what he was saying.

'Well . . . perhaps, as you say,' she replied, 'it is a good opportunity.' She had to keep a cool head; this was the chance she had been waiting for. If he left, divorce would be so much simpler.

'Well . . . in any case . . . I've made up my mind to accept and leave with Petros,' he said quickly and stood up. 'But I wanted to let you know.'

*

342

Katerina walked into the *saloni* holding the tea tray to find mother and daughter sitting side by side uncharacteristically cheerful. Anita looked up, a smile brightening her face; Katerina hadn't seen her like that for the longest time.

'I am obviously missing something good,' she said and put the tray on the side table. 'Will you tell me so I can smile too?'

'With pleasure . . .' Anita began.

Katerina listened transfixed, her hands folded in her lap, her brain working overtime. All of a sudden she leapt up, nearly knocking over the teapot.

'*I knew it!*' she cried, hoping she hadn't woken the children and making the other two women jump. '*I knew it*,' she hissed under her breath this time.

The suspicions she had been harbouring for so long about Petros had now been confirmed for her.

'But I had no proof, you see, just my own misgivings,' she started to explain. 'The only person I discussed it with was the padre and we agreed that since I had no evidence I should wait and see, and now *I SEE!*' she said, raising her voice again. 'This is all the proof I need.'

After independence, it was commonly known that many collaborators who had not already been disposed of by their own people for betraying the freedom movement were being offered the chance of a new life in England by way of repayment for their services, and apparently Petros was now about to claim his reward. Even if they had no proof, it became clear to all three women that Costas too was being rewarded for whatever part he had played as a possible informer.

'I *knew* that man was a snake! We should thank the Lord and the *Panayia* they are both leaving . . . they deserve each other,' Katerina said, and got up to pour the tea.

Larnaka, 2010

Anita looked at Adonis long and hard. 'When you were growing up we led you to believe that your father . . . I mean Costas, was dead. We didn't know what else to tell you. We despised him so much we wanted to forget all about him.'

'And is he dead?' Adonis asked.

'I don't know . . . most probably drank himself to death,' Anita replied with an expression of disdain at the memory.

'Did he ever try to come back?' he asked.

'No. We never heard from him again, nor did we want to. He might still be in England but I neither know nor care.'

'But did you divorce him? I *do* hope so!' Eleni added, looking alarmed.

'Well, because we married in the Catholic Church,

there were complications. But it didn't matter; he was as pleased to be gone as we were to see him go.' Anita laughed drily. 'Knowing him he probably married again in England, making himself a bigamist . . . In any case, if he had tried to come back he would have had to deal with my mother.' She chuckled again. 'He wouldn't have dared, and as you know your grandmother lived well into her nineties!'

'It's so ironic,' Adonis said, looking around at the others, 'I grew up knowing my father wasn't worth knowing, and now I find . . .' he took in a deep breath and stood up, 'that the exact opposite was true of my real father.'

Anita stood up too, and going over to Adonis took him in her arms. 'I wish it could have been different for you, my son.' She cupped his face in both hands and kissed his forehead. 'I wish it could have been different for all of you . . .' She looked at the girls. 'I wish life had been simpler for all of us, but it wasn't.' Weary and visibly upset, Anita sat down again. 'But we made the best of what we had,' she said, wiping her eyes and looking at the three tear-streaked-faces, 'and what we had was love! I hope you can all say that you lived in a house of women who loved you, and be able to forgive the mistakes we made.' With that, all three of them reached across the table and took Anita's hands in theirs. They stayed holding on to her for a long while.

They had all been sitting in the kitchen listening to the

old woman for almost three hours. They'd been oblivious to how much time had passed, their late hearty breakfast had kept hunger at bay and none of them realized it was well past lunch.

'Shall I make some tea?' Marianna looked around the table.

'Forget tea,' Adonis replied, 'I think what we need is food and a glass of wine,' and jumping off his chair, he made for the door. 'A walk on the beach and lunch at Stephano's will do us good.' He stopped and turned to look at the three women standing in the kitchen. A surge of love and tenderness washed over him. *How lucky we all are still to have each other*, he thought. Yes, the revelations of the last couple of days had been shattering and profound, and he wished some events had been handled differently. But there was nothing he could do about that now. They had to come to terms with what they had learned, and not assign blame to anyone. What had been done was done with the best intentions and with love. These three women and himself were all that was left of the family he cherished. Katerina had gone, but her legacy remained. He carried her genes and those of his father; he was living testimony of their lives and their love.

Stephano's fish restaurant down by the shore was another favourite haunt of Adonis and Robert when they were in town. As soon as the proprietor saw them he made his way to their table with a bottle of wine and glasses.

'May her memory be eternal,' Stephanos told them, as he filled their glasses. 'Katerina was a good woman, we will drink to her memory.' And so they did, not just with one bottle but two, or maybe three. They drank chilled white wine from the vineyards of Aphrodite and ate freshly cooked succulent red mullet, with chunky fried potatoes just like Katerina used to make, and the sea breeze and the sound of the lapping waves gradually began to soothe their souls.

After the table had been cleared and the coffee had arrived, Anita delved into her bag and took out three envelopes.

'Now my children,' she said, 'there is one last thing. When Katerina was in hospital she gave me these for you.' She handed out the envelopes. 'Each one contains a letter.'

All three wanted to tear open the envelopes as soon as she handed them over, then and there in the fish restaurant, but they restrained themselves until they arrived home. It was a stiflingly hot afternoon and the walk back from the restaurant had never seemed longer. They sat in the *saloni*, across from each other on separate armchairs, with the blinds drawn to keep out the raging afternoon sun, and the overhead fan turned to full speed though it only circulated hot air. Then they opened their envelopes.

As Adonis pulled out his letter, another little bundle fell out on his lap. They started to read silently, each lost in Katerina's final words to them.

Larnaka, 2010

Adonis, my beloved son!

I have called you 'my son' many a time but you never knew that I spoke the truth. Now you know. You are truly my child, my flesh and blood, my one and only son, and I have loved you and cherished you every day of your existence since the blessed day I gave birth to you. I only hope you have felt that bond flow from me to you. You cannot imagine how often I longed to hear you calling me Mama instead of dear Anita . . . But if she hadn't adopted you, you would have been taken away from me and I would have brought shame to myself and to those around me. The secret of your birth is the only regret I have in my life but my compensation was to see you growing up so close to my heart. I did the best I could to give you what I thought you needed in your life. We have lived together as one family with so much affection and tenderness pouring your way. I believe that you and I have had a relationship as close as any mother and child could have, and you have always rewarded me as a son rewards his mother. For that I thank you, and God, with all my heart.

*There have been many times when I wished I could
have told you the truth, but it could not be. Now I
want you always to carry the knowledge that you are
the son of a great man. My life has been blessed and
enriched by the gift of love your father gave me, and
you, my son, have been the most precious gift of all.
The secret of your birth was the burden I carried all
through my life. My regret and sadness was not only
that I couldn't openly acknowledge that which was true,
that I couldn't shout it from the rooftops, be openly
proud that you were mine, but also that your father
never knew. He went through life blind to the fact that
he had a son. A son that any father would be proud to
call his own. I am now carrying that regret to my
grave. I had no other choice. Your father was no
ordinary man, Adonis* mou, *I had no right to come
between him and his God. Perhaps I chose wrongly but
I did what I thought was best for all of us at the time.
Having you has given me the greatest happiness and
you were the most enriching experience of my life.*

*As my illness progressed Anita was adamant that
you should know the truth about your birth. I must
admit that I was less willing, perhaps through
cowardice, but as it is also Anita's secret, not only my
own, I have now agreed.*

*Another reason for my reluctance was that I did not
want to disturb the lifetime of stability that had been*

maintained since your adoption with the secret of your birth kept hidden. I thought, wrongly perhaps, that you might reject me if you found out the truth. I couldn't bear that. Perhaps it was also wrong of me not to tell you myself face to face; but by the time Anita convinced me to do so it was too late and you are so far away, my son. I am writing this letter while I still have some strength. Anita told me she will speak to you and the girls herself. She will explain, and I hope when you find out about your past you will not think unkindly of me and perhaps even understand.

You have grown into the most wonderful man and you, my son, have been loved not only by me but by four other marvellous women. Your grandmother Olga adored you, Anita has loved you as your legal mother, and you have been hero-worshipped by your 'sisters'. I am certain you have always felt that bond between us all.

I am as proud as any mother can be about her child and I have much to be proud of. I have loved you with all my heart and soul and I hope you can find it in yourself to forgive me for leaving it so late to tell you the truth.

I send you my blessings, my boy,
Your loving
Mama

After he finished reading her letter Adonis looked down at the little bundle of papers tied together with a faded yellow ribbon on his lap. With trembling fingers, he untied the ribbon and picked up the first letter. Holding the pale blue paper fine as a butterfly's wings he started to read the words written in faint blue ink.

My dearest Katerina,

The words I want to write to you, I cannot; the feelings I want to express to you, I must not; therefore I will speak of everyday things to you.

I was delighted to hear your news and to learn that dear Anita is doing well in her pregnancy. I pray every day for her. I was also glad to hear that you find Vienna to your liking. You describe the city so vividly that I am able to visualize the places you speak of. I have taken a book on the history of the city out of the library and while I read your letters I look for the buildings you describe. I have also started listening to Mozart in the evenings when I am alone. The music is uplifting and helps to raise me out of my melancholy . . .

Adonis read on. There were six or seven of these letters written to Katerina when she was in Vienna, and then at the bottom of the pile there were as many again written to her from Rome. These were slightly shorter but still tender and caring. None of the letters were long and all were written on the same fine airmail paper. Adonis folded them carefully and replaced the yellow ribbon as before. He sat for a long while holding them, knowing that he would be reading them all again, many times over.

The bible that Padre Bernardino had given him before he left Cyprus and these letters, Adonis realized, were to be the only mementoes he would ever have from his father.

Larnaka, 2010

Eleni, my darling girl,

You are the daughter I never had, and I have loved you as such. After your mama, my dear Sonia, died so tragically I vowed to take care of you and love you as much as I did Adonis. I pledged to look after you and make sure no harm ever came to you. Both you and Adonis were my joy and gave meaning to my life. Later on, when Marianna joined us the three of you brought me an abundance of happiness.

By now you will have heard from Anita many things that you had no idea about. I hope and pray that the mature woman that you have grown into will understand and forgive anything you deemed our wrongdoing. I am proud and humbled by all your achievements, Eleni mou; I had no education beyond the elementary school but I have lived to see you, my little one, blossom into a clever girl with achievements

*beyond anyone's imagining. A teacher, no less! But
what am I saying? A university professor, a great
academic! You are an anthropologist, my girl, so I hope
you of all people will be able to understand all that you
have learned from Anita. Over the decades, your aunt,
your mother, your grandmother, great-grandmother and
I have gone through a great deal. Much was good and
some painful but on the whole, we survived the perils of
life together. I salute you, Eleni – you come from a
family of great women. Go through life being proud of
who you are and remember the long line of wonderful
strong females you are descended from.*

Your loving
Tante

Larnaka, 2010

My darling Marianna,

*You are my alter ego. I have taken you into my heart,
my girl; I rescued you as I was once rescued. I promised
to protect and nurture you as I was once protected and
nurtured. Under the roof of the Linser women, and
away from the poisonous life of your early years you
have grown and flourished and found a loving family as
I did all those years ago.*

*The three of you have been my beloved children and
you have given me much joy. I die a happy woman*

knowing that you, Eleni, and Adonis are as close and as loving to each other as any three siblings, just as I have been with my dear Anita and Sonia. You will always have each other.

I am more proud of you than you can ever know. You came from nothing but have made much of yourself and your life and have become the independent young woman that you are.

I have loved you with all my heart, Marianna mou, *but none of this would have happened if it weren't for the woman who did all that for me, and more. Olga Linser and her heart of gold gave us both the opportunity to become the women we are. Having said that, many people get a helping hand to better themselves, yet they don't always achieve it. You have succeeded because of your strength of character, your intelligence and determination.*

Be proud, be noble, and always remember the women who shaped both of our futures; we owe them much.

Your loving

Tante

20

It was Robert who first put the idea into Adonis's head.

'Wouldn't it be great to go and see where you were born?' he asked when they spoke later that evening after Adonis had read Katerina's letter. 'Vienna is not so far from Cyprus,' he continued, encouraging Adonis. 'You're in Europe – now's the time!'

'I will if you come with us,' Adonis replied, knowing that Robert wouldn't refuse, and immediately started googling flights and hotels in Vienna on his iPad to show Eleni and Marianna.

'Could it possibly be that the apartment block where they lived has been turned into a hotel?' he asked the girls after one hotel in particular caught his eye. 'Maybe there's more than one Grashofgasse,' he wondered, scrolling through the website with the girls.

'I guess we'll find out when we get there,' Eleni replied, peering over his shoulder at the screen.

They arrived in Vienna in brilliant sunshine, having never expected to find it so vibrant, light and hot. Stories of cold winter days had led them to believe that Vienna's skies were grey and dull instead of the cloudless blue they now encountered.

In the taxi from the airport they entered a city as beautiful as its legendary Empress Sissi, familiar to them from Grandmother Olga's stories and from a Hollywood film made about her life.

'I want to go to Sissi's palace,' Marianna had told them on the plane, leafing through her *Guide to Vienna*, which Anita had slipped into her bag before they left.

'And you won't be going alone,' Adonis replied. 'I'm right there with you!'

Sissi's celebrated beauty had held a childhood fascination for all three.

'Me too!' added Eleni, remembering how the two girls had often competed to be Sissi during their dressing-up sessions. Secretly Adonis wouldn't have minded being her either, but thought better of it and kept faithful to his priestly robes.

They met Robert at the hotel a day later.

'This will make up for missing the funeral,' he'd said, after booking his flight.

'I wish Simon was free to join us,' Eleni moped, 'then it would have been perfect.'

The Hotel Karntnerhof on Grashofgasse was at the end of a cul-de-sac in the heart of Vienna, but to their disappointment it was not what they had anticipated.

The building had clearly not originally been built as an apartment block and later converted into a hotel as the address had led them to hope. It was a baroque-style palazzo, opulent and charming, probably built some 150 years before as the family home of a Viennese aristocrat. Adjoining the hotel, at the end of the cul-de-sac stood an impressive eighteenth-century bastion adorned with twenty-first-century graffiti.

Tired from their journey and a little emotional, the three friends agreed to meet in the lobby after a couple of hours' rest for an early-evening stroll in search of a suit-able place to dine.

'I think our first destination should be the American Bar for a cocktail,' Adonis had told the girls, squeezed together in the tiny art nouveau lift on the way up to their rooms.

'Perfect!' they both agreed.

They couldn't remember the last time the three of them had been on a trip together somewhere. The last time had probably been to Athens, so long ago now. It was after Eleni had graduated from the London School of Econom-ics, and she had arranged to meet the others in the Greek capital for a few days on her way to Cyprus. She had wanted to tell them that she had agreed to marry Simon and felt the need to break the news to them first, before announcing it back home. She and Simon were fellow students and had been together for a couple of years. She hadn't anticipated the relationship would turn out to be permanent, which meant she'd be staying in London after they got married. Anxious about the prospect of disappointing Katerina by not returning to Larnaka after her studies, and aware of her aunt's antipathy towards the English, she looked for support from her beloved Adonis and Marianna. 'They love you and they want what's best for you,' Marianna told her. 'It's not every English person's fault what the British did to Cyprus all those years ago. It's forgotten now.'

'It's true,' Adonis had agreed. 'Besides, my mother and Tante have Grandmother Olga to deal with,' Adonis joked. 'She will put them right.'

This trip to Vienna, which Robert had been right to suggest, was already having a similar healing effect to the Athens trip long before. The circumstances were less happy than on the previous one, but together they felt capable of dealing with whatever crisis they had to face.

'Which side of the bed would you rather sleep on?' Eleni asked Marianna, kicking off her shoes and flopping on the big double bed, once they were in their room. 'I hope you're not going to snore,' she continued teasingly.

'Excuse me, madam!' Marianna protested, laughing, and flopped down next to her. 'As I remember it, you're the one who snores *and* talks in your sleep!'

It had been a long time since they had shared a room,

let alone a bed. A sense of well-being washed over them; this felt like old times.

They found Adonis already in the lobby chatting with the concierge, a map of the city opened up on the counter as he took down notes.

'Hans here says that there is a superb restaurant on our doorstep.' He looked up at Eleni and Marianna as they stood looking over his shoulder.

'The Apfelbaum is very good, probably the best restaurant in town,' Hans told them in perfect English. 'It's been open for only a few months, we highly recommend it to our guests, but it is best you book.'

'Where is it?' the girls said in unison.

'Just behind the wall, through the gate,' he replied.

The gate in the wall, if fully opened, would have allowed access to a horse and carriage when it was first built. Adonis pushed the half-open door and walking through he entered a courtyard, followed closely by the girls. Oddly nervous as if they were trespassing they hesitated for a moment before venturing further into a little piazza flanked on all sides by a four-storey building.

The courtyard in which they found themselves was so familiar, so recognizable, that it stopped them in their tracks. Blinking in disbelief they stood looking around them.

'Oh my God!' Eleni was the first to speak. 'Looook!'

she gasped, pointing ahead and bringing her hand to her mouth.

'It's still here!' Adonis breathed.

'The . . . the tree . . .' Marianna started to say but her voice trailed off.

The apple tree stood in the middle of the little garden, now reduced to a fenced-off patch of green, leaving the rest of the square to be used as a car park for the residents. This, they instantly knew, was the courtyard of Grashofgasse of long ago, the place they had come to Vienna to find. The apple tree was a giveaway, even if all that remained from the floral garden were several rose bushes which competed for space with the tree. The four-storey apartments wrapped themselves around the entire square, just as Adonis, Eleni and Marianna had seen in the old family photograph albums. They stepped further into the yard and stood looking up. A sign read '1010 Wien, Grashofgasse Wohnung'. On the third floor on the right-hand side, they were sure they could locate Great-aunt Heidi's home and above that they could see a roof garden, tufts of greenery spilling over the tiles; someone was apparently continuing Nicos and Sonia's work.

'This is where you two were born!' Marianna suddenly shouted the words, shaking them all out of their reverie. Blinking again, Adonis and Eleni looked at each other; their knees seemed to go weak and a sudden fatigue took hold, demanding that they sit down. Across the way on the ground floor with its welcoming doors flung open was the Apfelbaum restaurant that Hans had recommended. Several tables and chairs spilled into the yard, and a big sun umbrella and potted plants signalled that the small area in front of the restaurant was its property. The three made their way to one of the tables and dropped on the chairs in a state of emotional exhaustion, stunned at their unexpected discovery.

'I think we need a drink,' Adonis said, calling the waiter who was making his way to them.

'I had a feeling this must have been *it* when I saw the address of the hotel,' he said looking around him, 'but I thought it was too good to be true.'

'After this past week nothing should surprise us any more,' Eleni said.

'It's incredible how we found it – no one will ever believe the coincidence.'

'I don't know, but I'm thinking . . .' Marianna hesitated. 'Who knows . . .' she started again, 'it was probably Tante and Grandma Olga who guided us here.'

'Who knows indeed,' Eleni said, looking up, and lifted her glass of wine towards the apartment. 'Here's to you, Olga, Katerina, Anita and Sonia, we salute your loyalty to each other, and marvel at your courage. You're all a hard act to follow!'

As it turned out, on that first night in Vienna they

ended up sitting under the stars in the Apfelbaum restaurant, whose name they learned meant 'apple tree',
unable to tear themselves away. It was a warm and balmy
evening and they sat in the square eating and drinking
and basking in the pleasure of their happy discovery
until it was time to take themselves off to bed.

They were still having breakfast when Robert arrived.
Tall, black and handsome, he cut an impressive figure
and turned everybody's head as he walked into the
dining room. At the sight of him all three jumped up,
overturning at least one empty coffee cup and noisily
threw their arms around him, causing further curious
looks from the other guests.

Robert's presence brought a sort of calm to their febrile
state of mind as always, and he willingly spent the day
listening again to all they had to say. Even though he
knew most of it from Adonis, the revelations of the past
days needed more discussing. Robert himself had had his
share of family complications when at the age of sixteen
he'd discovered that his biological father was not the man
who'd brought him up.

'Who hasn't had their share of family secrets?' he
pointed out, as they sat drinking coffee in the Café
Central later that afternoon. He looked around the table
at everyone. 'It takes time to get over them, and in my

case therapy too, but the good news is you *do* get over them. That I promise.'

'I've been thinking . . .' Adonis hesitated for a moment. 'I was wondering,' he tried again, 'if I should look for him.' He searched Robert's face for a reaction. 'You know . . . try to find out if he's alive?'

Robert let out a sigh and reached for Adonis's hand. 'I didn't go looking for my father because I knew he was already dead, but you have no idea. So I think you should do whatever you feel the need to do. I wish I'd had that opportunity.'

'I had a dream last night,' Adonis continued, swallowing hard to stop his tears, 'and I've been thinking about it all day. I dreamt of him. The way he was when we were young when he used to come and visit us at the house.' He looked at the girls. 'I dreamt that he was standing in the kitchen with Tante, and I called out to him; he turned to look at me and I ran into his open arms. I called out "Father," but in my dream I didn't know if I was calling him Father as in Padre, or father . . . as in *my* father. I woke up crying.'

'I have these dreams about my mother all the time,' Marianna said in a tiny voice, her eyes filling up. 'I'm always running into her open arms but when I get there she has vanished . . .'

'I have these dreams about my parents,' Eleni said, 'but the difference between you two and me is that my parents are both dead and I will never find them.' Eleni took a deep breath, exhaled slowly and carried on. 'But *you*, Marianna *mou* and *you*, Adonis *mou*, you both have a chance of looking for your mother and father. Since your mama hasn't come to find you then perhaps it's time you tried to find her . . . and you, my darling cousin, your father was never going to look for you because he has no idea who you are.'

The Natural History Museum of Vienna was grand, and majestic enough to have been a palace built for kings and queens; instead it housed old bones, fossils, dead animals and plants. But then again many buildings they encountered in the Austrian capital as they explored it looked grand enough to be palaces.

This time it was Adonis who came up with the idea they should visit the museum in search of their great-grandparents' botanical work. They had been so caught up with the discovery of the apartments that they had almost forgotten that this was the city where their ancestors came from and their story had begun, and that the museum itself was the reason why Josef and Eva left their country to go to Cyprus and start a new life there.

Adonis telephoned ahead of time to make an appointment and explain the purpose of their request, so when they arrived they were warmly greeted by a museum official who was to take them to the archive room.

'I believe your relatives contributed an important body of work to the museum,' the man said as he ushered them up magnificent staircases leading to rooms of gothic splendour full of cabinets containing a host of extinct species, some in bottles or glass dressers, dinosaurs on plinths, and prehistoric bones on display. He whisked them through room after room, and they resolved to revisit at their leisure once their tour was complete. Finally, they arrived at the archive room. In contrast to the elaborate palace of a museum they had just been through, this was a modest chamber whose walls were covered from floor to ceiling with shelves full of files and storage boxes. Apparently modernity and technology had not yet reached the museum's archive collections.

'You probably think we are still in the nineteenth century,' Professor Buchsbaum laughed apologetically after introducing himself. 'Of course,' he explained, 'we electronically record our collections too, but here we have the physical specimens and artworks which we must preserve. Works like those of your great-great-grandparents are fragile and must be protected. As you see,' he pointed at the rows and rows of shelves along the length of the room, 'there is so much material, since the museum opened in 1889 the collections are constantly growing.' He gestured around again. 'Josef and Eva Linser, your relatives, are two of our most valued contributors from the early days. They were among the first botanists to have been sent abroad for the purpose of collecting flora and fauna around the world for the museum – as you will see.' He signalled to one of his colleagues to join them.

'Many of Eva Linser's illustrations are in the museum,' the man informed them as he shook their hands, 'but here you will be able to examine them more closely.'

Lost for words, Eleni, Marianna, Adonis and Robert stood looking and listening in awe, while the professor began to explain and lay out with the utmost care, botanical documents and artworks that had been compiled and created over a century ago by two people so closely connected to them yet who had been so unfamiliar to them. In this room of antiquities and in these objects of beauty and rarity lay part of their own history. Objects that had travelled for thousands of miles from a land of sun and sea, and were as primitive as if they had come from another planet.

Arms linked, leaning over a counter that ran along the entire length of the archive room, the four friends continued to look in wonderment at beautiful, exquisite illustrations, botanical specimens as delicate as lace, preserved for posterity.

Names hand-written on cards by Josef and Eva categorized each rare species of flower and plant, names as elusive and enchanting as the man and woman who wrote them, who now lived in Eleni's, Adonis's and Marianna's imaginations through the stories they had been told. Standing in that room poring over their legacy they could almost believe that Eva and Josef had come to life.

They read name after name of wildflower that they hoped they might still encounter if walking in the hills and meadows of the island, and which thanks to Eva and Josef Linser had been plucked from obscurity so the world would know of their existence.

Cyclamen cyprium, Orchis anatolica, Crocus cyprius . . . a multitude of island species: exotic, exclusive, even mythical; here indeed were the flowers of Aphrodite.

As she gazed fascinated by their delicate beauty, Eleni's mind wandered off to the past and to those five women who had shaped her own life. They too, she mused, were Aphrodite's floral offerings. Her great-grandmother Ernestina, she thought, if she had been a flower, would have been a pious arum lily, whilst her grandmother Olga would have been a majestic rose. Her mother would have been a daisy, cheerful and capricious, and Anita a chrysanthemum, ardent and melancholic. Katerina, she decided, could only have been jasmine, the smallest, most modest of flowers, yet the most fragrant and potent of them all.

As they stood contemplating the work of their two ancestors they realized that this part of their journey was now complete. A few days ago Eleni, Adonis and Marianna had gathered together with heavy hearts to bury the woman they all considered their surrogate mother. They had travelled to Larnaka for a funeral, not knowing that the journey was to become the most significant they would ever take.

They had arrived knowing who they were and where they came from, and left with their history rewritten and the perception of who they were transformed. The revelations and uncovered truths they had learned in the course of these few days had redefined their past and changed the course of their future.

They looked across at each other and as so often when the three of them were together, each knew what the others were thinking. The look carried all the love and tenderness they felt for one another and told them how their journey to the past had helped them understand the present and prepared them for the future. A future full of new possibilities was now waiting for them.

Acknowledgements

My thanks go to my Greek Cypriot friends who first inspired me to embark on this tale. These friends, who were born and have lived in Larnaka all their lives, unveiled a face of this town I did not know existed. In conversation with young and old *Larnakides* I discovered a town with a past that I never could have imagined.

My thanks also go, as always, to my agent and good friend Dorie Simmonds for her constant encouragement and belief in me, and of course to my editor Caroline Hogg, who keeps taking a chance on me, and all at Pan Macmillan. I can't thank Ann Boston enough for her invaluable support and help with editing my first draft.

Among the Lemon Trees

By Nadia Marks

Anna thought her marriage to Max would last forever. They had raised two happy children together, and she looked forward to growing old with the man she loved. But when a revelation from her husband just before their wedding anniversary shakes her entire world, she's left uncertain of what the future holds.

Needing time to herself, Anna takes up an offer from her widowed father to spend the summer on the small Aegean island of his birth, unaware that a chance discovery of letters in her aunt's house will unleash a host of family secrets. Kept hidden for sixty years, they reveal a tumultuous family history, beginning in Greece at the start of the twentieth century and ending in Naples at the close of the Second World War.

Confronted by their family's long-buried truths, both father and daughter are shaken by the discovery and Anna begins to realize that if she is to ever heal the present, she must first understand the past . . .

'My book of the year. An utterly gripping
story of love and family secrets'
Vanessa Feltz

It's time to relax with your next good book

THE WINDOW SEAT.CO.UK

If you've enjoyed this book, but don't know what to read next, then we can help. The Window Seat is a site that's all about making it easier to discover your next good book. We feature recommendations, behind-the-scenes tales from the world of publishing, creative writing tips, competitions, and, if we're honest, quite a lot of lists based on our favourite reads.

You'll find stories and features by authors including Lucinda Riley, Karen Swan, Diane Chamberlain, Jane Green, Lucy Diamond and many more. We showcase brand-new talent as well as classic favourites, so you'll never be stuck for what to read again.

We'd love to know what you think of the site, our books, and what you'd like us to feature, so do let us know.

🐦 @panmacmillan.com

f facebook.com/panmacmillan

WWW.THEWINDOWSEAT.CO.UK

extracts reading groups
competitions books new
discounts extracts extracts
competitions events discounts
books new extracts events
events books reading groups
extracts new reading groups
new reading groups
interviews events new
events extracts extracts books
discounts events
new books events
events new
discounts extracts discounts
www.panmacmillan.com
extracts events reading groups
competitions books extracts new